I0817699

Also by Chloe Michelle Howarth

Sunburn

HEAP EARTH UPON IT

A NOVEL

CHLOE MICHELLE HOWARTH

MELVILLE HOUSE
BROOKLYN • LONDON

First published in 2025 by Verve

First Melville House Printing: December 2025
Distributed by Penguin Random House LLC, 1745 Broadway, New York, NY 10019
www.penguinrandomhouse.com

Melville House Publishing
46 John Street
Brooklyn, NY 11201
and
Melville House UK
Suite 2000
16/18 Woodford Road
London E7 0HA

mhpbooks.com
@melvillehouse

ISBN: 978-1-68589-253-1
ISBN: 978-1-68589-254-8 (eBook)

Library of Congress Control Number: 2025946682
Printed in the United States of America
1 3 5 7 9 10 8 6 4 2
A catalog record for this book is available from the Library of Congress

The authorized representative in the EU for product safety and
compliance is Easy Access System Europe, Mustamäe tee 50, 10621 Tallinn, Estonia.
gpsr.requests@easproject.com

For Ben & Chris

Prologue

OFTEN I WAKE TO THE sort of scream that permeates soil and rattles the coffins and fossils it passes by. The sort that even the birds and insects understand as pained. A sound so intense it has a texture and a weight. When that screaming comes to me, I wrap myself around it and cling on. There's something soothing about it; it's like having you around.

There's something about all of this that is easier to sink into than to break free from. The deadweight of grief. The small bliss of my stagnancy. Habits I cannot sense the evil in.

And yet, it hurts to think about you. About what happened. So I leave it in my blind spot and try to move on, and pull what comfort I can from your constant screaming.

Jack

DIDN'T THEY ALL TELL ME that this would come with time? Healing. Things getting lighter. Things meaning less. I thought it was just something people were saying to fill silences. But it appears that they were right. The trouble is running off me. I am moving on. Such quare liberation.

While the others sleep, I step out of the house to take in the last of Kilmarra. Knowing without really understanding that in the morning we will leave the place we come from and never come back again.

Big bloodied sky, yellow clouds hanging in the thick air. The bare winter trees reach up to be touched by lightning. I do the same. I wait for the weather to break over me. For the rumble of thunder. For God to make Himself known to me. But when the sky opens, no god or heaven is there. Only miles of navy dark.

And I realise that over the last year, I've been so focused on the darkness of my skies that I've let the rest of the world pass me by. I wonder have the others noticed this? I wonder have they seen the gloomy fire that cuts up my horizon, and know how gladly I have let it blaze?

I go back inside to start loading up the cart. To wake the rest of them.

Leaving the house for the last time, my mind turns away from you, and to the whole year that has passed. A year of things left unsaid, unacknowledged. As though their happening didn't ruin me.

*

I'm woken by the bumps in the road, the cart rolling on. All the rest sat up and awake. High time I sat up with them. A little birdsong. A clear evening. White fog lining the roads, smudging the town before us. And yet without the haze of mourning, I see clearly.

'How are ye now?'

Tom calls, nodding at two passing men. How he has strained to hold us all together. How well he has done. Say what you want about Tom, but thanks to him, we are now just an ordinary family, leaving our ordinary past behind as we come into a new town. When we're settled, I'll sort him out with a few pints. To say thanks.

'Fine morning.'

Tom smiles at the man and woman standing into the hedge to let us pass. His eyes widening. The woman smiles obligingly. It might seem like a small thing, but when she looks at me, I feel able to hold my head up and nod at her. Just yesterday that would have felt like an immeasurably big task. Anna mutters something to herself. I look at her for what feels like the first time all year. And although it makes her uncomfortable, I find it hard to look away.

Beneath a sky of soft clouds, we trickle into the square of Ballycrea. Our wheels meet their potholes, I taste the salted wind, and we are irreversibly here.

It looks just the same as all of the other small towns we've travelled through. Post office, shop, pubs. Weathered walls, horse shit, county flags. A girl in a miniskirt and her mother in a shawl. Donkeys and carts among Fords. Modernity is doing what it can to make its impact here, just like in Kilmarra. I'm not sure why I expected this new place to be any different from home.

The further our cart rolls into the town, the more heads turn to take us in. How perfectly dull this is. How wonderful you would look among it all. Warm skinned and blonde, in your pink frock. Glowing in the crowd. Smiling at everyone, wanting to be known, reaching out to shake the hands of the locals like some sort of pageant queen.

But there is none of that. It's just a quiet day, like every day. All achingly plain. Although I want to leave my sentimentality behind and embrace my new start, I cannot help but long for the immediate vibrancy that you brought to everything. The absolute wonder of you. Darling. Anyway.

A big, unexpected sigh leaves me. It feels good to let the shoulders drop.

'Hello, hello, folks.'

Ah, he's loving this. Tall, square-jawed Tom, who our mother would describe as strapping, trying desperately to catch the eye of anyone he can. Look how he holds himself, as though the world is watching. As though god himself has taken audience to see Tom bring us into town, holding the reins of the pony as though she is some unbroken stallion. Glancing out of the corner of his eye to see who is looking. The torn lapel of his coat, burying him with embarrassment. Even before all the effort he had to take to make us appear like a happy family, Tom was always obsessed with appearances.

And yet, here are Peggy's socks, browned at the soles. A pile of battered trunks and cases, and the chicken pressed against the wire of her cage. Anna in Mammy's faded red headscarf. My cap, low over my eyes.

'How are ye keeping?'

Tom asks through a stiff smile. So strange that he can't just drive the cart through the square without trying to connect with people.

They are all going to think that Anna is my wife, aren't they? Or they'll think that she's Tom's wife, and I'm just some poor, lonely bachelor that they have graciously taken in. I take Peggy's feet in my hands to warm them up, squeezing her little bones. Tom turns to look at me, and in the name of optimism, of healing, I pull a smile out of my mouth. I am not the same dreary old Jack that I have been. If this is going to be a new start, I need to be new.

'This is the crowd in Dr Desmond's place, I suppose.'

A woman says, as though we are too far away to hear her. Pure brazen.

'Isn't the town getting busy?'

Her friend says back. In ways I'm surprised, and in more ways I am not, when Anna calls down to her,

'We'll turn around and go so, will we?'

Peggy gasps, and laughs without meaning to. Tom's jaw tenses. And in a move of solidarity that I can't quite explain, I laugh too. Later on, I'm sure, Tom will have something to say about all of this. About how we can't waste our chance here by acting the fool. Later on, I'm sure, I will regret taking Anna's side. Tom will probably try to track those two women down and apologise to them. And I suppose he'll be right to do it. Already I'm sorry for laughing. But in that moment, Anna displayed a very rare version of herself. Somebody unbothered and happy, unburdened and funny. Healing will mean untangling the good parts of Anna from the rest of her. That'll be some job.

I open out my arms for Peggy, and she comes to sit with me. Her small head against my arm, vibrating with the gravel beneath us.

'Are we nearly there?'

She asks, getting restless, and I stroke the back of her hand. I have no idea if we are nearly there. 'Tis Tom knows where we're going, not me.

A little while out of the town, we trundle up the long grass of a steep hill. It seems cruel to let the pony pull all this weight. I suppose I should have considered that when we left home.

A white cottage, dark blue paint beginning to peel from each of its five windowsills and front door. A little beaten path starting from a seemingly random point in the grass leading up to it. And a fence around a patch of land adjoining the house. I suppose that's where the pony will live. The poor creature may never move again after this journey. Moss on the roof, moss on the walls. Suitably rundown. I can't express how much I am trying to gee myself up about this new cottage.

My knees crack as I get down from the cart, and for the first time in a long time, I am reminded of my age. I can't say I remember turning twenty-eight. And yet, here I am. This definitely isn't where I thought I would be at twenty-eight. A full, fresh start unfolding before me. A fresh start was never something that I wanted; certainly not something that I thought I would need. And yet.

Peggy is bouncing around the yard, burning off all the energy she stored up in the cart. She is happy to be here, and I try to mirror her enthusiasm. After struggling with the lock and working himself up, Tom lets us into the cottage where we are hit with the smell of dust and the look of disuse. Peggy dashes past us, unfazed. It's all on one level. That's the first thing that lands with me. No stairs, no ladder. All laid out flat here in front of us. I suppose the others notice this too. And it will be added to the ever-growing pile of things we leave unsaid.

Smaller than we are used to. All arranged in a completely different way to home. It isn't that I expected it to look the same. I just didn't expect it to look different. I wonder how long it takes to settle in somewhere new.

'There's no beds!'

Peggy shouts, running back out to me. Looking to Tom, I realise there that we don't have half the things we need to fill a home. Anna answers her.

'No, we've no bed yet. Sure we've nothing yet.'

'Obviously, Anna, I just said.'

'Don't start acting the brat the minute we arrive.'

'Era shut up will ye, girls? I'll sort ye beds. I'll sort everything we need in the next few days.'

Tom says, dragging in the two largest trunks. I stand at the window, allowing all this to happen. Peggy's lip trembles. I wonder if she has come to expect me to be passive. I lower myself to her height.

'Go on and get the chicken, will you? And we'll find a place to put her.'

Before we left, I tried to explain to Peggy it wasn't worth having only one chicken, that she wouldn't lay enough eggs for us all. But Peggy wouldn't leave her. She said a chicken isn't just for eggs. My girl. How could I refuse her?

As she turns to walk out the door, it hits me; I think it hits us all at once: we have left our home behind, permanently. There isn't a scrap of our past here. Nothing to identify with, nothing to hold on to. And so I will have to hold on to Tom, Anna and Peggy. It will be easier to keep my head above water if I am buoyed by them. None of us have the strength to stand on our own.

'Has he no shame at all, not to run so much as a brush across the floor before we arrived?'

She's only being judgemental. No bed, no curtains. A table and chairs coated in dust. No sign of life at all except for the turf, the loaf and the jam that Dr Desmond has left for us. That's something you don't get from most landlords. Tom and Anna stare at the doctor's offerings, presumably embarrassed and offended at the idea that we might need a little boost to get us started. Peggy opens the jar of jam and cleans the little blobs on the lid off with her finger, licking it away. A purple stain, sugar in the grooves of her skin. Tom pulls the jar off her and turns his face into a smile, while Anna lets hers fall into a frown.

'Wasn't that good of him? A great sign of the people here.'

He says, and Anna responds by rolling her eyes.

'God yeah, such charitable people.'

She looks around for somewhere to put herself, and her eyes fall on me. For the second time, I find I cannot look away from her.

'Have a look for a sweeping brush there, Anna.'

Tom says, and she breaks our gaze.

There isn't a brush. Peggy lets the chicken out of her cage and chases her across the room. We unpack the cart, arrange things and then rearrange them. We have an argument about it and then put things back where they were the first time. We light the fire, we all eat a slice of the bread, and, like every evening, Tom leads us in a rosary. Afterwards, he settles by the fire to count the cash in his money tin.

We're at the time of year when the night comes in fast, thanks be to god, because I can't face being awake at midnight, hearing the town ring in the New Year. Without a bed, we lie out on the unbrushed floor and Anna drapes a few blankets over us. Maybe tomorrow, I will talk to her.

And then, the first day is over. And the last of Kilmarra tries to leave us.

I wake to blonde light.

For a moment, there is nothing but this gleaming, pale yellow. What sweetness. What peace. Let me touch it. I chase it, trying not to come back to life.

But it's too late. I am suddenly awake. All the appalling colour of the world rushes back to me, and there is no more room for the blonde of you. I have woken to the day of your first anniversary.

The comfortable smell of the newspaper and cooking rashers. The crushing weight of three hundred and sixty-five days. The urge within me to mention your name and force my siblings to dissect every moment of your death.

I sit at the table, Peggy alongside me, asking Anna where her school pinafore is gone. Tom puts a hand on my shoulder and squeezes without looking up from the paper. It's hard to say how many times he has told me that time heals all wounds. Hard advice to be grateful for when you aren't something that I want to heal from. I feel every muscle in his hand and send the small bit of good that's left in me back to Kilmarra, back to you. Blessing myself, I take the heel of the bread the doctor left.

Do you know that I would have helped your sisters today? I'd be below at your father's house now with the cart, waiting to bring them all down to Mass. And then I would have stayed on and looked after him. I would have looked after him for the rest of his life. I hope that you know how much they mean to me. Yet another thing out of my reach. I butter the bread and try to find a way to make the best of this.

But sure look, I hear your voice telling me, look at all the good things that are here. And it's true, as the sun begins to show itself, I see that I've Peggy, and bread, and blackberry jam. Somehow, I've enough strength left in me to believe that 1965 could be good to us all. And in the mornings, however briefly, I have blonde light.

Tom

FOR A SMALL TOWN, BALLYCREA is an awful big place. It bleeds out for miles and miles into the countryside. The type of edgeless endlessness that could scare a person. There's always people to meet, townlands to memorise. All day, every day, I make my way around the town, shaking hands and introducing myself to the locals. Like a politician. A little bit pathetic, I know. But I do what I have to do. And it appears to be paying off, because today, at last, I have been invited to the pub with some local men.

Ger Doyle's pub is all dark wood, a wall of shelves lined with bottles, stained glass from Murphy's brewery, a typewriter and record player up on the bar. Ger Doyle lets his two girls pull the pints. I don't like to see a woman pulling a pint. They haven't the wrists for it. One stands behind the bar, only a few years younger than me. Smoking a cigarette, waiting for somebody to tell her what to do. Another girl, perhaps my age, comes out from behind the bar in the full bloom of pregnancy. She puts a shiver through me, which I choose to ignore.

'The price of pork is gone astronomic.'

Bill Nevan says, sitting his pint on the bar. Barrel-chested and going grey, he seems to be the oldest of these men. I agree with him emphatically; I would agree with him if he said the price of pork had gone through the floor, also. I try to somehow hide the sliced ham I bought this morning, though it's wrapped and left on the counter in front of them all. Whatever these men say, I will take on as my own opinion. Just until we're settled and they like us. Then I'll see about speaking my mind.

'Isn't it a great thing?'

Another man, whose name I haven't caught yet, replies. He is the only one drinking beer among pints of stout. Bill has the deepest, loudest laugh, which spills out of his mouth as he pats the man on the back.

''Tis well for you, boy.'

The unnamed man is some class of a pork farmer, I suppose. Their conversation moves fast, and they don't pause to catch me up. I do what I can to laugh along and act like I know what they are talking about, afraid to say the wrong thing in case they revoke the offer to drink with them and pour my pint out onto the floor. We stopped farming meat when I was a child, it's just as well they moved on from pork.

'What's your game, Tom?'

John Moore asks. I have already met his wife in town, but I don't mention this to him. The words 'medicine' and 'law' almost jump out of my mouth. The chance to make something of myself, here and now, is so tempting. But I steer myself back to something truthful. Better to be humble, to lie low. These don't seem like the sort of men who would be impressed with anything too extravagant, anyway.

'Turf.'

It's only the last few years I've been a turf man. It doesn't mean much to me, it's just the most recent position I fell into. The false smiles they offer let me know that Ballycrea already has a turf man sorted. The conversation hops on again. But I can't stop myself from interrupting.

'But I was never workshy. You know the way. I was always glad to do whatever came my way. Turf, farming, barkeeping, you know, I've done it all like.'

I get a sympathetic nod from Bill. They know what I'm getting at. I can't be the only man who has stood in this pub begging for a job. My God, it's mortifying to try.

'Con will give you a bit of work, I'm sure. I'd say he's overrun with all his pigs.'

John Moore says. They all start laughing again as Con rolls his eyes, all of us absolutely certain that he won't be giving me an ounce of work. And at my own expense, I have to laugh along with them. Well, at least I've learned another name. They start to talk about horse racing; a man from two towns away is a jockey, and they all have opinions on him. I don't know the first thing about racing. I don't feel like much of a man right now. When the pints are drained, all of us file out of the pub, and I let defeat take me by the hand.

This is the rhythm that most of my days have taken since we arrived in Ballycrea. Talking to whoever I can, wherever I can, so that I might get myself into a bit of employment before the money in the tin runs out. Mammy left us that money for our weddings. That almost makes me laugh now.

'Mr O'Leary, how are things?'

Dr Desmond catches me off guard. A tall, handsome man. Too handsome for the likes of Ballycrea. Seeing me walk out of the pub at midday, with no job to go to.

'Great! All great.'

I feel an enormous amount of pressure to impress him. Some part of me believes that if I am not funny, kind, or interesting enough, he will evict us from his cottage.

'Everything okay above in the house?'

He looks me right in the eye. Between the damp and the dust and my family, there is very little right above in the cottage.

'Perfect. All perfect.'

Surely he sees through this.

'Good stuff. You'll let me know if you've any trouble.'

He pats my shoulder and turns to leave without saying goodbye. Giving me no indication of how he feels about me.

It's almost a full week that we're here, and I still don't feel I'm standing on solid ground with people. Every day I've been in the pub, the post office, the shops and the square. Conversing, charming, appearing friendly without appearing overbearing or desperate. As though I'm only chatting for chatting's sake. And already, I have made an acquaintance of Mic Harney in the creamery, Ger Doyle and Bill Nevan in the pub. Frank Lennox, who stands nearly all day on the corner stoop of his home across from Doyle's, looking out on the town and commentating on all that happens before him. I know John Moore and his wife, and now Con the pig farmer. And while Anna berates me every evening for coming home without a job, at least I'm making a nice name for us in the town. At least I'm trying. And doesn't God love a trier?

'Tis no surprise that I'm the only one of us making an effort in Ballycrea. No surprise at all. Of course, Peggy goes to school, but besides that they only exist as rumours. Imagine, your Jack, afraid to venture out beyond the front door. Not the man you left. Not at all.

And in many ways, it's making my life easier. The less they are seen and known, the better chance I have at crafting a pleasing narrative for us. As far as Ballycrea is convinced, we're a perfectly lovely family. Not too grand, not too shabby. Jack, a gentleman. Peggy, an angel. Anna, a homemaker. And myself, head of the house. Perhaps the locals are beginning to suspect that I've made up all these siblings of mine.

'Tom, hello.'

Ciara Moore, John's fed up-looking wife, greets me as I come into her shop. The little bell rings, an old man looks up at me from the chair by the door.

'How are ye settling in?'

She asks, and I wonder if she already knows how poorly I just performed in conversation with her husband.

'Oh great, yeah, 'tis a lovely place. Lovely people. Just the paper, thanks.'

I smile, hoping I look genuine, while I take a newspaper from the stand and leave it on the counter. I want to mean what I'm saying, but I can't tell if I do.

'I've a few bits inside that might be of use to ye. Plates and things, and the old armchair in the backroom. We've no use for it.'

Her charity is surprising. I'm not above accepting it. She's nicer than she looks.

'Listen, there's a crowd calling down to ours this evening, it might be nice for you to come down and introduce the family around?'

Little things like this give me an enormous boost. They dull the feeling that every day is as hard as the first day. They take away from the sting of hearing a murmuring group rush to a silence as I approach. Knowing that people are talking about us, but not knowing what they are saying. Misremembering names and initiating unwanted handshakes, and lying awake at night thinking about it. Yes, for a while now I've felt stuck on the outside of an inside joke, but tonight, I am invited to John Moore's gathering. Now that's progress.

I nearly fall over myself accepting her offer, without a notion of how I'm going to get them three out of the house. All the trouble they could bring me if they decide to exist as people on their own, without my supervision. There's another problem now, another thing to deal with. I better get home.

Walking out of the town, the houses begin to thin. Ours is the only cottage up the hill. A lonely walk, but I like having the time to myself where I'm not meeting anyone. Ahead, there are felled branches, looking like spines dropped in the field. Pure eldritch. Perhaps Jack was cutting firewood.

Something grey and maroon, unmoving, just before me. A lamb in the road. Its insides out. Bloodied wool. Organs pecked away by crows that don't fly off when I come near. Warm, thin vomit fills my mouth, and just as quickly is swallowed down again. I'm glad we don't keep sheep. This little woollen carcass isn't my problem. I draw a smile on, and I walk into the cottage, thinking that my life is to become problem-free. At long last.

I'll say this, the people of Ballycrea aren't bad. The town isn't bad, not at all. And that's without the thick optimism I've been spreading over everything. It really is a nice little place.

And although I haven't found any yet, there's work here. There's always lads out bringing their wares to the mart, repairing walls in the square. Everything seems to be beaten by the sea wind, and they are incessantly fixing. It would be easy to give up when the wind keeps blowing. But they don't give up. Isn't that a great attitude to have?

Up at the cottage, as has become a routine, I find Peggy making a racket in the garden, Anna at the window, so far off in her thoughts that she might as well be back in Kilmarra, and Jack in the corner. Sitting in quiet contemplation. I could guess what he's thinking; I could probably speak it out loud as he thinks it. And while there are probably a lot of things he would like to do and say, I feel quite confident that he will remain in the corner, almost motionless.

As I come in the door, Anna comes clambering to me, as though I am vital air. As though I escaped and left her behind. She doesn't like me being out in the town for long, meeting new people. It's hard to say if she has noticed, but Anna has become incredibly dependent on me. In the mornings, she makes me promise that I will be home for dinner. As though I would leave and never come back. Anna is always preparing for the next abandonment; it's sad, and the reasons are too much to face.

'If I was going to leave, don't you think I would have come to Ballycrea alone rather than hauling all of ye along with me?'

She didn't laugh when I asked this. She never laughs too much. The trouble is, Anna doesn't realise just how many chances I've had to leave. A ticket to London with my name on it. A pub in Wexford that needed looking after. Countless other lives that I have passed up out of loyalty to her and the other pair. I use things like this to remind myself that I am a good man. I could have left when you came into the picture, you were good for keeping them all in line. A part of me wishes I had left then. All the disappointment I might have avoided.

How to convince them to come out to the Moores' this evening? How easily I could remind Anna what a lack of friends leads to. How deeply the loneliness sinks its teeth; the sickening slow pace with which each minute passes.

Perhaps if I was just honest and told them that I want to build up credit with people. That I want to have somebody to fall back on besides the family, because they are always falling back on me.

I suppose the truth of it is, I know that there won't be any convincing involved. If I tell them we are going, they will have to follow. The more of an effort we make here, the quicker we'll get used to it. I've found that, generally, people will get used to any situation they are put in, no matter how difficult. And the best way to settle into something new is to be immersed in it.

I have to remind myself that it won't always be like this. A day will come soon that we are all so busy with work and friends that nobody will need to be coaxed out of the house. A day will come when Kilmarra will just be a strange dream I once had, and the residual horror of it will drift off. I will stop thinking that the sunrises there are like Holy God putting watercolour across the sky, and that here in Ballycrea, He is just switching on the big light.

A day will come when I think of you less. It will, because it has to; because there was a time when I could think of nothing but Mammy and Daddy, and now there are weeks when I think of Daddy only once or twice. Fleeting thoughts of my mother don't hurt me much at all once they are gone. We'll get there. We'll get popular, and employed, and it will be like you never happened to us at all.

And while I wait for that day, I will distract myself with Ballycrea. They won't be tepid towards us for long. The brand-new family in Dr Desmond's cottage will soon be just part of the scenery, as though we have always been here. If I could just leash and muzzle the three of them and get them down to John Moore's house.

Forgive me, but I must say that there is something freeing about being away from Kilmarra; to be where there isn't a scrap of you. Nobody knows your name or your face. Nobody knows what happened, or what it did to us all. There's nothing left now but a hazy, collective memory to remind us you were ever real at all. My God, 'tis a year already. Madness. Just the thought of you makes me think of that sheep, and that maybe I should have had the mercy to at least kick its body into the hedge.

Anna

TOM'S GRIMACING FACE CAME UP the hill and blossomed into a smile as he came in the door. He thinks he's cute out, that I don't see him putting on moods.

Then again, all we have done for the last year is put on moods. I have drifted so far from the person I used to be, and lost total sight of the person I was trying to be. All that's left of me are the confused, troubled parts. Sewn together and draped over me as I skulk around the new cottage all day. Preparing meals and then cleaning up after them, so that I can prepare for the next. Wasn't a fresh start supposed to be liberating?

Jack seems to have less interest in leaving the cottage than I do. It could stay this way, myself and himself, never piercing the membrane of the front door. Maybe we could get back to the way we used to be. Always laughing and fooling like children. Or we could carry on as we have been all year, in a stagnant silence together. Trying to figure out whose fault all of this is.

I'm just not ready for the town yet. Picking up Peggy from school, meeting her teacher. Hanging around the square with Tom, being seen by people. I'm not ready to start all that. The best way to look after myself is to cut the stitches between me and the world. Letting myself escape somewhere easier.

Like to one particular Sunday afternoon, two years ago. A place I drift off to all the time.

Sky saturated blue, the air sweet and heavy with pollen. Lukewarm bathwater, steam filling the air. A glossy bar of Pears glistening in your hands. And me, pulsating in a church-cold breeze. I feel it stinging. I still try to dull it.

You, hunched, trying to get what heat you could from the water that your father and sisters had already washed in. You know we would have given you the first bath in our house, if you had just come over. The soft moss of your body hair. The veins on your chest spelling my name. A profane heaven, all obscured by the lace curtains. Why would I choose to put myself on display below in Ballycrea square, when I could send myself off to places like this?

'The price of pork is gone astronomic, lads.'

Tom announces himself at the door, taking off his cap and wiping his forehead. He lands slices of ham down on the table. So far, I've managed to avoid cooking fish, which Tom tells me is half the price of pork. More likely, it's just what's popular here, and Tom wants to be seen buying it. Jack looks up from the corner, listening without joining in. Just as I think Tom is going to tell me once more ''tis all fish here, girl', he launches into a new story.

John Moore, whose wife sells him the newspaper every day, is hosting a small gathering at his house this evening. Unfortunately, the invitation has been extended to the lot of us.

'He asked for me by name, did he?'

I ask, because John Moore doesn't know for certain that I even exist. What harm would it do him if I didn't attend? Only for a moment on Thursday, as we rolled into town, was I seen by anyone at all. Those who did see me are probably beginning to think that I was nothing but a trick of the light. A little flicker, there and gone. My god, to be nothing but a flicker of light.

'Too much of your time is spent sat on your arse, staring out the window. It's not healthy for a young person like yourself to sit inside all day.'

He stumbles over his words, not knowing whether to call me a girl or a woman, settling on person. He doesn't know what to do with me, he doesn't know what I am.

'Since when do you have a problem with people staying indoors all day?'

He doesn't respond to me, but adjusts his shirt and lets my comment hang in the air before dropping, unacknowledged.

'We'll go down for an hour. It's proper to go somewhere when you've been invited, and it's good to be seen out.'

His voice is a clever blend of curt and soft, so that I can't accuse him of being forceful, but I can't disagree with him, either. Peggy comes in from the garden and sits with Jack, under his arm. They talk together, quietly. She's the only one he ever wants to talk to.

'Ah Tom, can we not wait another few days, until we're settled?'

I try, more sweetly. I know better than to annoy him; I'm not stupid. And although he smiles at me, he says,

'John Moore isn't going to wait until you're settled.'

This obsession with John Moore. This obsession with all the strangers of Ballycrea. At his best, Tom is an insecure people pleaser. At his best. But he is also the oldest, and so he makes the rules. I don't know why I bothered objecting. I suppose it isn't often a woman gets a gleaming new chance. I might as well use it.

'One of us better stay here and look after Peg.'

Jack pipes up from the corner.

'Sure can't she come with us? It isn't a human sacrifice we're going to.'

Tom laughs, trying to get us to laugh along with him. Jack tries to hide the look of defeat on his face. I know Tom is only trying to make the best of things, but it feels like he's trying to distance himself from us. From me.

'Where are we going? Is it tonight?'

Peggy asks, and I let Jack take all of her questions.

I wish he would try to see things my way. If he would take in the view from the window and realise that it's a lovely place to spend every day, watching all the acres of the headland, the fields dotted with farmhouse roofs, and the little blossom of light from the town in the evenings. Trying to trace the road we took from the square all the way back home to Kilmarra. When Tom was a little boy, Mammy always knew exactly what to say to put him in his place. But then Tom grew up, and whatever way I angle my ears, I can't seem to hear Mammy.

'Will there be other girls my age there? Will the girls from school be there?'

He doesn't know. Sure he doesn't know anything.

None of this would be happening if Mammy was here. I miss her. I miss the time when she had all the authority. I even miss the time when she had less authority than me. She would let me stay at home if I wanted to. She would have told me to pack more jars and stockings and thread. All of those little things that didn't seem important when I was trying to fit my life into a suitcase. When I had cramps in the cart, she would have made Tom stop and get me aspirin from the chemist shop. Instead, I had to sit in a long, awkward fear; afraid to mention it, afraid to move in case cramping had turned to bleeding.

See, Tom says he is doing so much for the family, but he doesn't take very good care of me at all. He is doing all this for himself. I wonder would he be happier if we didn't come with him to John Moore's tonight.

'We won't be out late, Peg.'

Jack tells her, and I take this as a promise. He sends her back outside to see if the chicken has laid any eggs. Tom sits at the table and opens the newspaper, and I take it as my sign to start making the tea. I move without thinking, cutting the veg and boiling the water. All the time, I am trying to get back to you in the bath. But I can't get there. I am in the cottage, without escape.

One summer's day, months from now, everything will be better. Today will just be a piece of a past I can hardly remember. I know it will, because I have felt the hardest time in my life fade to nothing but a little fog beneath my eyelids. One day, you will be nothing but a smear across the back of my mind. Jack will stand up straight and seize his life again. We will be happier than we ever were before, one day. When I can't get quiet, when I can't get myself back to your bath, I think of this.

When Jack gets quiet, he thinks of you. A soft drizzle of rain on your eyelashes in the spring. A drizzle of honey on your fingertips while baking. A drizzle of blood on the banisters. Lillian, I am pained to know this.

Dropping the carrots into the pot, I scarcely feel the boiling water splash on my arm. I scarcely realise I am speaking when I call out,

'Shake a leg, Jack! We're all going out tonight.'

Jack

IT POURS WITH RAIN THE entire walk to John and Ciara Moore's house. Let's see is it enough to put a dent in Tom's determination.

'Such a bad impression, to all land on soaked.'

Anna muttered, as we left the house, even though I gave the one umbrella we have to herself and Peggy. I don't know what kind of weather she was hoping for in January. Doesn't she realise that if we land on soaked, everybody else will land on soaked?

'Should we not turn back?'

She calls out through the rain, the umbrella struggling against the wind. But Tom only throws his hand up to her, shrugging her off. Then she pulls Peggy's arm along, so that it doesn't seem like she is the one who is slowing us down. It must be exhausting to think the way she does.

And as expected, we arrive drenched, the smell of the rain soaking through our clothes. I can see the steam coming off Tom, raging that this is how his family is to be debuted to the parish. Anna did warn him.

Too late, I am worried that Peggy may well be the only child here. Tom said it would be fine. I wish I hadn't listened to him. The poor child will be exhausted by the time we're done. And Anna will look like an unfit mother for bringing her out so late. How humiliating for her. All I can hope for now is that there will be an old woman here that we can put Peggy with. Someone whose mind has gone to water, who is just dying for something small to dote on. Perhaps she would have room on her lap for all four of us.

'No getting pissed tonight.'

He points at both myself and Anna, but only really means for me to take it in. Years ago, I might have gotten carried away with the lads, drinking and messing. I might have overshadowed him. Better able to make conversation and be told I was so like our father. Tonight, I know he isn't warning me out of jealousy, but because I have become a different class of drunk: unsettling and sad, hellbent on flushing you out of my system. Better to avoid those sorts of antics for the evening.

At the door, Tom straightens his collar, and then mine. He takes Anna's chin in his big hand and looks sternly into her eyes. My hand on Peggy's shoulder. Tom letting out a breath. On our best behaviour, we go inside.

Into the amber of a fire crackling, a small hive of people. Layers of talking and laughing, and against expectation, nobody turning to look at us. It's more dignified than I thought.

A fiddle starts, a bodhrán follows, and a man sings 'The Holy Ground'. It draws a sharp pain from me, it's so long since I heard a fiddle. The bodhrán somehow beats within me.

Silence falls across the room for the music. The singing man doesn't open his eyes to see Tom's long shadow fall across the floor, his tall frame stooping under the door. Strapping is right. Making room for thinner, lesser me. And then Peggy, hand in hand with Anna. Not another child in sight. I want to lift her up onto my hip, I hate that she keeps getting older. There is little stir as we come in. Once more, we move unnoticed among them.

As we slip through the room, Tom whispers to us.

''Tis Noreen Doyle there at the fire. And against the wall is her brother, Ger Doyle, who has the pub, and Jim Ryan with him.'

He goes on with his hushed roll call until somebody shushes him. One of the many great shames of his life, no doubt. We stand still until the song is over. As the music ends, a big man makes his way over to us, his voice thunderous.

'Tom, how's things? This is the family so, is it?'

He asks, smiling. His two big, warm hands over mine.

'That's right, Bill. This is Jack, and my sister Anna, and little Peggy.'

Bill hardly looks at me and Anna, all his attention falls on Peggy.

'Peggy! Tom is always telling us about you, Peggy. And he never said you were so big!'

Bill acts like he has known us all our lives. Like he has known Peggy since she was born and is surprised at the height she has grown to. Partly unnerving, partly comforting. I find it hard to believe that Tom has ever mentioned Peggy.

'Did you know that the Moore's dog had pups a few weeks ago? Will I show you?'

He offers Peggy his hand and she takes it, unafraid, glad to be led off to wherever the pups are. Tom allowing it all. And I have to let it happen, and try not to be concerned. As though a stranger hasn't just stolen my small treasure away.

Without Peggy to watch, I take in the room. And yes, that fiddle has brought you back to me. There was never anything so gentle as your fingers on the neck of a fiddle. Nights like this remind me of you. But don't all nights remind me of you? Sitting by the fire, playing 'The South Wind'.

The door opens behind us abruptly, letting in a moment of the rainy night. Shocking me away from you. Two girls come in from the dark. Pretty. I suppose both of them are pretty. Almost blonde in the dim light; but in the sun, I'm sure, they are nothing but muddy, pale brunettes.

'Mary and Teresa Doyle,' Tom whispers to me. 'Belonging to Ger who has the pub. Mary is the, the one who's, you know, expecting.'

He fumbles through it. The Doyle sisters look at us as they pass by, with Teresa turning to look a second time. I catch the caramel of her irises. I like it. She smiles at me, and lingers for one warm second, and then she's gone. Leaving me floating in her wake. It's so long since I noticed a pretty girl.

But it's nothing. Just one person noticing another person, that's all. It's being acknowledged as a man, not just a brother. A feeling I had forgotten. How quare. What an unexpected thrill. The exact sort of thrill that I want to ignore.

Anna ushers us away nearer to the fire. Tom nods at the Doyle girls, offering a faint smile. I would imagine he is already analysing it in his head and wondering if it was too much. It's a strange thing that Tom hasn't more luck with the women, because he isn't a bad-looking man. He takes after Daddy; the classic, broad sort of look that women go for. If he was born in another place, he might have been a film star. But there are so few women that Tom thinks are worth his time, and as soon as those worthy women get to know him, they go off him. What harm though, it always left me with more to choose from. He was always green when I would be dancing with girls in Regan's. But sure it never meant much to me. I was only ever trying to have a bit of craic, to hold up the O'Leary name, be social and charming, like Mammy and Daddy were. When I first met you, I never ever saw a man so jealous. The secret to women is that they want to be treated like people, not tameable creatures. That's the secret that Tom doesn't seem to know.

Anna pretends not to have seen either of the girls. Did you hear Tom stifling his sigh? Annoyed at her already, but not wanting to seem annoyed. When I stand back and look at my siblings objectively, they're fairly entertaining.

'How's the form? How are ye now? How are ye getting on?'

Tom offers little greetings to everybody he passes, dying for somebody to stop and answer him. And then, to my surprise, somebody does. A woman and her husband. The Moores, I learn, whose house we are in.

'Where's the small girl?'

'Ye keep the house gorgeous.'

'Did ye get something to drink?'

'Áine, is it? Annie? Anna! Sorry, Anna.'

'Everybody is coming in drowned wet!'

I don't know why I assumed we would be standing alone in the corner all night. Tom has been out in the town every day, working his magic. Of course he knows people, of course the hosts want to talk to him. I watch their back and forth, smiling where they need me to, nodding and mumbling along without really adding much. Ciara Moore puts a drink in my hand, she touches my shoulder. Warm. It's good to be touched. It's good to remember that there is life beyond the cottage, the family and the past I've been stuck in.

A little crowd appears to have gathered around us. Tom has made us interesting. I suppose he is waiting to be asked for a song.

'Little Peggy is around somewhere. Jack is two years below me, and Anna is a year below him. Our mother had her hands full, God rest her.'

People are laughing around us, chatting around us, to us and about us. I'm sure that until Tom mentioned our mother, half of the locals were still wondering which one of us was married to Anna and which of us was Peggy's father. A part of me would like to clear my throat and let them know that any chance I had of getting married is dead and buried, and as far as anyone is concerned, I am Peggy's mother and father.

'There's a book club, Annie, you might like to come along.'

A woman says to Anna, and I see her biting her cheeks and looking straight through the woman, not responding. When she has the chance, Anna slips away to the other side of the room.

And while watching Anna, I catch the Doyle girl looking at me again. Whispering to her sister and looking right at me. The flood of heat. The thrill that I wanted to ignore comes back to me. Instincts re-emerge. What she sees in me, I don't know. You used say I was like a hare. That was fine at the time, when I had found a woman who wanted a man like a hare. If any of these strangers meet me on the road home tonight, they'll be telling everybody they saw the púca; a ghoul. The state of me. The perfect way you used to laugh at me. Ah darling, would you ever laugh at me?

What I wouldn't give to be back in Kilmarra now, instead of looking at a room of strangers. For the first time, I wonder why Tom chose Ballycrea as our new home. Or whether any thought went into it at all. Maybe he just closed his eyes and pointed to a village on the map. Maybe he let the pony lead us wherever she wanted. And with all these people around, potential friends and pretty girls, I realise that I don't know how to start again. I don't know what to do.

'Miltown.'

Tom tells his little crowd.

'We were there all our lives, until our mother died. We packed up then. It was just too much.'

He is offered sad sighs. A woman's hand comes to his arm.

'The Lord have mercy on the dead.'

Anna watches from across the room. I've never heard of Miltown. Why is he making things up? Why is he pretending to be completely heartbroken over Mammy, when he hasn't cried a tear for her since 1956? The dirty liar. I wait for the mention of you, for the real reason we're here. But it doesn't come.

With a sharp breath, I realise he won't say your name. He isn't going to mention you at all. Somehow, he is happy to let you go. Suddenly I feel sick for looking at the Doyle sisters.

We've had this conversation a hundred times. I know we agreed it would be better if nobody knew about the way that you died. I just didn't realise that meant we would pretend you never existed. I didn't think there would be any harm in acknowledging you. Maybe I was stupid to think we would go on remembering you the way we have. And I understand what he is trying to do. To get us all to move on. But I don't know. I still call you mine.

I try to settle it in my mind. But it doesn't settle. In just a few words, Tom has made you a secret. And in my silence, I have allowed it. In this moment, I hate Tom.

Anna

HE HAS THEM ALL IN the palm of his clammy hand. The meagre social skills I once had seem to have vanished, but not Tom's. The desperation is radiating off him, but they all appear to like him. It was always Jack who did the charming, before.

Once, we were a very social family. Mammy and Daddy used to always be out. I remember the smell of Mammy's nail varnish taking over the air as they were getting ready to leave. She always did her nails last. Peach Gloss. It made her look so grand. She never cared that other women thought she had notions, or that it would all chip off the next day when she was setting the fire or pulling up weeds. My Mammy had standards.

'Turf, back home I was the turf man. But there's plenty other things I'm capable of.'

'It isn't often we get a capable man around here!'

Even after Daddy died, she kept herself very well, and she was always out. None of that black shawl business. Mammy was only a widow on pension day. By that time, the style had changed, but she still wore her Peach Gloss. Now and again, at Easter and in the summer, she would paint my nails. I was old enough to buy my own nail polish then, but I always liked her doing it. She was gentle.

After she died, I really wanted to be a Peach Gloss sort of woman.

To keep it up in her honour, I suppose. But I wore it only once, because the sight of it made me cry like a little child. My hands were so like Mammy's, but also, so frightfully different. A taunting reminder that she would never really be close to me again.

The Peach Gloss I had was left in Kilmarra. I can still smell it, though. Still see the sheen of it on her nails. Your nails were always bitten. Jack never seemed to mind. I tried to tell you a few times about how nice Mammy's nails were. But you didn't take it as advice. You just smiled and told me how good I was to remember little details about my mother.

'And will you give us a song tonight, Tom?'

'Betty, I'll give ye a song when Mrs Moore wants the house cleared!'

I was never much like her when I was out; tonight has confirmed that hasn't changed. Mammy was a real social woman. She could talk to anyone, you know, and everyone wanted to talk to her. The same gift that you had. The same gift Tom is trying to prove he has now. That Jack seems to have lost track of. Mammy knew the name of every person in every family in Kilmarra. I found I could barely make it past small talk. I stand with my handbag clutched to my side, and watch as the conversations happen around me.

Although it feels like another life entirely, it really was very recently that we were known by everyone. That Tom had a career. That Jack had the town in his pocket. Yes, it was all so recent. How quickly things change. How well you know.

Another woman goes to sing. The same one who asked Tom for a song. Was it Betty he called her? I don't want to stare at her, but where else am I to look? She rocks back and forth while she sings. These slow, minute movements. Almost imperceptible.

It puts me in mind of you. But doesn't everything? Always singing. While you were clearing up after the dinner, and running around in the yard with Peggy, and reading the paper to your father. Humming away to yourself. I remember thinking that you were such a beautiful singer, but looking back, maybe you were just persistent.

It doesn't need to be considered, this woman before me really is a beautiful singer. Somehow she is able to put emotions into the tune. Maybe she is a professional.

While I watch her, I feel the heat of the fire warming up my damp clothes. Stay here, Anna, don't float off. I look around at everyone, to keep myself from drifting into faraway thoughts. The shapes of people come in and out of my eyeline, but this singing woman always comes back. Betty, did he say?

I listen dutifully, slowly, lightly tapping my foot along with her, and wonder why music has never moved me in the way that it supposedly moves other people. I always seem to be one emotion away from what everyone else is feeling. I want to be on the same page as everyone. To have an identical experience of reality. To be moored to the same comprehensible and solid emotions as they are. I wish I didn't have to float away to safe places all the time; to you in the bath, or Mammy painting my nails. I wish I understood enough about my feelings to feel safe anywhere.

Peggy finds us again, she is frenzied over the puppies. Jack bends down to lift her and sits her on the table, whispering something in her ear. For a moment I am so deep in this woman's curling voice that I forget to shush him. Just for a moment, I forget a lot of things. Almost everything.

Black hair lit by the fire, like countless black electricity wires you'd see in Cork city. And her cheeks reddened by the heat; freckled red apples, fit for horses. I smell the rain drying on my dress. Right now, I don't feel like a novelty at all. I am just a collection of senses, near a song. A singing woman. Amber coloured. Damp and warm. Perhaps this is what it is to be moved.

When the song ends, that feeling goes with it. And it is replaced by the heat of tears, as I remember all of the things that I let myself forget.

A ripple of clapping for her, Tom's the loudest. He's delighted that she has stopped, so he can get back to talking.

A new surge of confidence comes to me. All night I've heard about this supposed life we had in Miltown. And with nothing to gain or lose, I start telling people the little details I pick up.

'You've probably never heard of Miltown. Or maybe you have. I don't know, it's only small.'

'Would that be Miltown Malbay, in Clare?'

I have no idea. What county did Tom say we are supposed to be from?

'I better check on the small girl.'

I say, and turn back to Peggy, asking her question upon question about the puppies. Leaving somebody who I pulled into conversation all alone. Mortifying. I'm sure it's fine though. There must be a hundred Miltowns in Ireland. I'm not questioned any further. 'Tis mad; whatever we tell the locals, they believe. How easily it's all washed away. My whole life and everyone I ever loved, all gone. Sorry, girl.

The night ends up being much longer than the hour Tom promised it would be. Of course it does. That's the way that things go with Tom. It's always just a little bit longer, I always need to try just a little bit harder. It's always just a little bit different from what he said it would be. Well, it got me out of the house. It made me a little bit less afraid of Ballycrea. Now I've seen the town and met its people, I know they're all ordinary. Ordinary thoughts and opinions, more or less. None of them with any extraordinary power over me.

It ends with myself and himself up at home, standing in the frame of the back door, looking out onto the empty night. He told me to wait until the others were gone to sleep, so we could talk, just the pair of us. Many of my nights have ended this way.

Peggy curls up like a cat against Jack. Over my shoulder I see them, sound asleep. I wonder when she will grow out of that. I wonder when he will let her.

Only myself and Tom, watching as the wind moves through the long grass on the hills. Rising and falling. Like standing at the sea's edge.

He produces Daddy's pipe from his pocket. Although he likes to think he doesn't have any vices, one pint and that pipe is stuck to his mouth. Oh, Tom has vices alright. The dark of the night and the depth of the silence come together, creating the perfect stage for us to address them. If I only had the nerve to start, I'd stand here all night, confronting Tom.

He offers me the pipe. You used to hate smoking. Once you told me that the smell of smoke reminded you of old men. That's when Jack gave up the fags. He was so cross for two weeks after, do you remember? I wished he would just take it back up. But he was mad to impress you.

Tom is smiling at me, as though everything is fine. Right now, I want to dig up all that he has done. To exhume the memories he has buried, peel back their flesh and have him witness their bones; not even beginning to decay. But he smiles at me. And I don't have the nerve to stand up to him. I take the pipe.

'You'd all that Miltown business nicely stitched together, hadn't you?'

My feeble attempt at confronting him falls flat. I want to mention Mammy. He shrugs his shoulders. I pull on the pipe.

'Sure 'twas just to move us along. To cover the tracks. That's all.'

When will Tom stop trying to cover tracks? When will he settle into the life he has created for himself?

'I hope you're okay, Anna.'

He hasn't asked me that for a while. It makes me forget about what we had been talking about, about what I have been feeling. It makes me think that I might not be okay; or at least, that I might not appear okay. Sure why else would he be asking? I'm not sure what he wants me to say, or how honest he wants me to be. So I just nod, and try to keep my face from souring. But I feel it happening. Slowly, the smoke leaves my mouth, white against the night sky.

Of course, I know that it's hard to come up with pleasing answers for where our parents are, or why none of us are married. Stringing together a simple, plain backstory for ourselves will probably help us more than the truth would. Sever the cord. Keep looking ahead. I understand what he is doing, he has helped me to understand it many times. It just hits harder than expected when the plan is actioned and is no longer only a thought.

'Don't worry about it, girl. It's done now. Let the locals spread it, and we just go along with it. It's a small enough detail, really. It won't be hard.'

Miltown is forgivable. Even your erasure, I could come to forgive. But what he said about Mammy sits like a stone inside me. I can't move past it. Of all people for Tom to pull into his self-serving tangle of lies. You'd think that after everything, I'd be rather numbed. But moments like this remind me that I am an endless, expanding collection of exposed nerves. Constantly being touched and trapped.

'I'm sorry if I upset you.'

He sounds genuine, and yet, I wonder whether I should believe him. I link his arm, squeezing, and give him back the pipe. I hope he'll understand, I hope he'll hear me without talking. Please, Tom, let's just enjoy the quiet.

The breathing of the world, the howling of a far-off dog. On a hill in the distance, a house flickers its lights, winking at us both. And before us, two or three more houses light up. Life everywhere.

It's always like this with Tom. We are always building to a crescendo that is never reached. I fall away from the fight, just like he wants me to. And it remains within me, dull and deep, like a toothache.

Thinking over it again, I manage to find the humour in it. He is so eager to move on from the past that he has created a second past for us, and now we have two of them to manage. Beyond this, there will be no more mention of Miltown. Tom will sort it out with Peggy and Jack. It will just be another thing that we never talk about.

I take in the night. I watch the navy world come alive with electric light. The cold air and the taste of it. For the longest time, the only constant in my life has been the dark blue of the night sky. Looking down on me as I woke up. Filling the gaps around me as I slept. The edges of clouds, the edges of my body, coloured navy. Inescapable, soothing darkness.

A sudden tingle starts in the back of my mind and races to the front. That woman's singing voice echoes within me. Acting as a harmony to each of my thoughts. The shapes of her mouth. The flex of her tongue. Only something to think of. A fizzing thought to end the night on. Yes, for a long while there was nothing besides the navy sky.

But tonight, stars.

Betty

'AH GIRL, WHAT KIND ARE they, arriving in a donkey and trap?'

Ciara runs the Hoky over the carpet, not looking up as she speaks to me. Since her guests arrived, she has been waiting for them to leave so that we could dissect them. To Ciara Moore, the O'Learys are nothing but a bit of fresh meat. Once she gets the measure of them, her interest will dry up.

'It was a pony, not a donkey.'

I feel I need to stand up for them. I can't say why. The majority of Ballycrea has been subject to Ciara's opinions, it's harmless really. She helps the housekeeper at the local convent most afternoons, making tea and sandwiches for the nuns. Her way of making up for all of her hissing gossip, I suppose.

'Small difference, what year are they living in? Very strange people, I think. I'm staying away.'

Of course, she isn't going to stay away from the O'Learys. Nobody is. Nobody could, in a town of this size. When she realises I'm not going to indulge her, Ciara changes tack.

'You're very good to stay and help with the cleanup.'

From the moment I walked in the door this evening, we both knew that I would be staying late to clean up with her. When the crowd started to thin, Bill and John stepped outside. I suppose they think

they're doing us a favour by keeping out of the way. At my house it would be the very same, with Ciara staying back to help, and the two lads stood outside.

'He wasn't bad looking, was he? The oldest lad, Tom.'

She smiles, watching me from the corner of her eye. As though her husband isn't only a wall away from her.

'I thought you were staying away?'

Tom wasn't bad looking, but they're all good-looking when compared to John Moore.

'That child was only gorgeous. She was weak for the pups, Ciara.'

I say, carrying the chairs back over to the kitchen table. It's hard to put an age on the little girl. It's hard to put an age on any of them, really, they all look a little bit older than they say they are.

'Well, it's the first time I was grateful for any of those pups. Otherwise what would the poor girl have done all evening? What were they thinking, bringing her out so late?'

The youngest of Ciara's children is seventeen now, and heading for Bessborough in September. I suppose she has long forgotten the years when she would walk through the square with three of four children hanging off her. I suppose she feels fit to judge the O'Learys, now her own children are finished with her. Having never had a child myself, I feel it isn't my place to speak.

'They're probably up to ninety with moving house and didn't think. Or maybe she's too young to be left on her own. Tom is a nice lad, alright.'

'He was tense though, on edge like.'

'If you've nothing nice to say, Ciara, then say nothing at all.'

I don't know where I picked up this way of talking like a teacher. Like a mother. She puts the Hoky away and folds her arms, sighing.

'He was a nice fella. A bit too glad to talk about himself, but he was grand.'

I hear Bill outside, laughing with John. Smoking, no doubt. I've asked him a hundred times not to smoke.

'I never had a chance to talk to the other two. Are they twins or what?'

'They could be. Ah, but the child was beautiful, wasn't she?'

Rather than answering me, she lets a silence sit between us. The sort of silence that anticipates somebody saying something awkward.

I wouldn't say I've taken it too far. She takes a breath in, but lets it out without speaking. She is building up to something. How embarrassing, I really hope I haven't taken it too far talking about the child. I hope we aren't about to dredge up all my failings once more. The cleanup is more or less done when she comes out with what she is holding in.

'Do you think Bill would have a few hours' work to give Tom? John says he sounds desperate enough.'

All that anticipation, for this? I suppose not everything is about children, having and not having them. I suppose Ciara doesn't pick up on all these subtleties, the way I would have expected her to by now. Or perhaps she does, and knows better than to mention them.

'Well, he could probably give him a few hours alright, but not enough work to support the family. I wouldn't want to insult him.'

'Sure three of them are adults, can't they all get a bit of work?'

How easily we move on from the little girl. Although a part of me can't move on from her. A child without a mother, such a shame.

'What did you make of your one, Anna?'

Ciara asks me.

'Era, she seems harmless enough.'

Jack

THE EVENING SKY HAS BEEN brewing all day, and now it sits, lilac and dense on the town. Low and close. It feels like, in a minute, the sky will leak in the window and flood the cottage. The Sacred Heart of Jesus framed next to the door. The flame of his heart. The black inferno in his eyes. And I, every day, scalded by this heat. Tom, every day, blessing himself and sending a kiss to the heart. Anna, sighing into the electric bulb. Peggy sits alongside me, doing her lessons. I want to help her, but she doesn't seem to need it. But I can no longer let my eyes drift between the impending sky and his burning heart.

'Explain these sums to me, will you, Peg? You're a great girl for the maths.'

If I can't help her, perhaps she can help me. She really is so clever. I hope that it will carry her out of Ballycrea. She is too focused to answer me, it seems.

Anna is huffing her way around the room as though she can hardly breathe. Daddy used to say she was prone to tantrums. You'd think at twenty-six she'd be grown out of that. You'd think at twenty-eight, I'd have the nerve to tell her to cop on. A part of me would like to give her the attention she's after. I'd like to say what we are all thinking, and shine a hideous spotlight on her. One so bright and so focused, it would reduce her to ash.

Tom sits next to me. She puts a bowl of porridge before him. The same colour as your hair.

'How's the head now?'

I ask him, hoping to get away from my own thoughts. Maybe he has something funny to say about last night. Maybe he met some nice people. He's the one who wanted to go out, after all. But he ignores me. I'll try Peggy again.

'Tell us about school, Peg, what kind is your teacher?'

Although she has already told me twice, Tom and Anna don't seem to have asked her about her new school at all. I want Peggy to feel important, because she is a part of the family. I don't want her to grow up feeling like a consequence that we were burdened with, the way she is so often treated. I want somebody to talk about something, so that I'm not responsible for my thoughts. Just as she starts to speak, Tom cuts across her.

'Daddy's birthday today.'

He says softly, nodding to Anna's back, he pushes his bowl away and lights a cigarette. I squeeze Peggy's hand and realise that all day, I didn't think of Daddy. I forgot. Isn't that scary? I suppose that's a part of moving on, isn't it? I got over Mammy and Daddy at a normal rate, I did. There is so much standing in the way of me getting over you.

I suppose Daddy's birthday is what's wrong with Anna. Hopefully now that Tom has mentioned it, the sting has been taken out.

'That's right. Bittersweet.'

She says without much feeling, probably just something that she has learned to say. She puts my bowl of porridge down for me.

'Nearly sixteen years he's dead, imagine.'

Tom exhales, not caring whether Peggy understands.

'God help us, hard to imagine.'

I miss Daddy, I really do. It seems that, these days, all I do is miss things. And I miss so much. The smell of the fresh, cold morning air in Kilmarra. The sky in June, raspberry-coloured sunsets bursting with rain down over us. Your sister's plum pudding and my fingers trembling on the buttons up the back of your dress.

The most exquisite green grass, filling a thousand fields before me. My parents' graves. Having potential. Having patience. Your shadow on mine. Daffodils on the kitchen table in spring. The wreath on your door at Christmas. And you. Above everything, you.

Today, I miss my father. And suddenly, I miss the caramel irises that struck me yesterday and reminded me that I am a man.

'It was a good night, wasn't it?'

I try again to keep some momentum going, so that I am not lost to memories for a minute longer. Let's try to have some fun, and talk about last night. Let's hear why Tom left you out of our story.

Anna starts to cry. Quiet at first, but she allows herself to get louder. And then she encourages herself to get more animated. With such a fresh sadness, it's as though Daddy only died this morning, and not all those years ago. Almost as though she knows that I'm going to mention you, and needs a way to avoid it. They think I should be over you by now. How could I get over you when I'm hardly even allowed to mention you?

Anna was so happy coming to bed last night, whispering to Peggy that she was excited about Ballycrea. Look at her now. Tom lets out a big, rumbling sigh. The type he lets out before a fight.

'I've made four friends at school already.'

Peggy tries, and I feel bad for her. All this up and down, she is probably seasick from our unpredictability.

I remember when she was only a thought. Before she became a living person. When the big shame came over our family. Daddy was seven years dead, and Mammy was newly pregnant. I was nineteen then.

It was all too much to handle at the time. Tom went off the deep end when he found out. Ballistic doesn't begin to describe it. He was determined to stick Mammy in a convent, like she wasn't our Mammy at all. There were long, late nights spent fighting back and forth about it. About her. For Tom, it was simple. Mammy had committed an unforgivable sin, and ladened us with an unthinkable shame. The only solution was to send her to the nuns. I understood that, I suppose I still do. But there was something about it that I just couldn't move past: she was our Mammy. The same woman who changed our nappies and fed us and looked after us after Daddy died. Who were we to exercise any authority over her? If another family had made the decision, I could have justified it for them no bother. But I couldn't do it with my own mother.

Obviously, Tom felt differently. He was never warm with Mammy again. I suppose he couldn't cope with the idea that she was a person, a woman, beyond his mother. Beyond his control. Look, it didn't sit right with me either, but I knew we had to get on with it. I was better able to navigate the situation. Better able to take on the shame. But it took over Tom. Existing under the immense weight of that shame, I later realised, was existing under the immense weight of the church. 'Twas around that time I fell out of step with god and his son.

If she wasn't going to the convent, the only other option was for Tom to stand in complete control of her. Making her pay for her mistake every day. He once told me that her situation had caused difficulty with his deep-set belief that anybody can be granted salvation. If he had dug a little deeper, he might have realised that the real difficulty was believing that he could be the one to grant that salvation. As he demonstrated on Mammy.

It hit Anna the heaviest. Seventeen years of age, always the baby of the family, suddenly, not the baby anymore. It's safe to say she has spent her life looking for something to fill the void of Mammy's undivided attention.

She sat permanently at the foot of Mammy's bed for those nine months, and has not forgiven Tom. I doubt she ever will. I doubt he particularly cares, when he accomplished what he set out to do: bury the shame of Mammy's transgressions deep, deep in the ground. She lived for seven hours after Peggy was born. Tom refused to call for a priest or a doctor.

And while he might feel some regret for the way he treated her during her last months, I can't imagine his stance on the whole thing has changed much. A part of him will still be ashamed of her.

I was never particularly close with Tom again; until you died, and he was one of the few people who could take my weight. My forgiveness in exchange for his support. It got us past a rough patch. It's bringing us back to each other.

When I think back to that time, I remember the stress of being found out the most of all. Voices in the pub asking where Mammy was gone. Rumours that she was in hospital, or in hiding, or with cousins in Tipperary. Father Lynch peppering his services with the outcomes for unmarried mothers, the fate of bastard babies. Our feeble attempts at pulling together a story, wondering whether it was easier to lie for Mammy or just cast her aside. I wish I knew you then. I wish you had been around, to be good to my mother in the ways that I never was.

We never found out about Peggy's father. Whoever he was, he never owned up to it when Mammy was alive, so what good would it have done him to own up to it when she had died? I had my suspects, of course I had, but my nerve always buckled before I could confront anyone. Anna has still never acknowledged that this man exists somewhere in the world. As though Peggy was born of some immaculate conception. As though our mother wasn't capable of sin. That's the sort of attitude that Mammy wouldn't have discouraged. That pregnancy really was made to be the shame of her life. She was the pious sort of woman who might have seen dying in childbirth as a harsh, but ultimately fit, punishment. It's all so heavy to think about. 'Tis times like this I would like to find a bit of solace in god. Oh well.

'Put on the radio there, Peg.'

I say, unable to cope with the silence anymore. Unable to think anymore. Let me be the child's father. I'll look after her. She leans into the radio, fiddling with the dials, trying to escape the static.

'Era Tom, that thing is fecked.'

'Why don't you fix it, so?'

The form is bad. Maybe tomorrow, I could go down to the town with him, and we could inquire about renting a television. Then, we could bring the whole world into our house, and bring ourselves into 1965, and leave everything that has passed behind us. I think Tom would be glad to hear that I want to come into town with him. I think they would all be glad to get a television. Maybe I'll ask him now. If everybody gets riled up over it he won't be able to say no.

But just as I open my mouth to speak, he puts out his fag and gets down on his knees, and calls us for the rosary.

'Would anyone go down to the pub?'

I ask, willing to go and socialise to avoid praying.

'We offer this rosary for our father, Joseph O'Leary, on his birthday.'

With steel in his voice, he begins his show. I've no choice but to get down on my knees and join him. And the girls have no choice but to follow me.

This ritual puts me back in your house, something I know I'm better off avoiding. Praying the rosary or the angelus, with one of your sisters leading and your father taking it all at a different pace to the rest of us. Ivory candle lit and dripping. White rosary beads from Knock Shrine passing through your fingers. Cream walls. Yellow flame. All leading me back to blonde.

I open my eyes and find myself very much in Ballycrea. Anna grits her teeth. The sky behind her churns. Peggy quickly closes her eyes and lowers her head, hoping I didn't catch her. Praying every word so carefully. I wish you hadn't taught her that. Lately, Tom has her saying extra prayers every night, trying somehow to wash away the guilt of her birth.

I wish that I had something else worth teaching her. A shame I never took on a hobby or a trade. But I never needed anything like that before. It was always enough to go out in the van with Tom, and down to the pub with the boys, and call into you in the evenings. I didn't need to know anything when my life was perfect.

You were the one who knew everything. Happily teaching Peggy to play the fiddle, and keeping Anna in the group with your friends, always calming her down. Indulging Tom in his deep conversations, making him feel clever. And giving my small life meaning.

We reach the end of the rosary, and while Tom remains in silent prayer, Peggy opens her eyes again and looks to me. She wants to be told that it's over.

The poor child is exhausted, but she won't go to bed without the rest of us. I suppose she might be afraid in the new house. When I nod at her, she rushes off her knees and to the sink, where she strokes the chicken.

'How about that drink?'

Anna says, reaching for her handbag. I forgot that I offered to go to the pub.

'There's a bottle of something behind the oats, I'm sure.'

Now that I don't need to get out of praying, going to the pub is the last thing I want. Somebody has to bring Peggy to bed and clear up after the dinner. I know Anna never asked to be a mother, but she is the nearest thing that Peggy has to one. I wish she would act like it. It's disappointing that she hasn't taken to the role better. It's a shame that I cannot be everything that Peggy needs. She deserves a proper mother, not Anna's cold indifference, not my male shortcomings. Little Peggy, my Peigín. She deserves an awful lot more than she gets.

Anna sighs, seemingly upset we aren't going out. Since when does she want to be out and about? I can't keep track of her. All I want to do for the evening is think of you. It's terrible, and I'm sure you'd hate it, but all I do is think of you, darling. Of you in the morning, and you in the afternoon. You in your black dress, that used to move like water around you. You sprawled across the sofa, your knees apart, forgetting your manners. Of where you are now, and where you are not. To tell the truth, I think of you far more than I ever did when you were still here. So much that sometimes, it's like you never left. If I put my hand out in the air, I swear I almost feel the swell of you against it. I remember you so, so well.

Or rather, I remember you often. And I worry sometimes, because I can't be sure which of my memories are true to life, and which are just lovely exaggerations that I have conjured up to keep myself going.

Let me say something awful. Sometimes I wonder if I love you more now than I would if you were still here. If your memory is a better woman to me than you ever really could be. Because a memory is a very easy-going thing, you know? A memory can't be let down, and it can't let me down. I loved you, sure you know I loved you, I just wonder if I love you better now.

You'd kill me, but if you were here now, I'm sure that I'd forget to appreciate you. I would probably have my head turned by pretty girls now and again. I'd probably stay out drinking with the boys and leave you at home, alone. I'd spend money where I shouldn't, and I would disappoint you. What had we, two summers together? Two years. Long enough to know you were my soulmate, not long enough to make a mess of things. Oh, all the beautiful ways we would have let each other down. Isn't it silly? I want so much to have the chance to disappoint you.

Anna

A LACE CURTAIN OF FOG is pulled over the town. It makes it hard to know what time it is. It must be about two weeks since we arrived in Ballycrea, because we've been to confession twice and the market twice.

Tom puts a bowl of veg down for me to wash, humming to himself. He seems to get happier every day. I wonder how happy he will get before he bursts.

While waiting for his enthusiasm to infect me, I pass the time watching the way the light changes on the fields and feeding oats to the pony. It doesn't really make me happy, but it keeps me going.

I've started walking down to the town with him; to pass the time, to stop him from asking. I've come to accept that we are in Ballycrea to stay. At least until we get a car, because the only way I'd go back over the Healy Pass on the pony and cart again would be in my coffin. But sure I haven't even a bed at home, I've no hope of seeing a car pull up anytime soon.

I haven't let Tom take the pony out again. 'Tis all cars now, he knows that. Everybody else has one. Why shouldn't we have the fine things that everyone else has? Why shouldn't we have the life that Tom pretends we have? He better get a bit of work soon, so that he can buy us things, and stop humming around the house with all his happiness, and leave me alone.

As deeply as I dreaded it, being in town is okay. I don't mind it. There isn't a great deal in the town to mind, to be honest. A few pubs, a few shops, a tailor and a little library, all of which double up as people's homes. The convent on the hill, thick, broad walls that you couldn't penetrate with a cannonball; each window a dark eye, watching. A lot of grey and white houses with colourful doors and windowsills. A man fixes some eroded bricks with cement. A woman waters pink flowers in hanging baskets outside her door. They're keen on improvement, it seems. I could find reasons to dislike it, but really it's no different from any other place. Wherever we ended up, I would have felt this way, homesick for a place that is no longer home. This is home now.

Something I cannot get used to is the fish. Boats with chipped paint and half worn names bringing it into Ballycrea every day. Big crates of it on the pier, lofted raw through the town, wafting their sea smell all around. Imagine how bad it looks when I gag as the fishermen walk by. I'm meant to be blending in here, assimilating with the locals and their ways, not bringing up bile as they pass.

It's just that I'm not used to fish, that's all. We usen't ever have fish in Kilmarra, not even on a Friday. Mammy was allergic to the scales, or so she said. I never questioned it. I never questioned her; not about anything. But it's what's popular here, and so Tom insists that we buy fish today.

'When in Ballycrea, do as the locals do.'

My god, he is incessant. I let him into the fishmonger on his own. I can't imagine how well I'd fare in there. It strikes me that I never walk around the town; I always wait outside whatever building Tom is in. They will think there is something wrong with my legs.

The fish is wrapped in paper and landed in my hands, and I can do nothing to get rid of it. I wonder how much he spent on it. This reeking dead thing, heavy in my arms, no doubt leaving a smell on the sleeves of my coat. And even though this is a fish town, and they are all eating it every day, I'm embarrassed by it. They'll all think the smell is off me. Imperfections aren't charming on me the way that they were on you. A dirty face or sweat stains were things that you somehow managed to make endearing. I'm sure if you were here now, smelling of uncooked fish, it would only add to your appeal.

Just when I think it's time to go home, Tom stops us, insisting that he introduces himself to Brendan O'Donovan, who he wishes he had spoken to the other night.

A flock of pretty women pass me by, as I am suddenly left alone in the street. And I feel each of their eyes move over me. Strawberry blondes and brunettes, all a little bit younger than me. I want to go where they are going. I want to be one in a two, and I want to know what they think of me. Let's not bother with all of the reasons that I'm one on my own. As they pass me by, in their perfect, shiny pairs, I feel more lonely, more embarrassed, than I have for a long time.

It reminds me of you and all your countless friends. It was so rare to catch you on your own. Wherever I saw you, at the window of the butcher's, in the doorway of the pub, from the field behind your house, there was a sister or friend in your shadow. I was so embarrassingly insecure to see you in constant company, and to be a solitary thing, viewing it all from a distance. I can admit that now.

Those passing, pretty women remind me of all the friendships that I've misplaced. Those close connections that always fell short of lasting. Where are all of those girls now? Do they remember me ever?

Before they are out of sight, one of the women turns to look at me again. Only a quick glance, but I feel a bolt of urgency strike me. I want her to know I've caught her looking, to dethrone her, to humiliate her. I pull a face at her. It's all I can think to do. How juvenile. But then, isn't she juvenile too, walking around with her clique, staring me down? She turns away, probably unsure if I really did pull a face, or if she's just imagining it. I bless myself and say sorry to the air.

The boys have told me that tunnelling this far into my thoughts doesn't do me any good. I'm always being told what not to do, without being given alternatives.

Tom comes back after talking to Brendan. At long last, we make our way home, the road rising and dipping below us so frequently that I feel I am out on the sea. The big dead fish in my arms does not help.

'I met Bill Nevan there with Brendan. Did you meet him the other night?'

He asks, fully knowing I won't remember who Bill Nevan is.

'He's going to call up this evening with his wife. They'll eat dinner with us, we can play cards maybe. A dinner party!'

A dinner party? 'Twas very far from dinner parties he was reared. Where does he come up with it? I don't know how to respond. And then I realise that even if I did know, there wouldn't be any point in responding. Tom has made his plan. There is no backing out now. These strangers will come to our home and judge us and inspect us, and I will have to make them feel welcome while they do it.

As I sit down and try to write out a plan for the evening, I feel Jack's heavy eyes on me. Staring at me. Or perhaps, staring through me. Perhaps he was already deep in thought, focused on some point in the distance all day, and I sat in his eyeline. I write down what food I know we have, and try to think of a way to stretch it to dinner for six people. The house gets dim around us. We don't have enough of anything, really, unless we all have slightly different meals. Outside,

Peggy is shrieking, laughing, playing with the pony. If she would only shut up for a minute so that I can think. If I could only get a break from Jack's staring.

'That'll be beautiful.'

Tom says, tapping the wrapped fish with his knuckle. And I realise that Tom intends to serve the fish for dinner. If I could only get a break from his relentless happiness and his big notions. If the three of them would just leave me alone.

And then, an unwelcome wave hits me, and I feel that the menstruation I have been dreading and unprepared for has arrived, late. I would have been worried if I wasn't so laughably single.

Wordless, I take myself to the bedroom. I lean against the closed door, so that none of the others can follow me in. What good are two brothers and a child to me now? It can be so hard to be a woman without the company of other women. I'm not sure you ever knew what that was, with all your friends and sisters.

I remember wanting so terribly to know your cycle; to make my own less alienating, just to avoid any trouble, just to feel close to you. Just to have something shared between us.

But it was just another thing you wanted to keep from me. Wasn't it? Just another way to put space between us. And how you loved your precious space.

Maybe it sounds stupid to you, but you don't know what it would have meant to me to feel like somebody was on my side while I was aching and bleeding and alone. Remember, I never had a flood of sisters or friends. I didn't have anybody. But you knew that, didn't you?

How pathetic, I still don't have anybody. Soon, I will need to explain all this to Peggy. Where to begin? You would have done it so gracefully, so easily.

I remember once spying a bloodstain on your bed, and you asking me not to look in your room anymore. Oh my god, I loved you so terribly. Even bleeding, I adored you. I remember the day Jack told me you were pregnant.

The shock of it all. The dread and the fear. The isolation of knowing that I really would have to bleed on my own. That horrible cycle, beginning again.

Jack

A STUPID IDEA. I'VE WARNED them all that this is a stupid idea. But Tom is nearly doubled over with the desperation of having people up to the cottage. To show off how well we're doing and prove what a wonderful family we are. To confirm to himself that people like him. It doesn't matter that I don't want the Nevans calling up; it's all about Tom. Isn't everything? When people include him in a round in the pub, he thinks it's because they are dying for him to drink with them. In Mass, he likes to think that people are shaking his hand because it's an honour. When they say 'peace be with you', what they mean is 'good man, Tom'. He would have invited anybody up this evening. The Moores, the Doyles, any eejit who was willing to be hauled up the hill and sat down at our table. And the Nevans are the fools who said yes. As if we don't have enough to be tense about. It's pure Tom to draw people on us like this, into our home. Right into the eye of the storm.

'Nobody helps me in this house.'

Anna says under her breath, hoping to be heard. Since she came back out of the bedroom, she has been like a dog. Fighting with Tom over the dinner, screeching at Peggy to get out of the kitchen. Wanting to be pitied, I'm sure. But not actually wanting any help, because then we couldn't pity her. She is scrubbing a fork, trying to take all the worn-in stains out of the handle.

'I can help, Anna.'

Peggy says, crowding her. Any minute now, there will come the threat of the wooden spoon. But Anna takes a steadying breath.

'Not now, Peggy. I haven't the patience for you.'

Tom is milling around, setting and resetting the table. Hiding shoes in the bedroom and trying to make the house look both grand and ordinary at once.

'Feck this.'

Anna mutters, dropping the fork into the sink. The house smells of heated fish. And I must admit that I feel sorry for her right now. Since I was born, we have had the same three or four meals on rotation. Boiled veg, tough meat. I'd be sucking the fibres of it out of my teeth for two days following. Mammy never passed any passion for cooking onto Anna. A shame. And now she is expected to prepare a fish, which she has never done before, and serve it as dinner to strangers. Sweat collects in the bow of her top lip. Her eyes, lightly twitching, focus on the stove. I wonder when would be the right time to suggest opening a window and letting the smell out.

'Why do you do all the cooking, Anna, if you don't like it?'

Peggy has a real talent for asking the wrong questions at the wrong time. I would laugh if Anna wasn't so tense. Maybe Peggy is after some attention.

'If I didn't cook, ye would all starve.'

There is gravel in Anna's voice.

'Peg, why don't you go out and pick a few flowers for the table?'

I shoo her out the door, and breathing deeply, I try to remain detached from the stress of preparing for our guests. I want to watch all of this like a film, objectively, not like my real life, unfolding before me. I think that will make it all easier to digest.

Anna

IT ISN'T THAT I THINK cooking makes me indispensable, it's just good to remind them that there are reasons to keep me around. If they ever did think about leaving me somewhere, bumping me off, one of them would need to learn how to cook first. It's like a little alarm I've set for myself.

Tom lands turf onto the fire. I am so hot already. I haven't changed my clothes yet, the Nevans will be here any minute, and my stomach is cramping.

This isn't fair; it was Tom who wanted a dinner party, but it's me who has to create one. With no notice, I've had to cook a fish and clean the half empty cottage into his vision of perfection. Like he's a spoiled child. Like I'm the mother that spoils him.

Peggy bursts through the door, weeds and wildflowers in one hand, the Nevans on her heels. Jesus christ, they're here already. All smiles, letting the fresh air flood in, and I see them. The singing woman, her dark hair, cake tin in her hands. Bringing all this cold, bright air into my home. This is Betty Nevan, and her husband shutting the door after her. And here I am, fish blood in the creases of my fingers, with the threat of a leak from my underwear, damp with sweat.

'Hello all!'

She comes into my cottage like it's her own. Taking off her coat, taking in the layout and all of our things, making long, fluid strides around the room. Her hair catching the yellow of the big light, as she admires what little there is to be admired. Bill starts talking to Tom, she starts talking to me. It's a lot to listen to at once.

'Ye are so good to have us!'

''Tis years since I was up this hill.'

'You've the place lovely, Anna.'

'Who's for a drink?'

For just a moment, I wonder whose home we are in. They move around with such familiarity it's like they once lived here with us. They take their places at the table and talk among themselves. I can't keep up with them and the dinner at once. Peggy nods along with everything, as though she understands. Now and again, she interjects with something about her day, without the manners to know to be quiet when adults are talking. Her shrill little voice, piercing the conversation with news of a baby doll she made out of sticks, or a dress that she saw a girl wearing in town. At her age, she can't separate her interests from everybody else's. But astonishingly, Betty is interested.

'Is that right? A doll from sticks? And an orange dress! Would you wear an orange dress?'

This woman is all but lifting Peggy into her lap.

'Do you know Ciara Moore?'

Peggy asks her, and Betty brightens further.

'I know Ciara Moore well. She's a great friend of mine.'

'Because I was at her house and I met her puppies, and I was hoping to go again.'

'Now that's a lovely idea! I'll sort that out for you, pet.'

Betty puts a hand on Peggy's shoulder, both beaming. For a moment, I am jealous of the attention they are giving each other. Then I realise I have to serve the dinner. And I'm not sure how to announce it. Usually, I would just put the food on the table, but this evening, I feel I need to say something.

'It's my first time attempting fish, so.'

I want to tell them to manage their expectations, or ask them to go easy on me. But I don't know how to finish the sentence; it trails off into a silence for them to absorb.

'I'm sure it's beautiful.'

Bill says, but I see his eyes go straight to the potatoes. I don't even know what to serve fish with. Tom and I fought between cabbage and potatoes for nearly half an hour earlier. Betty smiles at me across the table. With a shaking breath, I smile back at her, and I try to settle. But there is no settling. The Nevans are all questions.

'What do ye make of the town so far?'

'Did ye get down to the strand for a walk yet?'

'And what age are you now, Peggy?'

They are charismatic, the sorts of people who know the right things to say and to ask. And they have a way of nodding along with our inane answers that makes us seem interesting. Bill, talking with the confidence of a politician. Betty's laugh sparkling up out of her throat like Christmas lights. Happily, Tom takes their lead in the conversation. It was never made clear what he wants them to know about us. He gives them a little about Miltown, a little about our parents, and how much we adore being in Ballycrea. All lies.

'Actually, Tom, you might be just the man I need. I've a fence below that I need a hand with. There's cows need to go in there in the morning but 'tis knocked down.'

Jack straightens in his seat. Presumably offended that Tom was asked instead of him. He chews his food for a long time without swallowing, as though he is afraid of it. Jack is afraid of everything.

Tom looks so pleased with himself. There's probably plenty of men in the town who could help Bill out. He's only trying to get the measure of Tom, that's all. To see what sort he is. That must be why they're here tonight. To see what sorts we all are.

'Oh, absolutely, Bill. No bother at all. Sure we can head up after we've eaten.'

I give him a warning look, but he ignores me.

'You wouldn't let the Nevans have their evening?'

I try to sound unbothered.

'Sure you heard him, there's cows need to go in the field in the morning.'

Tom wants to sound relaxed, but his voice is grating; he is annoyed. Betty shifts in her chair. We are making her uncomfortable. He grunts, dismissing me. Can you believe that? Grunting, in front of these special guests of his.

'What do you like to do, Betty?'

I ask, surprised at myself. What a good question to move things along. She is pushing the food around her plate.

'Oh, all sorts, really. Book club, the bingo, sewing circle, I go walking with Ciara Moore most evenings. And then, of course, there's the soaps! Did ye watch *The Riordans*?'

I think she might talk all night if we let her. She doesn't seem to have noticed that we don't have a television. I don't want to be the one to point it out. The chicken comes out from under the dresser. What year are we living in that we have a chicken in the house but no television? I chase it outside, mortified.

'So you'll give me a hand with the fence?'

'I will, of course.'

'We'll be an hour at most.'

Bill says to me, as though they need my permission to go. I want to clarify to them that I am nobody's mother. How controlling, how uptight

I must appear. Tom smirks. It takes all I have not to throw my food at him. Betty looks around, trying to think of something to say to clear the air. I wish I could tell her I love whatever programme she was on about.

I nod at Bill and Tom. Let them put up their stupid fence if they have to. I put a piece of fish in my mouth. To my horror, it's centre cold.

'Oh, Mammy, look at the state of this.'

I say to her under my breath, sighing. Mortified. I can't help it. It's a natural response. I cough to try to cover it up, and hope that Betty and Bill are as polite as they seem. Nobody acknowledges it. They've warned me about this before. It makes them uneasy. Tom clears his throat, pretending he didn't hear me. I can't be bothered with this anymore. I want to ask the Nevans to go home now.

'Ciara Moore is your friend, so? I met her there last night. Lovely woman.'

Jack offers. It turns me cold. Why should Jack have noticed the loveliness of that woman? What has he seen in her? And why would he mention it to her friends?

'She is, yes. She's great for dancing, you know.'

Betty smiles, teeth gleaming.

'Is that right?'

Jack is yet to swallow a bite of food.

'And John, did ye meet John? He's a pure gentleman.'

Peggy scrapes her fork along the plate. Tom flinches.

'I loved *The Riordans*, the best thing on television at the moment.'

'Well, I sold most of the land years ago, 'tis only a very small farm I keep now.'

Rain pelts against the windows.

'Did ye see Lemass went off to meet himself in Belfast?'

'What's the pony's name, Peggy?'

Everything they're saying glides past me, faster than I can manage.

'Christ almighty, when I saw that fence knocked.'

'This isn't cooked at all.'

Little Peggy is the last to speak. It all comes upon me. They all have so much to say, so loudly and so close together. They always have opinions. I'm never allowed to have an opinion. I'm never allowed to be right. They expect me to be a mother, but only give me the respect of a sister. They are all allowed to tell me how they feel, with no regard for how I feel. Before I know it, I have stood up from the table, and I growl at Peggy.

'Don't eat so!'

Betty's hand covers her mouth, and they let me sit in the silence of what I have said. Tom's eyes are black; he might jump across the table at me. Instead, he waits for an inevitable surge of shame to take me, for the collection of thoughts, the apology.

I always say sorry, if they wait long enough. But they won't say sorry for provoking me. Watch. They don't even consider that they might have pushed me. It seems they are always, always looking for an apology, for me to take the blame and make everything better. I have to laugh, or I'll look mad. Slowly, I lower myself back onto my chair.

'I never cooked a fish before. Not once!' I giggle, hoping it will all seem funny. 'Sure how would any of us know that it's cooked?'

Tom is the only one to speak. He puts a hand across the table for me to take, which, for the sake of my dignity, I feel I have to ignore. My god in heaven, was there ever such a disgraceful scene at a dinner party?

'Sorry, Anna, it's lovely.'

And suddenly, I am moved to take his hand. Such gorgeous warmth. Such a gentle soul. I hate to have startled him. I don't want him to fall out with me.

'Don't eat it, pet, you'll get sick. Sorry, lads, I'll clean this away.'

And as I move to take the plates, Betty stands and takes charge, bringing over her cake tin.

'I know what we'll do; we'll have the cake! Folks, life is too short not to have cake for our tea.'

She is laughing, like everything is fine. Maybe it is fine. Maybe it was funny, and I'm just too aware of myself. Loosen up, Anna, take a breath. I throw my eyes up and laugh at myself. It's sometimes unnerving how quickly my moods can shift. I get up and put the water on to boil. Peggy bounces in her seat while Betty presents the cake, shaking off my outburst. In fairness to her, Peggy never gets too upset. Something in me wants to let everybody know that Daddy was dead with years when she was born. I don't know why this thought comes to me. A shifting mood; ammunition, I think. We've had a few discussions about whether we should tell Peggy all this. While I think it might do her good to know the truth, Jack says it's best not to have a child know just how extravagant their original sin is.

''Tis all fish here, isn't it? I suppose I better get used to cooking it.'

I hoot with laughter. It's best to keep it all light and nice, and not pay attention to Peggy, in case she brings something bad out of me.

And then Betty gives me the biggest, warmest smile. She saved me this evening. It would have been easy for her to walk out with Bill and tell the whole parish that I am a madwoman. But she is kind, and gentle, and she brought cake.

'You wouldn't come up to ours with Tom this evening? I might show you a few tricks.'

She asks, winking, smiling, glowing, and handing me a plate of her cake.

'You know, I heard in Japan they eat all their fish raw. Did you ever hear that?'

Bill asks, trying to make us all feel better. Aren't they good? I breathe in all the fresh, bright air she brought into my cottage. This evening, I'd follow Betty anywhere.

Tom

WE STAND FACING THE FENCE, myself and Bill. The rain turns to wet mist around us, cold air holds onto me. It looks like it was flattened by an animal, whatever happened to the fence. I don't want to ask.

Why did he ask me to help him, of all men in Ballycrea? I don't want to ask that, either. I don't want to ask him anything at all, in case I offend him and he changes his mind and sends me home. I stand stiff, still and silent. There is still some colour in the sky. The sticky evening light, clinging to me. Honey on my coat, light that will stay with me all night. A sure sign of spring. Bill stands against the fog. His silhouette the shape of a prayer.

'Was it Ballygarron ye said ye came from?'

Bill asks, as he heaves up a plank. I take its weight from him.

'Miltown. We were all born there.'

I am almost alarmed at how naturally I have taken to lying. I hardly know Bill at all, and yet I know I should not be lying to him.

'My father's cousins were in Miltown until 1934. Long gone now.'

A stone in my throat. He is coming too close to my story. How do I remain grateful while telling him to mind his own business? He goes on.

'They had the same idea as yourselves, I suppose. And who have ye left there now?'

'Nobody, really. Our parents are both dead.'

He softens. He understands.

'God rest them.'

It feels like he is about to ask more. Like he wants to make me feel comfortable, and so wants me to talk about my parents. Nothing would make me less comfortable.

It's a funny thing, because if Bill was to ask me what made Daddy and Mammy so special, I wouldn't know what to tell him. I don't have a definite reason, or any particular examples. Really, they were just people, probably no better than anybody else. But there was a short time where they were perfect. Better than anybody had ever been. Before I grew up, I suppose, and realised that even parents are people. Capable of sin and disappointment.

Oh, but there was a time when Daddy's warm hands were always open, and he had the answer for every question. Always making me laugh, always teaching me something, making me better. There was a time, however distant it now seems, when Mammy smelled of baking, and was never too busy for me. When she was the light I looked to, never dimming. Sweet patience and relief, she took all my trouble off me.

And while that time came to a crashing halt, it's how I choose to remember them both. When I felt like I belonged to them both, in a way I've only ever felt with my family. I don't know what it is, but we are all linked together in a way that can never be undone. That's all a bit much to be telling Bill Nevan, I suppose. And maybe he senses that I am on the verge of divulging something to him, because he takes the conversation away from all I am thinking.

'It must be hard on your sister, always with you two lads.'

Of course, this is in reference to her little display this evening. But he is gracious enough not to mention it directly. I never considered whether Anna finds it hard to be with me and Jack all the time. Sure isn't it hard on me, with the three of them always depending on me? Isn't it hard on all of us, always surrounding each other?

'Well, she has Peggy.'

He shakes his head, as though I'm wrong for saying this. As though I haven't a notion what I'm talking about.

'A child isn't proper company for her. I'm sure herself and Betty will take to each other.'

It's as though he knows how well Anna takes to a bit of female company. As though the Nevans know exactly what we need.

Anna

INSIDE, THE NIGHT LOOKS SO close. The sun is about to drop. The very last of its light is pointed at Betty's kitchen counter. There lies the knife and the fish. For now separate things.

'Well, what do you make of Ballycrea so far?'

She asks me, and now that I'm close to her, in her home, I smell her. Talc and perfume, Imperial Leather. Something I didn't expect when I saw her singing by the fireplace in John Moore's front room. Her purple apron, dotted with little lavender flowers. The rose colour has not yet gone from her cheeks, I don't know if it ever will, and her speaking voice isn't too far from her singing voice. It's like everything she says is a line from a song she knows by heart, she sounds so assured. I am, in part, afraid of her.

'Yeah, it's nice. Different from home like, but it's nice.'

I hope that she won't ask me how it is different from home, because I don't have any examples except for the constant reek of fish and the pairs of women who stare at me in town. But she doesn't ask. Instead, she smiles and moves us on without a word. Taking the fish in her hand, undisturbed by its staring eyes, its gaping mouth, or the odour that fills her kitchen, masking her scent.

'Alright, 'tis this way, look.'

She holds the fish out towards me and begins running the knife along its belly. Up and down. Without leaving a scratch. The lightest noise of the blade against the scales, hardly heard over my trembling breath.

The lustre of its flesh in the last light of the day. Slowly, she drags the knife, demonstrating something unnamed. We are too close, this feels too much.

Breaking the tension, she pulls the knife back sharply towards herself. Wordless, I watch as she descales the fish. It seems to come to her as naturally as breathing. As though she has done this all her life. Perhaps she has.

The scales fall like wedding confetti onto her counter, sticking to her hands. She makes it look so easy. But then, unexpectedly, alarmingly, she offers the knife and fish to me.

I wait for some reassurance, but it doesn't come. It appears she thinks I am perfectly capable of this. Strange, to consider what I am capable of. A fearsome thing, really. Something that I try not to let myself think of too often.

Slowly, I move the blade to the skin like she did, only without managing to remove any scales. She takes my hands and puts them where she wants them.

'Like this.'

She says, and I realise when she motions down to the fish that I have been staring at her. Once more, I begin to draw the knife back towards myself. Now and again I go in too deep and leave tiny cuts. The smell in my sinuses. Flaccid body in my hands. I have to focus more on steadying my breathing than I do on the knife in my hand. And still I gag. The noise of my throat jumping, of my saliva rising and catching. What a personal thing for her to have heard. Heat rises under my skin. Blood pours into my cheeks. The indignities of my human body, exposing me as immature and unversed in something as minimal as the smell of fish. I don't want to seem rude or ungrateful.

'Sorry.'

'Don't worry, you'll get used to it.'

Choiceless, I have to keep at it. The little cuts ooze. And I wonder about the shades of my own blood. Of Betty's. What temperature it takes, and how thick it flows. The eye stares up at me, watching as I peel away its body again and again. By the end of it, my hands are glittering with scales, glossy with plasma. When Betty takes the fish and knife back off me, all this lovely gore is transferred to her, and I feel suddenly afraid that she will know I am menstruating.

'Now, watch this part carefully.'

She says, gently, and without warning, sinks the knife into the fish's belly. I don't mean to, but I gasp. How childish I must appear. Unable to handle anything visceral.

Softly, easily, she runs the knife up through the body, slits the gills and pulls the fish apart. Dizzy, I watch and wait for Betty to tear the thing's head off.

Instead, she reaches inside, into the unknown universe that exists within a fish. Isn't she fierce brave? Isn't she merciless? Out with her hand comes everything that once kept the fish alive. Little organs, pulled out and dumped on the side. I expect to see small, distinguishable kidneys and lungs coming out. But it's just bubbles of unidentifiable flesh in lilac and red, which Betty severs with the knife. The head removed, the body cut in half. It seems much less of a fish now. The indignity of its body.

'Offal.'

She says. Awful, was it?

And then, just when I am sure that I can't handle another moment, Betty pulls out the fish's spine. And I swear I feel my own spine being pulled out, too.

It's all too close. Too intimate. The gagging, the blood, the teaching.

By the end of the dissection, I feel that the development of my relationship with Betty has been accelerated. We have almost become one thing. As she cuts what's left of this fish into fillets, I want to run outside and throw myself into Tom's arms. I want Betty to wash her hands and put the knife away. Please let all this be over and let me never see another fish again.

'I know, it isn't nice. But you'll get used to it all, I'm sure.'

A whisper of goodness, isn't that soothing? Isn't that lovely?

'I've had fish before, it's just I never made it myself.'

'That's alright.'

Betty says, smiling. How good it is to have a woman smiling at me. Telling me I'm alright. I forgot what that was like. As she turns, I catch sight of the freckles dotted at the top of her neck. Like daisies crowding the edges of the road. Like stars clustered at the highest point in the sky.

The sun is about to disappear.

'Now, the job is done. That's ready to cook.'

She says, satisfied, and I look at the counter. The knife, bleeding. The spine, pale yellow. The eye, still staring. I am nervous to say another word.

'You know, you've lovely hair, Anna.'

She starts, almost absentminded, moving past what we have just done as though it didn't faze her at all.

Outside, I see the shapes of Tom and Bill driving the last of the piles into the earth. The fence is up again. The horizon goes from orange to blue in an instant. The last clouds of sunset are here.

We head home, Betty and Bill wave from the door as we go. The walk is dark, but I don't mind. The fog is freezing, but I feel fine.

'That was so nice.'

I say, and surprise myself because I really mean it. Now it's over, everything that just happened seems so much nicer than it was disgusting. And suddenly, a little bit more joy than the borders of my body can contain picks me up, and I float next to my brother. The colour of the sky is changing – mottled lemon, sugar and endless blue. And I feel myself change with it. Uncontrollably. For a moment, my feelings lift, and I am sweet and blue and endless.

'It's great to get out, isn't it?'

It feels good to socialise in these small doses. To feel myself slowly beginning to enjoy people. I am learning. I am normal. Just like anybody else in the world, walking along with my brother. Tom tells me that Bill might have a bit more work for him, and I smile, I even squeal and squeeze his arm. And guess what? I am excited to try to cook fish. I think this evening was all I needed to feel real again.

Cold comes up through the cracks in the wooden floor. Peggy is the first to drift off, safe among us all. Then, there is a long while of silent thought for myself and the lads. Impossible to tell whether it's hours or minutes passing us by, waiting to fall asleep or to see the sun heave itself up.

Sighing and grunting, and wondering if we should try to wake each other up to talk about things. I wonder about the Nevans, about Betty's kitchen. Tea cosy and painted cups. Bursting dresser. Wooden crucifix over the door. I wonder when I'll be called down again.

'Goodnight Mammy. Goodnight Daddy.'

Betty

THE LITTLE RADIO ON BILL'S locker mumbles out the news. Normally, I would be glad to listen, but after our evening with the O'Learys, I just need a bit of hush. The heel of the moon comes in and out of view over the hill. Bill keeps saying he'll hang the new curtains, but I like being able to see the moon. Sure we've no neighbours, it's grand. When the back of my foot touches our bedroom floor, I'm glad of the new slippers Bill bought me last week. I'm grateful for everything in our house. How warm and clean and proper it is. Oh, their dusty little cottage, so bare and cold. The food on their plates uncooked, the mood in the air so stale. It isn't their fault. It isn't my fault; but it lingers with me as though I should solve it.

'God help us, you could have cut the tension with a knife.'

I say to Bill, layering on my night cream. He is sitting up in bed, listening to something about Fianna Fáil that I decide not to engage with tonight, but which he is intent on hearing. It's as though the evening never touched him. Like it was never strange at all. Bill is never affected by things the way that I am.

I watch him in the mirror, looking for any signs that he is listening to me, or feeling what I'm feeling. But he is deep in the news. The little yellow light of my lamp falls on his left side. Bill is the lucky sort of man that suits ageing. Deeply handsome. Without much to say about the O'Learys, it appears.

I bless myself.

'Lord God, thank you for the abundance of food in our house. Thank you for our happy, healthy home. And please, God, look after myself and Bill tonight. And please look after the O'Learys as they settle into Ballycrea.'

I kick off my slippers and get into bed beside him.

'Couldn't have said it better myself.'

He blesses himself, counting my prayer as his.

'Aren't we lucky, Bill, that we have enough food to spare that I was able to show that young girl how to prepare a fish?'

It's only when I see people with so little that I realise how much we have. I try so hard not to be too proud or boastful that all of my small luxuries end up going unnoticed.

I twist the front of my hair into rollers. Bill nods in agreement. Always so chatty when out and about, but so quiet when it's just us at home. I think he likes to be able to switch off, without the pressure of keeping a conversation going.

'Ah I felt for her this evening, Bill, I really did. It can't be easy, looking after everybody with nobody looking after her.'

He isn't convinced, I know by the way he shifts in the bed. But he says nothing, leaning over to switch off the radio.

'Imagine being above in that house tonight. I'd hate it! I feel so sorry for her.'

'It isn't Anna I feel sorry for.'

He says quietly, turning his head in the yellow light. Looking at me as though I should have thought of this sooner. The child. The poor, gorgeous child, who only wanted somebody to act interested in her. So full of life, with so much to say and so many questions. It takes nothing at all to smile and nod along with a child. Why wouldn't they do that for her? Yes, Bill is right; Anna isn't the one I should be feeling sorry for at all.

'Poor Peggy! What can we do for her, Bill?'

He opens his arms for me.

'There's nothing we can do for her. Only put manners on the rest of them, I suppose.'

I put myself under his chin, and I feel home again. A big sigh leaves me. The whole day leaves me. For a second, I wait for him to say that we can take Peggy in and look after her. Just a small second of foolishness, before I realise that Bill knows better than to suggest that. He probably knows that I'm thinking of it. Maybe in another world, we could do all that. In another world, I suppose, we might have had a child of our own. There might be a noise in the house besides the sound of my expiring. I pull myself from my thoughts.

'You sort out the lads so, and I'll take care of herself.'

I tell him, patting his chest. He laughs and squeezes me, and kisses the top of my head. But he knows that I'm not joking, and that the O'Leary boys are to be his new project.

Bill falls asleep, and I lie awake, with the four O'Learys walking around in circles in my mind. I can't imagine what Peggy has been through. First thing in the morning, I'll call to Ciara and arrange for Peggy to go down and see her pups again. Maybe I'll even arrange for her to take one home with her. On a heavy breath, I fall asleep, and dream that the devil comes in and washes his hands in my sink, and lies down on my spare bed. And I watch from the doorway, and let him at it.

Jack

I SHOULD HAVE GONE DOWN to the Nevans the other night. Tom and Anna came home so energised. I was sick with the jealousy, I was. They always seem to be one step ahead of me. Already digging themselves out of your grave. Turning to face the sun, moving past our old lives like they never happened. And I am still working out the difference between wanting to move on and actually moving on. Stagnant, perhaps even moving in the wrong direction.

Anna sits across the room from me, a sewing needle between her lips. She has given up making curtains for now and started fixing a tear in my shirt. Each time the needle pierces her thumb, I feel it. Fat flesh, filled up with her life, just waiting for a puncture to break the tension. Some of the blood she sucks away, some she lets stain the shoulder of my shirt. Perhaps she is trying to show the world that I belong to her; to the family. Perhaps she is trying to show the world that she has so little regard for me that she would bleed onto my clothes. Really, it doesn't matter much what she means to say, because what Anna means to say is seldom what comes across.

She was so chipper after meeting the Nevans, but every day since, she has become more diluted. And with each passing day, it seems less and less likely that we'll hear from them again. I suppose we were terrible hosts, really, serving them raw food over an argument. Now she is reverting to the way that she was before meeting them, which must be even harder than it was before, because now she knows that there are good things here, which are out of her reach.

Look at her now, frowning at what's left of her thread. She is so like Mammy when she frowns. When Anna goes quiet like this, I know exactly what she's thinking. It's the same thing that I sometimes allow myself to think. That we should go back to Kilmarra. That we should stop forcing Ballycrea to feel like home, because it doesn't, and it never will.

All that we left there. Its pink evening skies. Our home. Make a sound, love, and I'll follow your voice back. And I'll tend to the pigs and look after your auld lad. I will see a real sunset and feel innately that I belong.

Anna sighs, because just like me, she knows that we aren't going back to Kilmarra. I'm trying to remember how I felt when I saw things through Tom's eyes, and I agreed that a fresh start was just what we needed. I'm really trying to get back to that feeling. Perhaps if we had something to look forward to. Perhaps the issue is that we aren't counting down to anything, or excited for anything. We are just moving further and further away from when things felt good. From the garden, I hear Peggy begin to sing 'I Feel Fine', in her little Cork accent, with the words half right. I can't listen to it. Okay, let me try something. Let me be energised by people, as she was by Betty Nevan.

'Here, Anna, did you meet anyone nice at John Moore's? I thought the Doyle girls seemed alright.'

Her big, glowering eyes stuck on me, as though I will slip out the door while she considers the Doyles. I want to tell her not to worry, I want to tell her that I'm going nowhere. I want to tell her a lot of things.

Mainly, that I'm too fragile to be cross, and that for the moment, I forgive every bad thing she has ever done to me. I want her to make me strong again. So strong that I could hate her.

'They're just a year or two younger than us, I think. They seem nice enough.'

She swallows the spit in her mouth like it is thick as mud. Normally, I would be prepared to settle into her dismissal, but not today. It's not easy to look at your siblings and realise that you've all grown up, and grown apart. I don't know when it happened, but Anna changed; I don't know how to talk to her anymore. Once, I was her closest friend. Now, I feel like an annoying guest in her house, outstaying my welcome.

'Maybe we could all go out together? I could ask them. It might suit us better than sitting in the cottage all the time.'

She is trying to ignore me. I can see it in the whitening tips of her fingers on the needle. If she wasn't my sister, I would be humiliated trying to fight for her attention this way.

'He has my heart broken, Mammy.'

She whispers. I absolutely hate it when she talks to Mammy like that. We would all like to have a conversation with Mammy, of course we would. But all Anna is doing is talking to herself. I don't consider myself a violent man, but enough of that whispering could certainly incite violence in me. I have to hurry past it.

There is a small part of me that is keen to meet the Doyle girls without Anna there. A part that would love to go out and meet two pretty sisters. The rest of me, the most of me, is just afraid of what will happen if I stay isolated forever.

'Don't ask them, Jack. You can't be asking a pair of sisters to go out with you. It wouldn't look right.'

She doesn't want me getting close to anybody. It's like she knows I want to move on, and she wants to stop me.

'No, we could go out the four of us. Make a few friends like. We can leave Tom and Peg here.'

Always the victim, tears in her eyes already. She makes it hard to talk to her. Wouldn't it be sweet to lash out and show her what she's like? To remind her that if you had asked, she would have jumped at the chance to meet the Doyle sisters. It isn't that I'm after romance, just a bit of company like. Can you blame me? I want to feel the buzz of meeting people, but she doesn't want to let me.

'Don't ask them, Jack. Just don't. Alright?'

Like she's trying to protect me from myself. Like she knows something I don't. But then she smiles at me, this funny little sneer, just like she had in the cart when we first came into Ballycrea. And I see that true version of her once more, briefly. Glimmers of who she used to be remind me of who I used to be. She comes and goes; and when she is here, it feels like the sort of day when winter suddenly becomes spring. Reminding me that I grew up feeling wildly inferior to her, and that all of her excellence still lingers, somewhere. How I miss that inferiority. How I miss my sister. I don't mind the humiliation of trying once more.

'Why can't I ask them?'

If I push my way to the centre of her, perhaps all that she has built up will crumble. But just as I start to bring myself close to her, and consider asking her an honest question, perhaps even confronting the real issue, I see Tom coming up the garden path.

'Leave it there now, Jack. You know what he'll say.'

Anna

I WAS NEVER SO GLAD to see Tom's face at the window. Haven't we only just had your anniversary, and Jack wants to go out meeting women? I shouldn't have to tell him why that's inappropriate. The old Jack is creeping out again. The way he was before you, a divil for the drink and the women and never without the boys. We all thought that the time you had Jack was the making of him. It slowed him down, grew him up. He dropped the bravado, you know? It was a relief to see him settled. These days, it seems he is unmaking himself. Regressing to the half adult he was before you matured him. I suppose he doesn't know what to do with himself anymore.

'Well, well!'

Tom bursts through the door, announcing himself and throwing a pound of wrapped ham down on the table. Not fish, but ham. Something about that hits me harder than I would have imagined. I was looking forward to attempting fish again, to use what Betty taught me. I suppose Tom might not think it's worth the money to let me practise.

He starts telling us about what's happening in town. Small, tiresome gossip that doesn't mean anything to him, but that he pretends to be scandalised by. Nothing about Bill or Betty Nevan. I was hoping we might have been called back down to their house by now. It's embarrassing to be waiting for an invitation that might never come. How terribly I want to be shown ways to hold the knife against the belly of a fish. How to pull it through with such poise that it appears to be art rather than slaughter. How to do anything with the grace and fearlessness of Betty Nevan. Like I said, it's embarrassing.

Tom wipes his hands on his trouser legs and sits down at the table. Enlivened from the socialising. Inwardly, I'm sure he is imploding over the silence of Bill Nevan, who he was half counting on for a job. However, as ever, he doesn't allow himself to become derailed.

'Come here to me, girl.'

He calls, his arms out to Peggy. Occasionally, he decides to switch on his heart for her. Jack throws his eyes up to heaven. Maybe Tom is trying to put some truth into his lies about how close a family we are. If he was to be honest, I think the nicest thing Tom could say about Peggy is that he is indifferent to her. Perhaps it's the shock of his attention, perhaps it's knowing that she is too old for this, but Peggy hesitates before sitting on his knee. Jack's face is decidedly still as she leaves his side.

And even though I know it's contrived, my heart softens to see them like this. Tom is right to stay positive. He never lets things swallow him up. I wish I could be the same way.

'Ah, aren't ye lovely?'

I cannot help but say. Tom bouncing Peggy on his knee, and Peggy letting him, acting younger than she really is. He starts singing a song I don't recognise. Something he made up himself, probably. Suddenly I realise how lucky we are to have each other in this new town. To have people we are entirely comfortable with, and a place where we can be ourselves. Right now, with the four of us together, it's like we never left Kilmarra. It's like nothing ever changed. Equally comforting and heartbreaking. What great, sudden love I feel. My heart liquifies, the blood rushes out of me. Out of control.

'Sing me a song, will you?'

Tom says, softly, smiling, right in Peggy's hair. She recoils, his breath in her ear. It seems, for now, he has decided to love her. Daddy used to sit me up on his lap when I was little. He used to bounce me up and down and treat me like I was the centre of the universe, the way Tom sometimes treats Peggy. I was so loved by my father. Nobody loves me that much anymore. Nobody tries to, and I suppose nobody could. I want to get to a place where I appreciate those things without feeling hurt. I want to be asked to sing, too.

Peggy starts, her little voice high up, bringing life to the room. 'Weila Waile'. It makes us laugh. What a song for a little girl to sing. I pretend not to care where she learned it, because right now, we are all happy. It has been so long since we were all happy at the same time. Tom has done his job. It's good to be here, just for now it's really good. If you could see us. If you could just come up the garden path and knock lightly on the door. You'd be so welcome, if you would come.

And just as suddenly as my heart melted a moment ago, it has solidified again; it almost ceases to beat. It's hard to see Tom do this to her. A sudden outpouring of the love that she is famished of, which he will take away again without thinking. It's hard to see Peggy loved. She is the last piece of Mammy that I have. She is the reason I have no Mammy. Complicated.

Whatever was within me a second ago that was letting me enjoy myself has disappeared. I can't help but get lonely for you when I'm supposed to be happy. It feels inescapable. If I can't even enjoy myself in the good times, then when am I going to enjoy myself? When is the weight of all this going to go away?

The anxiety comes over me. I don't think I'll ever feel right again.

The fear takes up every thought. It fills the spaces between my clenched teeth. I try to put it all to the back of my mind, but you're already there. You're everywhere.

Yes, what a song for a little girl to sing. How horribly inappropriate. I've lost the humour in it. Tom encourages Peggy as though he really is entertained by her. As though he is mad for her. He seems to have stepped into the perfection that he is always trying to create. Like nothing bothers him anymore. The claws of his bachelorhood don't sink in as deep as they used to. The shame of his past doesn't hang as heavily. It seems like he has it all sorted. I just don't know if I believe it.

Such a pity that happiness isn't actually contagious. Such a hard thing to be the odd one out, not feeling what everybody else feels. Not enjoying what everybody else enjoys.

It's just January, that's all. I'm sure. The cold and the headaches of the season. Everybody is irritable in January. It's just that I feel disappointed we haven't heard from the Nevans. That's it.

Come on, Betty, knock on the door and solve me. Solve it all.

Tom

DUTIFULLY, I WAIT FOR BILL'S word.

And each day, I act like I am not wounded by my own hopes. Outside, with Jack, I clean up the yard. Anna insists we stay busy. The Devil makes work for idle hands, and all that.

'I've big plans for this place.'

I tell Jack, pushing the shovel into the earth. Pushing my positivity into him.

'Peggy will plant sunflowers for me here, and I'll get us a wheelbarrow and bicycles. I might get myself a little writing desk, and we'll have a bed each. And whatever else we like.'

Jack makes no signs to say that he doubts me, but he doesn't seem to believe me either. I want to feel he's on my side.

'We'll go out for a few pints soon, just the pair of us. Scope the place out properly.'

And though he tries to stifle it, I see a smile coming to his eyes. There was a time when Jack couldn't be kept out of the pub. Always in with the boys, after the women. The women were weak for him. Not boorish, he was charming. Able to read people and understand them. It suited him. I'll coax that rogue back out of him. It would suit me.

'There might be a dance on or something.'

Now we're making progress.

'We might meet a few women.'

As soon as this leaves me, I wonder if it was too far. If he isn't ready to talk about women yet. But he takes the shovel from me, forcing himself to have the craic. The earth crumbles off it through the air, as he spins and dips it as though it's a woman he's dancing with.

''Tis like this, look. You were never a natural dancer, Tom.'

He tells me. As though he would ever dance with a woman like that. And what if we were to meet a pair of women? What then? I laugh with him. The sky is turning to a pale purple. Soon, the fine weather will find us. For a minute, I feel like we are boys again. Like we are young. Like any minute, Daddy will come out of the house and tell us to stop fooling and get back to work. It could be. Is he in there now, alive all this time? I feel like I am alive.

Yes, I would love to go to a dance. Oh, for the days when we were a social family. Always out, always meeting people and invited places. I bite my cheeks, unable to consider all the many reasons we dropped that. There is so much I want from this new start. More than anything, I want to hold my head up high in the town.

Just as I am beginning to consider forgetting all about Bill and his farm and moving onto other ventures, on Sunday, he asks for me after Mass. And then Monday he asks for me in town, and on Tuesday. By Friday, I have stopped waiting to be asked.

Daddy might have said I was a fool, waiting on Bill Nevan like this. That I should try to make a go of things on my own, without answering to somebody else. Even sixteen years on from his death, I still feel I need to impress him. Today, I realise that it doesn't matter very much either way if I impress Daddy. The world goes on turning, and I need to put dinner on the table. Having somebody to answer to suits me. This job may be the bettering of me.

Anything at all to start the bettering of me, because there is so much I want from life.

I want to be everything that, currently, I am not. A well-off man. A purposeful man. More important, less imposing. Oh, to be anything but this, Tom O'Leary, broad and burdened. Let me work my way to the top. I follow Bill around his field, taking in everything that he tells me. There isn't a terrible amount of work between the two of us, just more work than he can manage on his own. Paddy Murphy used to help him, but he's getting too old now. He talks about work and trivial things at the same time, so I have to keenly gather every word he drops.

'Did you ever see *Sixty Five* broadcast on the television? They'd a thing on last night, *Heart of Thy Neighbour*, all about the North.'

He knows I don't have a television. It's nice to be caught up on what is being shown, so I don't feel behind on things.

'There was a man on saying that the Protestants up there are actually afraid of the Roman Catholics! Now can you credit that?'

I know about as much as any other man does on the topic, but it doesn't feel like enough when talking to Bill. I'm only guessing, but he seems well-educated. I don't want to say the wrong thing, to seem ignorant.

'They don't seem very afraid to me.'

I offer, and he laughs. Sure I don't know where he stands on the whole thing.

'*On the Land* is what I like, 'tis a farming programme. Betty hates it.'

He goes on laughing, telling me about the presenter and the topics they cover. How it's the best thing that Telefís Éireann broadcast, besides the news.

Isn't he lovely to listen to? I never thought I'd be chatting to a man as clever as Bill Nevan. No, for a long time, I thought that a man is born into the life he is to live. Some men are born to go to the likes of Trinity College, and study law and politics. To occupy dignified spaces and make money, and to cultivate culture. And then there are those like myself, born to turn turf and plough fields in a never-ending loop. Sharing our grand ideas and opinions with the animals and the soil. I always thought it was the luck of the draw which side you ended up on. And I have resented my side, until I met Bill: a good man, with a good life, who wants to give me a start.

The days are starting to stretch out, making space for me and my ambition. The sea air is filling up my lungs, cleaning me. And the dark weeks of January are so close to being behind me as I push a shovel through Bill's land. I am well on my way. I will make this work for them. For myself. Peggy will grow up here as though she never lived anywhere else. By the time she is my age, Kilmarra will be such a far-off memory that we will question whether we were ever there at all. The poor bastard child will never know what trouble she caused us.

Without people always asking us about you, Jack will find his rhythm again and get back to himself. He will lighten up and find things to keep him going. More than that, he will be happy. All the trouble will lift off Anna, and she will know such sweet, holy peace.

What a wonderful chance he has given me. Yes, I'm well on my way. What a charming family we will be. Admired by everyone, with the finest of everything. The happiest people in Ballycrea. We will shed the people we have been. Leave it to me. Our dignity reclaimed. Our trouble forgotten. Yes, watch will you, and give me all your strength while I smother the O'Leary name in glory.

The last few days have reminded me of how young I really am. I realise that it doesn't matter that I haven't made it yet, because I am going to make it now. It doesn't matter if people think I'm clinging too tightly to my siblings. Let us cling to each other if we need it; what harm does it do to anybody? If it makes us feel better, then it makes us feel better. We all latch onto people now and again. Don't pretend you never did.

Each morning at seven, I wait for Bill at his gates, and we get to work as the world turns from dark to light. It seems that he is glad of the help. I think he might be glad of a new man in the town. Bill says that I have refreshing ideas, an interesting way of seeing things. Isn't that a fine compliment? I recite poems from memory for him, I sing songs while we work. Sometimes, if I can get away with it, I pass things off as my own. Sometimes, I will attribute something I've written to Yeats, and take his belief as a compliment.

''Tis on the stage you should be, Tom. Not working out on the fields.'

I don't know what to do with this but nod and laugh.

In the evenings, I see Anna and Betty come to the door. Brightly, joyously, every evening Anna comes down the hill to walk me home. How lovely it is to see her lightening up. Often, she sits in with Betty for a half an hour, and they talk. It gives her a chance to be a woman.

Such a fine house, bigger than two people need. They stand in the doorway, looking out at us. Isn't it all so quiet? So soft?

Anna

'HAVE YOU ALWAYS LIVED HERE?'

I ask Betty, from where we lean against the door frame, watching the lads in the field. The sky, gone the colour of buttercream and rose. The night will be in soon. A tiny birdsong starts, and the chickens are clucking in the coop. A yard cat passes us by, here to walk around in the last colour of the day. Briefly bewildered by the beauty of it all, I take a moment to breathe deeply. I didn't realise how badly I needed to take a proper breath. A minute of quiet, in a perfect place. A pretty evening and somebody good by my side. I feel like I could fall asleep. I feel safe. A feeling I had forgotten.

The more time Tom spends on Bill Nevan's farm, the more time I spend in Betty Nevan's kitchen. This half an hour at the end of the day, drinking warm tea, watching the sky and talking quietly with Betty. Knowing that every day ends with this half an hour is knowing that life will end with peace. What peace it has brought me. I had forgotten how good it feels to have something to look forward to.

It's a nice life. Imagine. Something has come into my grey world and settled me. This isn't the sort of happiness that thinking of you could interrupt. How lucky I feel, here in the slow pace of Betty's kitchen. The music on the radio and the sea asters painted on her plates. Talking to her makes me feel interesting, like I'm two pints deep, all the time.

I don't know her age. Forty-four, I'd guess. Maybe forty-five. A very beautiful, well-looked-after forty-four or five. I'd forgotten I had even asked her a question when she answers me.

'Not always. I was once a blow-in, too. I came here when I married Bill. But that was so long ago, it's hard to believe I ever lived anywhere else.'

How reassuring, to know that a woman like her was once just like me. A total stranger in Ballycrea, making a new start. Look how well she has done, with her farm and her friends and her sanctuary. It makes me think that perhaps being in Ballycrea could be an opportunity, not a consequence. Isn't it funny, how easily she has reframed things for me. Without even realising.

'I would have thought you were always here. Just that, the town seems to really like you.'

She takes in what I've said. It's good to be considered, not just answered. She unties her apron.

'Well, I like the town. What's left of it anyway.'

If I stay quiet, she might go on talking. If I listen to what she says, I could learn what she knows. Then I could do what she does, and live as she lives.

Even now, just leaning up against the doorframe with her, I feel closer to calm than I have in so long. Perhaps it's being in the company of a woman. Perhaps it's getting a break from my real life. Perhaps if I stay here for long enough, she will heal me. As long as the evening is coming down around me, as long as she will have me, I will stay here with her.

Raking her fingers through her hair, she rolls what she loses into a ball and lets it float off. A bird will use that in its nest. How nice is that?

Looking at me sideways, she realises I'm not going to say anything.

She clears her throat and keeps going.

'Well, you know the way. There's always youngsters immigrating, there's always shops closing. Things changing, you know? Bill is always saying I'm no good with change.'

Although she says it in a light, jovial way, there's nothing light about the way she has seen into my head and spoken my thoughts back to me. Everything is always changing, I can't cope with it, either.

'Don't get me wrong, I understand it, 'tis just sad to see so many going. Did you ever think of it? Immigrating?'

She asks me, presumably wary of me not saying anything. This time, I have every intention to answer her, but just as I open my mouth, I notice the ball of her hair caught on the grass. It takes me for a moment. That is exactly what I want to be. That is the level of peace I have been trying to reach. To exist as nothing more than a loose tangle of hair. Her hair. In the breeze, and then on the grass. Just waiting for a bird. So still and so easy. I am brought back by Betty's humming.

'Would I immigrate?'

I try to centre myself again, to bring my mind back into my body, because I'm not a tangle of hair. I'm a person, being spoken to by the creator of the tangle.

'No, no I couldn't. Sure who would look after my lot?'

There was a short while when my life was filled with effervescent conversations about going to America with Milly Hayes, the milkman's wife. We were very good friends, at one time. If she had really wanted to go, I would have gone with her. But, obviously, she wanted to marry the milkman more. It's a shame when things are one-sided like that. I used to pretend to talk to her sometimes after that. An unhealthy habit, I suppose, that I should never have allowed to develop. It was the loneliness that did it. I must admit it's come back a bit since you've been gone.

After that, with Milly, I never gave any serious consideration to moving out of Kilmarra. But look at me now, long gone from there, and only rarely thinking about Milly and all she once meant to me.

I wonder if Betty would think I was pathetic if I said I can't envision living anywhere but in a cottage with my siblings. Would she think I was pathetic if I said that I want to move so little that I would be glad to simply stand in this doorway for the rest of my life?

'The three of my brothers went to New York after I got married. Declan, Michael and Joe. Twenty-five years since I saw them last.'

Betty says, almost sighing, and it feels like I am being fed by the details of her life.

'I know they're all there together, sure they've all wives and children out there now. But I still get so afraid that they'd be lonely. If I knew one of them was lonely for even a minute my heart would break.'

'Don't men always break your heart?'

Something sincere, which makes her laugh. The sound of her soul. When those brothers of hers left, I wonder did they consider her loneliness as much as she considers theirs.

Every day she says a prayer for them, and although it's been years since she saw them, she says that she knows she will see them again. When you're lonely for a person in that way, you'll believe anything to keep yourself going. This would be the right time to tell her that I know what it is to miss somebody, to know that you won't see them again but to go on behaving like you will.

Bill is the only family she has left. Isn't it sad for her? But now, she has me. Somebody who understands exactly what she feels. What a blessing.

'Sure they might as well be on the moon, they're so far away!'

Once more, she echoes my thoughts, and somehow manages to laugh, even when she is sad. When people are far away like that, how can we be sure that they even exist anymore? Perhaps she has an answer for that. Perhaps she could let me know whether anybody from Kilmarra is still in Kilmarra, if it exists as it did, or if it still exists at all. You know? Like does the butcher still open for an hour on Sundays, and do your sisters still remember my name? I look at her for a long moment and allow myself to move a little bit closer to her warmth.

Betty shifts her weight, moves away from me, out of the doorframe to step onto the grass, bending down to stroke the yard cat and then leaning against the house.

'If you were to go, I'm sure Tom and Jack would look after themselves. They might be encouraged to be married.'

Something about this puts a twinge of insecurity through me. As though Tom and Jack don't really need me, as though they could replace me with any woman they came by. And I'm sure it means nothing, but I feel it as something.

No, she wouldn't want me to leave the country. As unknown as we are to each other, she would miss me calling down in the evenings. This new and precious routine is all that is pulling us out of the winter. She would miss me. And I would miss her.

'Tom used to talk about going off somewhere, I don't know why he never did.'

This seems to intrigue her, but I don't want to tell her all the reasons that Tom's life hasn't worked out the way that he wanted it to. There isn't time. Moreover, I don't know if I'm allowed. Before she can ask about it, I put the topic of conversation back to myself.

'I wouldn't want to go all that way just to find myself in the same situation as I'm in here. Cooking and cleaning and looking after people. Even if it was as someone's wife.'

Surprising, how quickly that came to me. It seems rather a fully formed opinion to have spat out. I didn't know I felt that way.

'What harm is it being someone's wife?'

She asks, and I wonder what other opinions would come out if I let myself speak. The truth is too embarrassing. That I've never had a chance at being somebody's wife, and so the idea of it has made me bitter. I wonder if she would still want to be my friend if she knew what a failure my romantic life has been.

Would she understand it if I said there was never anyone with enough patience for me? That there was never anyone worth my patience? When I can scarcely hold on to friends, what chance have I with a lover?

There was one short week with the father of a holidaying family from Leitrim. I thought that I would have to fight myself not to fall for him. That I would want so much more than a week, and that when it was over I would think of him all the time; that I'd be crying into my pillow, trying to feel the last of him on my lips. But in the end, a week of being pressed up against him was more than enough. Besides the very odd occasion that somebody mentions Leitrim, I don't think of him at all. That was the closest thing I've ever had to a relationship – what do you make of that?

I couldn't really count the afternoon with the man whose name I can't recall in Cork city.

Or the scattered winter nights I shared with Niall Schumaker, an unmarried schoolteacher in Fernmore. He was good to me, he really liked me. I could tell. But there was more passion in five minutes of conversation with Milly Hayes. More love in just the suggestion of your smile. Imagine. Pathetic.

I don't remember these affairs often, or with any particular fondness. They were exciting when they were happening, but as soon as each one ended I was just embarrassed.

Just things that happened, void of romance. Void of meaning. I try to convince myself that I used those men in the same way that they used me. I wouldn't want Betty to know that I had so little regard for my virginity that I threw it at the first man that came my way.

It's too much for me to think about, and so I know it would be too much to tell her. Instead I wait for myself to reveal another new opinion.

'There's nothing wrong with being somebody's wife. I think I just want to try being independent, that's all.'

It sounds like an impressive, forward-thinking idea; at the very least, it smooths over my mistake. So I commit to it, even when, really, independence is the very last thing that I want. What I actually want is for somebody to hold on to me so tightly that we become one thing, never separating. To be married with children tying me to somebody. To have a sister, the bond of blood keeping us together. To have anything more than meaningless sex and adulterated friendships.

'You could have independence, Anna. Of course you could.'

How quickly and easily she validates me. That's what it is. I realise now, Betty validates me. She makes me feel like a person. That's why I want to be around her so badly. She sees me as new, without my siblings and without my past, and makes me feel like I am my own clean thing. My own woman. That perhaps I don't need to lean on my brothers so much. Perhaps they don't define me. Perhaps my past doesn't need to follow me. Exhilarating. Betty could show me how to leave everything that happened behind me. How to close the door on it and start living a new life.

'But I'm glad to hear you've no intention of immigrating. It's nice to have a new family in the town. The young people are always leaving, it's good to have a few coming in for a change.'

Betty could be the person I've been looking for. Somebody with patience for me. Somebody worth my patience. Who could give me more than a few scattered nights, more than a week of her time. Who might want to stay in my life, always. Don't you think that I deserve that? Suddenly I want to hug her, to have her wrapped around me. So tightly that I would melt into her skin, and stay warm inside her for a while.

'Would you ask your small girl to call up to me after school on Monday? I want her to make a few Brigid's Crosses for me. 'Tis a way easier for little nimble fingers.'

I nod, in awe. What a good woman. Taking my worry off me. Taking my responsibility off me.

Leaving her house, I feel a foot taller than everybody. Ready to enjoy myself, to be a new person.

And I think of her hair caught on the grass. If she ever does that again, I will catch the hair and keep it in my pocket.

The sky is darkening as Tom and I go.

'Would you ever immigrate, Tom?'

When I ask, he rolls his eyes. But he surprises me with an honest answer.

'I used to think of it often. New York. Boston. Philadelphia. Those kinds of places. The big wide skies and the skyscrapers.'

He looks up at the sky. It's years since he talked about leaving Ireland. I thought he had it all forgotten. But perhaps it's lingering inside him. I didn't expect this.

'Wouldn't you feel lost, so far from home?'

I would feel lost without him. Tom is one of the great weights in my life. He keeps me on the ground. I can't believe the idea is still in his head.

'I would. Absolutely.'

He smiles. I can't understand why that would make him smile. The idea of being one little Irishman among a million Irishmen among millions of Americans. Such startling insignificance.

We come into the warmth of the house. Tom blesses himself. Jack is nudging the fire back to life, telling a fairy story of some sort to Peggy. I realise now that he must be the one who taught her 'Weila Waile'. I suppose he thought that was funny. I suppose he didn't consider how it would reflect on me. I think sometimes we have to remind ourselves that Peggy is a person, not a pastime.

Jack

I MANAGED TO GET MYSELF out of the house and down to Doyle's pub, where Tom said he would meet me at six. But 'tis twenty-five past now, and there's no sign of him.

Just as I draw up a sigh, Teresa Doyle passes me and my breath halts. The same green dress she wore in John Moore's front room. The same eyes, glinting for a second as she moves by. I sit up straight. I want to talk to her.

It's shocking to think that I should want to talk to a girl when this time last year I didn't think I would ever speak to anybody, ever again. When only last Christmas I was gearing up to become a father. How fast it all changes. If I think about it for too long, I feel taken over by a panicked happiness, as though you have just told me that you were pregnant.

Teresa pauses before me, the bar between us, looking at me while she touches a match to her cigarette. She puts the box between us.

'Help yourself.'

Her voice comes with an unexpected rasp. A small thrill. And I hate that I have to push the box back to her.

'I'm not a smoker anymore.'

She looks embarrassed. I feel embarrassed. You'd think that my greatest regret was telling Anna you were going to have a baby. But, to be honest, my biggest regret is giving up the smoking. Things are very bad when a man can't even enjoy the brief peace of smoking a fag. There are times when I feel as though everything within me is about to boil over, out of my mouth and eyes, and I wish to god that I was in the humour to smoke a fag. But you didn't like smoking, and so I didn't like it, either. Then there are rare times like this, when a pretty girl puts a box of Carrolls in front of me, and I have to refuse her. Rather than staying to chat, she takes the box back and goes to clear glasses from the tables. I breathe in the smoke she left behind, and get nothing from it.

At last Tom lands on, giving me a shy wave from the door. Behind him comes Bill, and as soon as they're in, several other men flock to them. Teresa appears again, ready to pull their pints. She looks at me only once. I want to apologise to her, but I'm not sure what I would be apologising for.

'Jack, how's the form?'

Bill asks, before Tom has even opened his mouth. Now that Tom is here with all of these men, I realise I am here on my own. I wonder what Bill thinks of me, the unemployed brother, drinking alone.

'No complaints. How are things working out with himself?'

'He's a credit to ye.'

Bill laughs, and calls for a round of drinks. Rather than facing all the men he has met, he turns to me again.

'And what would be your trade, Jack? If you're anything like your brother, I could get you sorted with a job very fast.'

Tom's face stiffens, like I've taken his favourite toy for myself.

'Oh, a bit of everything. But I worked in the pub most often. I could pull five pints a minute.'

It's easy to make Bill laugh. He's easy to read; most people are. The flush of Tom's cheeks deepens. Right now, he hates me. But I'm only treating him the way he treats me. He turns to the other men and starts reciting a joke or a limerick, something unfunny that will earn him a few seconds of attention.

'I'll bear that in mind.'

Bill says to me, before turning back to his group, laughing along with Tom's fooling. I don't need Bill's attention. I just wanted to remind Tom that I could take it away from him, if I wanted to.

And once more, I am on my own.

And I think about how different all of this would be if I had been married to you. I should have proposed the moment I met you. I had the ring in my pocket the day you died. Imagine.

Tom puts a pint in front of me, widens the circle to let me into the group. I smile along with what the men are saying, doing what I can to remain present.

Anna hated me when I gave up the fags. She said I was like a dog. She was the one like a dog when I told her your news. Looking back, perhaps it all reminded her too much of Mammy, dying as Peggy came to life. Maybe she was afraid the same thing would happen to you.

'Holy God swapped Mammy for Peggy. Didn't he?'

We used to all say, smiling, as though that little line would make things alright. The day she died was so silent, despite the new baby crying. It was the deepest silence I've ever known. And while the rest of us slowly let the sound back in, I don't think that Anna ever did.

'How's your sister getting on, Brendan?'

'Oh, Tom, I keep out of it. It's the Bon Secours one day and then the Sacred Hearts the next.'

Perhaps we didn't give Anna enough time to grieve Mammy before making her a mother to Peggy. Perhaps I shouldn't have celebrated Peggy so relentlessly. It was only so we didn't grow to resent the child who suddenly made parents of us all.

'I suppose a nun is a nun, at the end of the day.'

'Try telling her that. The decision has her driven demented.'

It was happy news, you being pregnant. I know we weren't married, but we would be married. Sure everyone knew we weren't far off it. 'Twas just that things came in the wrong order. Baby first, marriage second. I don't understand why people get their backs up about that sort of thing. It sickens me, actually. There were too many good things tarnished by a pregnant woman without a ring on her finger.

Despite all my odd feelings towards god, when I think of the baby I am compelled to bless myself. In ainm an athar, agus an mhic, agus an spioraid naoimh. Isn't it strange, what your emotions draw you to?

I'm ready to go home, I can't keep up with what these men are saying. Just as I am about to suggest it, Tom says to Bill,

'Sure we'll have one more for the road, will we?'

All the men agree, and so I am staying put.

But it's alright, because Teresa stands before me again, this time without her cigarettes, but with a bag of buttermints. I take one from her, and smile. Turning away from the lads, I take a deep breath of her.

'I'm Jack O'Leary.'

'I know.'

Betty

'I WAS WORRIED BECAUSE WE haven't any reeds collected at home.'

Peggy tells me, sitting at my kitchen table. Today, we had the first cold kiss of February. White light coming in on the table, a pile of reeds spread out before us. Her legs dangle from the chair.

'I thought we'd make them in school, but we just watched while teacher made one. We used always make one each in my old school.'

Such a great talker. I suppose it could be that she doesn't get much of a chance to talk at home. Now that I've got her started, she may never stop.

'I was afraid that there would be no reeds left in Ballycrea, and I wouldn't get to make any cross.'

Later on, I will have to show her the pond, and how many reeds grow there, so that she doesn't need to worry in the future.

'What do you make of the school? Do you like the other children?'

She is at such a lovely age. So keen to talk and share opinions, so eager to know things.

'It's better than my old school.'

'What was wrong with your old school?'

'They used call me bastard.'

Oh, I didn't expect this. She says it like it still hurts. A girl her age shouldn't even know that word. I assumed Peggy would have been popular anywhere she went. Thanks be to God that she has been given a new start.

'Nobody should call you that, Peggy. Sure it isn't your fault what happened to your mammy and daddy.'

I reach out, tilting her face to me.

'I told my teacher they're working in Áras an Uachtaráin. Just so you know.'

I take this to mean she wants me to spread the rumour on her behalf. I nod, and hope that she believes me. Those awful brats. I've half a mind to ring her old school. I squeeze her arm and try to get her mind off it.

'Would Anna normally make Brigid's Crosses with you?'

I ask, but Peggy doesn't look up at me again. She is focused on bending the reeds as evenly as she can.

'No, Anna can't make them. She hasn't the patience for anything like this. None of them at home would.'

I wonder what things Anna has patience for at home. Whether she is the closest to Peggy, or whether it's one of the boys. I carry a hot, heavy teapot to the table and sit with her, sorting the reeds by size. She admires the crocheted tea cosy in the shape of a hen. I tell her that I made it, that I can teach her how to do it one day. But she seems more interested in the woolly hen.

'I love all animals. I'm going to be a vet when I'm older.'

'Oh, you'll make a brilliant vet, Peggy.'

And I wonder where she got the patience from, if not from Anna or the two lads. I'm not being nosy, I only want to find out more about the family.

'So who used you make Brigid's Crosses with before, if it wasn't Anna?'

'Lillian.'

Hold on now. Nobody has mentioned any Lillian to me before. Peggy sighs.

'Is that your friend from home?'

I ask, and immediately regret asking. Ballycrea is her home now, I shouldn't be putting other ideas in her head. I'm sure it's been hard enough to get her to settle here, without me reminding her of the home and all of the people she has left behind.

'Lillian was Jack's girl. She used look after me all the time.'

Now there's a bit of gossip. Jack has left a girl behind in their old village. What happened there, I wonder? And has Tom mentioned anything to Bill? I don't know why I never considered that they might have left women behind them. Sure they're good-looking lads. It just seems like they are an isolated unit, the four of them, with no ties to anyone else. I'll have to tell Ciara.

'We used make them every year at her house, on the first day of spring.'

Maybe I shouldn't encourage her to keep talking about this woman. Especially if she is Jack's ex-girlfriend. Peggy needs to be present where she is, not half here and half there.

'What are you giving up for Lent, Peggy?'

It's easy to change the subject with a child. She starts listing all the sweets she is going to give up. Lent is more than a month away, but she doesn't question it. I pour a cup of tea for her.

'Lillian used always say she was giving up sugar, but then she would take sugar in her tea on Sundays and eat fruitcake with it. Are you allowed to break Lent on Sundays?'

'I'm sure even Holy God takes a little break on Sundays.'

I'm not sure what else to tell her. If this Lillian was breaking Lent, I don't want to tell Peggy that she was wrong. I wonder if it was a bad end between herself and Jack. Maybe she could come and visit, or maybe we could arrange for Peggy to talk to her on the telephone. Or maybe that's all totally inappropriate. I'll have to ask Ciara what she thinks.

'That's what Lillian would say! But Jack would never laugh because her daddy never laughed, and he wanted her daddy to like him.'

'Hurry up and finish that cross now, like a good girl.'

There's no taking Lillian out of her head. Once the first cross is finished, I hold it up to the kitchen window, to the sunlight, and pretend to inspect it.

'Peggy, this is perfect! Oh, it's so neat, you'll have to do me a few more.'

She smiles and keeps going. I ask her to tell me the story of St Brigid, and help her where she leaves gaps. But she knows the story very well. She is a smart girl.

When she has a few crosses made, I tell her to put on her coat, and wrap one of my scarves around her. Holding her hand, we walk down to Mrs Deer's house. Every year I bring her in a cross, which she keeps in the rafters. Living all on her own, Mrs Deer's house is dark and quiet, and I can sense that Peggy is half afraid to go in. I am so glad to have found a child to deliver crosses to the elderly with me, because every year, I fear that somebody will suddenly deem me elderly, and have a child drop a cross into my house.

We stand at Mrs Deer's door while she praises the cross from the threshold. Her warped posture and sparse hair scares Peggy. It isn't fair really; Mrs Deer is a lovely woman. Peggy holds my hand tighter until we leave her door.

'She's a very nice person, she's just very old.'

'How old is she?'

I laugh, and don't scold her for being cheeky.

'She's as old as the hills.'

I say, when we are far enough from the house that we won't be heard.

When Peggy was scared, she held onto my hand tight. She needed to be looked after, and she wanted me to do it. Thrilling heartbreak. She chose me, but she isn't mine at all. She's only the sister of somebody I barely know. I wonder if I will spend my whole life trying to mother things that don't need me.

Still, I bring her down to Ciara's door to give in a cross, and we spend an hour with the puppies. I keep the neatest cross for myself and show it off to Anna, and to Tom and Bill when they come in. Anna fidgets, and for a moment I wonder if I have crossed a line by spending the afternoon looking after Peggy. I hope she won't feel like I'm trying to step on her territory. I've to keep Anna sweet if I want to spend time with Peggy.

But things seem alright when we all sit down together for cake and a pot of tea. I'm just dying to ask them about Lillian, but I let her go unmentioned for now. To hear Peggy's laughing fill up the house is so sweet. And it's good to have new friends. To eat warm fruitcake with them on the first evening of spring.

Jack

'WELL, MAMMY, I DIDN'T KNOW what to think!'

Anna says, facing our only framed photograph of Mammy and Daddy. She is telling them about her day, the Brigid's Cross that Peggy brought home and the fruitcake she had with Betty Nevan. Not in prayer, or even in a conscious way. It was like she just thought of something that Mammy would have found entertaining and started talking to the photograph. I suppose there's nothing wrong with that, really. Sure don't I spend every minute talking to you?

But there's something about the way that she does it. Losing herself to these conversations. Pausing as though she can actually hear Mammy responding. I wonder sometimes if she sees Mammy before her, wiping down the side and sweeping the floor. It makes me uncomfortable. Once more, I feel consumed with the want to put a stop to Anna. It builds up from the pit of my stomach until I am close to trembling.

I sit up. Moving to stand. To strike her. With one blow, surely I could end her. One fine crack of my knuckles against her delicate little jaw. A tooth in the sink, marbled drool and blood. A mess I would happily clean up. But then as I close my eyes, I see you, sudden and gentle and good. This fleeting thought of you is all that stops me from catching and throttling her. The flashing promise of meeting you in heaven. The most rational feeling I have had in months – the strongest feeling I have had in months – stopped by something brutally irrational.

If heaven is there, I'm sure, it's nothing but a disappointing party full of the plainest people I know. And yet I am doing all that I can to get there, back to you. So before I do something I will regret, I get up and leave the house, and take myself down to evening Mass.

Before all this, it wasn't often I'd find myself pulled down to the church more than once a week. Now, I find it's one of the few places I can go to escape from everything. There's something about the routine of it, of being spoken at without the expectation to answer with an original remark. The anonymity of worship, melting my thoughts away. Converting them into a manageable cluster within me, that I can put aside for a little while.

What's more, today the first day of the month came to me again. I pretended not to feel each second of it grinding against me, but it was there, undeniably. Cruel. Sure what else am I to do but go down to the church, saying prayers I know by heart but don't understand. Talking to a god who may or may not even be there. Cruel alright.

'Tis all cruel like, but here is the true cruelty: whatever I feel about it, and however it has damaged me, I must carry on believing in God. That He is good, and that He loves us and is merciful. Because if there is no God, then you're not safe in Heaven. You aren't anywhere at all. You would really be gone, and I would be talking to myself. So I've to keep on praying, believing in Heaven and its many beasts.

It's a dark evening. Aren't they all dark evenings? I go down through the town on my own. A bit of quiet, thanks be to God. Already, I have my hands thrown into a lazy prayer at my crotch. And for now, I am nothing but a man walking down to Mass. It's alright. It's nice to just be a passerby, without thoughts or a history. Just somebody walking past somebody else. The black night reaching its arms out, every star a wild eye pointed down at me. The light of them swallowing my shadow, until I am entirely alone.

The steep stone steps up to the church. The burning just beginning to bloom at the bottom of my lungs as I reach the top. And as I enter the church I have to wonder, why don't I have any original ways of processing my feelings? Why do I always turn to prayer? Perhaps it's a custom ingrained too deep in me to ignore. Perhaps it's something to do with being under the surveillance of Himself; old 'holy God', and feeling I have to share everything with him. Whatever the reason, I'm here now. Take a seat, Jacky.

'Tis a rare thing now that I get a moment to myself. Ah darling, tell me, are you sitting with me? Tell me why you never sit with me. For months now I have been waiting for some sort of sign that you are here. The cold of your ghost. A hallucination. A delusion. Anything just to keep me going. I search and search for a sight of you, for the smell of your hair, the smell of your sweat. For anything. Going mad with the vision of you before me would be far better than going mad without you here at all. My angel, torn from my side.

Often, like right now, I fake the feeling of your hands on my shoulders, the click-clacking of your shoes on the ground. I might as well fake that you are here with me, since you don't seem to be calling down on your own. If I could only reach up to the awful, endless navy sky and tear through it. To put my wondering to rest. To reveal Heaven, or its absence.

I have to laugh at myself. Heading down to Mass, on a Monday, on my own. Imagine. If the boys could see me now. The church is quiet. A good handful here. Enough people to fit into the hand of God, I suppose, if your scale of Him is the same as mine.

Out comes Father O'Brien to kick us all off. I must say I'm dreading the vernacular Mass. 'Tis better in Latin, when none of us know what the priest would be saying. I fear that soon, I will be the only one who doesn't understand.

When he starts to sing, I am lifted.

'A Thiarna Dean Trocaire.'

Now that's something new. I never once heard an Irish song in Mass. It seems Father O'Brien is trying to get ahead of the game. And we respond, exact mimics of every crack in his voice. I fall into it all. Sitting, standing, kneeling. Something about it is so wonderfully automatic. And while the people around me are no doubt receiving immense comfort and joy from the experience, I am almost moved to tears by the emptiness of it all. I don't understand it, I don't know if I ever will. And that is fine. A palatable way to feel nothing at all. Something I can cope with. Something that means so little to me and yet I know so well. Nothing, everything. How sweet it is. A Chriost Dean Trocaire. I have found my flow state.

Lillian, if you're anywhere, you're probably not here. Do you know what, I really hope you're not here. I don't want you ever coming to a place as dreary, as empty as this, watching as I find semblances of comfort in nothing. Communion commences, and I find I want to take the chalice and bite it. I want to put my teeth through the eucharist. I want to hurt god and his son the way that they have hurt me. A thiarna dean trocaire, you merciless fucker.

Leaving, walking home, I catch a glimpse of something glorious in the night. My heart, at once soaring and plummeting, when I lose my breath at the sight of Teresa Doyle, emptying the bins beside her father's pub. I walk faster, hoping she hasn't seen me. It isn't that I don't want to talk to her, it's just she would be too much right now. I'm supposed to be missing you, I can't handle the creeping interest I have in Teresa.

'Goodnight, Jack.'

She calls after me. As I ignore her, I feel the sort of shame I often felt after making love, or shouting at Anna, or doing anything to express myself. It's embarrassing, to embrace the feelings so intensely.

At home, Peggy sleepily strokes the chicken, Anna is boiling eggs. Tom sits up against the wall, and I sit in alongside him. I let my head fall on his shoulder, and he welcomes me. No questions. No worries. This unusual proximity is no hassle to him at all. Just a brother minding his brother. I let myself relax, and smell the tobacco off him, and remember a time when I smelled like that. Maybe I'll take up the smoking again. Maybe that would put me back in touch with who I once was. It might at least take the edge off evenings like these.

I'm alright, amn't I? I've my brother and a familiar smell. I've a place to put my head down. It's more than I had back in the church. It's more than some people have in their whole life.

'Roll me a fag there, will you?'

I ask, lifting my head just long enough to see the hair in his nostril twitch, and he puts on a stern face and shakes his head.

'Not a hope. You've fine clean lungs now.'

And while I drop a big, heavy sigh on his shoulder, I feel such great love in his denial. He's looking out for me. For a moment, he puts his arm around me, squeezing and slapping my shoulder, reassuring me.

'You're alright, boy.'

I suppose he knows where I've been tonight. He doesn't bother plastering on a smile, but he is here for me now. From this angle, he is the spit of Daddy. In more than many ways, he is just like Daddy. I suppose, in many ways, he is my daddy now.

'I'm alright.'

And I let myself sink further into his shoulder, forgetting the cigarette and the embarrassment I felt walking home. Forgetting the sting of your absence, and the sting of Teresa's presence. Feeling only the fire before us and his rough geansaí on my cheek. If Tom wants to look after me, I'll let him.

Tom

PICKING STONES FROM BILL'S FRONT field, I cannot help but think of Daddy. He used to have me picking stones from dawn on Saturdays. I'd leave his land without even the dust that would one day form a stone. Spotless clay, sparkling crops. He would sit Jack up in the cart and let him do the ploughing. Even though I was older. Even though I wanted to do it.

'Jack wouldn't pick half as many stones as you, Tommy.'

He used to always say. That was it then; I wasn't allowed to argue with that. It always seemed stupid to me that a buck of my size would be reduced to the childish labour of picking stones, while a little rake like Jack was allowed to command the plough. I wonder did Jack realise how much it bothered me. I wonder did Daddy.

I see the back of the postman, Rob Keating, as a flash of colour cycling away up the hill.

'You've a delivery here, Bill!'

Betty calls out to us from the house. It's a glittering sort of day. Normally, Bill wouldn't stop for the post, but today he seems excited. As though receiving post is a new and radical concept. He drops his pick and motions for me to follow.

A crate up on the table, stuffed with newspaper. Bill beaming at it. Obviously it is something he has been expecting. I feel wrong watching, as though his wonderful crate is private and should be enjoyed when I am gone home. Perhaps I should offer to leave.

But Betty pulls out a chair for me. She puts the water on and makes us all coffee. Bill takes off his coat, sweating in the cold.

'Bill, will you leave those boots at the door and don't be walking dirt into my house!'

Her shrill voice. I kick off my own boots before she starts at me. Bill uses a bar to pull the lid off the crate. We are faced with clothes, jars of tea, marmalade and lemon curd, and three pieces of a glowing fruit that I have never seen before.

'This is what James sent over!'

Betty peers over his shoulder into the box, from Bill's brother in Northampton, reaching in to feel the fabric of the clothes that have come. She reads the note to herself, and then a portion out loud to us, which says,

'The peppers may be on the turn now, though hopefully the airmail was quick enough that you'll get to taste them. In any case, they are filled with seeds which you should try to cultivate.'

'You can't get these in the shops at all.'

Bill says, and I never saw him happier, or prouder, as he reaches into the crate for one of the peppers. Feeling, for a moment, connected to his brother, all the way in England. And I suddenly feel inferior to this foreign food, and I aspire to be it. Isn't that sad?

'Peppers,' he says, taking one in his hand and turning it over. ''Tis veg.'

James grew them from seeds, which were sent to him from Texas, America. To be honest, they look to me like they are gone past their best, slightly wrinkled at the surface. But they aren't mouldy either. What do I know?

I suppose James envisioned the peppers being eaten in a meal. However, between us, we can't think of what to put them in. Betty says the best thing to do is boil them, but they seem too special for that. Surely there isn't any harm in eating them raw.

And so, we sit around the kitchen table eating these peppers, uncooked. Not saving them for anything special, rather, making this ordinary moment into something special. Bright yellow and green. James wrote that they can grow to a ripeness that turns them red. It's a sweet, sort of earthy taste. Not like the pepper you'd sprinkle onto the dinner, not at all. These are the size of a hand, maybe a little bit less, and very light on the stomach. I suppose that is what they want in the hot weather of Texas, I'm not sure how much call James would have for them over in Northampton.

I wouldn't be in a rush to try them again. But isn't it amazing that I've come to a point in my life where I am tasting imported vegetables that started as seeds all the way in America?

'The lads must eat this sort of thing all the time in New York.'

Betty says, talking about her brothers. Her face fills up with happiness, and immediately then with sadness. Although I try to keep to myself, and to remain immersed in the flavour and crunch of the peppers, her face is more captivating. If I had to distil women to one thing, it would be a face like this. The intense and easy union of joy and despair. What would Mammy have made of these peppers, I wonder.

It's hard for me to believe that these are real people and that this is real food. That this is my life, you know? How quickly it has all changed. I never met anybody so generous. I never felt more grateful. It's Bill, glorious Bill. A genius of a man, so genuine and generous, giving his time and life and peppers to me. It's as though he wants me to know everything that he knows, and to have every luxury that he has. If I only knew what good deed I did in my life that paired us up. Perhaps he is my guardian angel. Perhaps he has the spirit of my father guiding him, looking after us both.

And I must say, it all brings me back to you. Not in a sad way. I'm just aware that peppers are something you never got to try. Something you never even knew existed. It brings me back to the kitchen in Kilmarra, with you and Jack. On days when Anna wasn't feeling right, you would come up and make our dinner. It all looks so warm in my memory, even though it hurt at the time. Washed carrots and parsnips scintillating on the side, bread batter in your cuticles.

Every time, you would show Peggy something new. Even if it was just something small, just to keep her involved and learning. You made her feel so special.

I can still see Jack peering over your shoulder, unbothered when you batted him away, asking to be shown a certain technique for peeling again. And you would show him, always, even when you knew he would never do the peeling and he would never really take it in. I think he used to just let on that he wanted to learn so you would slow down and make it all last longer. He was good for you, I think. Now that you're gone, I really do know that ye were right for each other. His hand on the small of your back. The golden sun coming in the window. A shame.

I was green watching ye, I can admit that now. Absolutely green with envy. I'll say it once: clearly, I was never in love with you, Lillian. But my God, I was head over heels for the idea of you. How swiftly it was all torn to the ground. I wonder will you get the chance to taste a pepper where you are. I blink away the slight pool that has gathered at my lashes and bring myself back to the small paradise of Betty's kitchen. Hot coffee in my cup and a seat saved for me.

Loose tea, lemon curd, peppers. These are the wonders in my life today, all granted to me by Bill. I want to write a poem about this moment. I want Bill to grade and praise it. I want to write him music and prayers.

It isn't that I worship him, just I want him to feel worshipped. I want him to feel how grateful I am. I want him to know what a good man he is, and how, in such a small amount of time, he has begun to repair the irreparable within me. I take another bite of the pepper. Isn't it sweet to be here? For twenty-nine years I've been alive. For the last half an hour, I've lived.

Anna

HEAPS OF GOLDEN ONIONS, SOFT stalked carrots, stacks of eggs and bunches of flowers. A bright morning. The Saturday market here is much larger than in Kilmarra. Women call out to each other. Men knock into me as though they can't see me. Peggy snatches her little hand out of mine. And Betty is just up ahead, moving in and out of sight. I like to keep an eye on her when I can. I like to take note of when she drops into Doyle's. When the car is missing from her driveway, and if she comes back with groceries or new clothes in the boot. I notice when she goes on her evening walks with Ciara Moore. I watch from six pews back in Mass, and although I can only see the back of her head, her face is clear to me. Her thoughts are clear to me.

Everything moves fast. It's hard to feel settled when she is out of my line of vision. All the big men smell of sweat, and somebody steps on my foot as I try to catch Peggy's hand again. We push through the people, and I feel her trying to pull away from me. Among the crowd I realise how small she is. I hate the uneven line between being her sister and her parent. If I was only her sister, I could shout at her, I could push her down and run off without her. But I am not only her sister. There were days when I could drop Peggy over to you while I came into the market. You'd spend the afternoon reading to her, singing with her, showing her how to play your fiddle. Jack used to say you were snooty for not sitting her in front of the television, remember? And you would smirk and tell him to feck off, that clever girls like Peggy shouldn't waste their time with television. There was a time when you would smirk at me like that. Something got in the way, though, and then came the sad time when you only gave me polite, obliging smiles. Like you didn't know me at all.

Betty appears in the crowd again, much closer than she was before. Too close, perhaps. I don't want her to catch me, I just want to know what she's up to. Who she's with. Where she goes.

I lift Peggy onto my back. She is too big for this, we look stupid. She kicks me, but I hold on to her.

'We'll be faster like this.'

I say to her, and she buries her face into my hair, presumably mortified.

'Faster to where? Where are we going?'

The benefit of being her big sister and her parent at once is that I can ignore her when it suits me. She stays quiet up on my back, as I wander around the market, seeing who Betty buys her messages from, who she makes small talk with and who she avoids. I just want to learn her better, in the ways she won't tell me in words. A mass of people separates us. Wide backs and big coats, boots and caps. And then, a gap in the crowd. And Betty's face, looking right back at me. She jumps back. Like she has seen a ghost.

I drop Peggy onto the ground, and she races to Betty.

'Hello, pet!'

She says, kneeling down to Peggy's height. Fussing over her. Pulling the cardigan up over her shoulders and rolling her sleeves down. It's embarrassing for me to realise how scruffy Peggy looks, and know that Betty probably thinks this is my fault. Why doesn't she fix my cardigan, too?

'Anna, would you let Peggy come with me down to mine for a while? I've a big, long list of jobs she can help me with. We might go and see Ciara's puppies!'

She says, and winks at Peggy. And I feel the wink like a knife through my muscle. But no, actually, no it's fine. Peggy is bouncing at the thought of the puppies, the thought of an afternoon in Betty's perfect home, and time away from me, I presume. I'm not jealous of how mad Peggy is for Betty; sure I'm the same myself.

'Absolutely! Sure we'll all go, will we?'

I say, and Betty hesitates for a second, but only to think of what Peggy can do first. The whole walk, Peggy holds Betty's hand like a tiny child. They talk about baking and school and clothes. Things that they seem to have spoken about before, private jokes between the two of them that jump up to hit me in the face.

Down at Betty's house, I take my usual seat at the table. And I relax.

'Right so, Peggy, will you fold these sheets with me?'

Betty asks, lifting a basket of washing onto the table. The chaos of the town leaves me. The high-up, dizzy heat begins to dissolve. I would be alright if Peggy wasn't here. This scary feeling comes over me, that I am being forgotten already. This crucial new friendship of mine doesn't hold the weight I thought that it did. The ache of this is too familiar, our relationship being underplayed for the company of a child. For the company of Tom. I feel I am coming in last again. Like Betty will soon stop smirking and start offering obliging smiles.

Her headscarf catches my eye, thrown on the table. Cerulean blue. Thrown down like it doesn't mean a thing. She gives Peggy a set of sheets to put in her bedroom and takes some bits down to the hot press. I hear them in the hall, Peggy asking Betty if she has ever been to Dublin Zoo, and Betty suggesting that they go together someday. Christ almighty. While they occupy each other, I am left alone in the kitchen.

Only me and the perfect afternoon light, and her headscarf. And I am taken, pulled, overwhelmed by an urge to try it on. To stuff it down my skirt. To hold on to it, and not let go.

She could come back any second and catch me out. But I feel if I don't put this scarf on now, I'll never be right again. So I put it on, just quickly. Why deny myself? Just for a minute. Just long enough to admire myself in the gleam of her sink. The threat of being caught is softened by the sensation of her against my cheeks. The smell of her all around me. The feeling of being enveloped by Betty Nevan. Who is surely about to catch me. Here she comes.

Snatching her scarf off my head, I feel her being ripped from me. Quickly, I put it into my handbag. Two of her black hairs, now laying on the shoulder of my dress. She notices nothing missing. She doesn't even notice as I take her hair from my dress and plait it into my own.

Betty

'LAST ONE!'

I say, giving two corners of a sheet to Peggy. I look back at the table once more. Did I not leave something there to tidy away? Maybe I've it done already.

'Who's your best friend in the town?'

For just a second, I think it was Peggy who asked me. It's the sort of question I would expect from a girl her age. Not from an adult. Not from Anna.

'I think I'm a bit long in the tooth to be having best friends.'

I try to laugh her off. Although there's nothing wrong with asking. Maybe I'm being unfair.

'Is it Ciara Moore?'

She persists. And I realise it isn't the question that bothers me, it's the insistence that I should share the details of my life with her. Anna is always prying, unabashed. I know I'm often prying myself, but I have the cop on to do it with some subtlety. There is a depth to her tone, as though she is asking something gravely important.

'I suppose Ciara is a good friend of mine, yes.'

I feel stupid for answering. Anna nods, like I've given her something to consider. I turn to Peggy, only wanting to engage with her.

'Peggy, what sheets do you prefer? I've to get a new set for the spare bedroom and I don't know what to choose!'

All of this flies out of my mouth to stop Anna from saying anything else. I'm not annoyed at her, I just want a minute where she isn't at me. Peggy brings the corners of the sheet towards me.

'I like either of them, they're both nice. We've no sheets at all at home.'

'Peggy, stop.'

Anna cuts across her. Something about all of this is so embarrassing. All of us trying to stop each other from talking. Anna must think I'm annoyed at her. She must think I'm so rude for not indulging her questions about Ciara, and she must think that I want to use her little sister for free labour. This is the last time that I'll ask Peggy over, it's not right for me to be getting attached to her.

Oh, but could I stay away from the child? Why should I stay away? She is obviously starved of attention. Leave us have each other. It's not right for Anna to be getting jealous over this. We would have had a nice time together, this evening, when she called down for Tom. But she pushed her way in. She made me feel bad, and now it's all just strange.

'Do you want to make a pot of tea, Anna?'

I ask her, smiling as politely as I can. Since she isn't going to give us a hand with the sheets, she might as well do something useful. It's funny that she is so different from Peggy and Tom. He had us roaring laughing the last night when we were watching *The Late Late Show*. Himself and Bill drinking bottles of porter, doing his Gay Byrne impression. I can't imagine Anna having the craic like that. With the last of the sheets folded, I send Peggy outside with scraps for the cats.

'You know what?'

Anna surprises me, breaking a silence that I didn't realise had formed.

'I have such a nice time with you, Betty. It makes such a difference to spend time with a woman. I'm always trying to translate myself for Jack and Tom.'

Such a lot to break a silence with. I wonder if she was waiting for Peggy to leave to say that, if it has been building up inside her for a long time. Or if she just said it without thinking. I wonder if she realised that she had soured the tone, and if she's trying to mend it. Whatever her intention, I believe what she says. It's touching. I sit down and put a hand over hers.

'Ah, Anna.'

I want to say more, to tell her that I understand. But I'm not sure what to say. To be honest, I'm not sure I can empathise, I've never felt like that with Bill. Never. He always understands me. It must be so hard to live that way, always trying to make yourself more palatable. The most vital parts of you, always taken with a degree of misunderstanding. And then me, the one woman she thinks can understand her, misunderstanding. Lost for words.

'You can always talk to me. The women have to stick together.'

I say, squeezing her hand, and then quickly getting up to make the tea, hoping it was enough. She's a nice girl, she's just different. I want to move things on, but I'm not sure how. I look out the window and see Peggy stroking the cats, and I feel my heart melt.

'Isn't Peggy as good as gold? Such a dote.'

As I turn with the teapot, I see Anna rolling her eyes. I pretend not to have noticed.

'Did you ever want a child?'

She has a real talent for catching me off guard. She must hate me for wanting to spend time with Peggy. She must want to tell me that I need to grow up, to remember that Peggy isn't mine. I don't see the point in lying to her.

'I always wanted a child. Always.'

I pull my eyes away from Peggy and go back to the table. She seems surprised by my frankness. Well, if she's going to be startling, I'll join her.

'Why haven't you had any so?'

She should know better than to ask that. But there is something refreshing about the way she just speaks her mind. It makes me feel like I could do the same. I take a deep breath.

'It just never worked out.'

Such a short sentence to sum up so many long years of disappointment. And while such a short sentence betrays everything I've been through, I find it is all I can manage. And she surprises me once more.

'It could definitely happen yet.'

By the look on her face, she really means it. And I find myself relaxing with her again, because I didn't expect to reveal so much of myself to her, so readily. Maybe she isn't as bad as I thought. Maybe she's refreshing, in a way that I need.

'Would you want a few of your own?'

I ask, realising that with Anna, I have no idea what is coming next. She laughs.

'I'd be scared to.'

Afraid of the most natural thing in the world. Isn't it funny? She goes on.

'Oh, it's all of it. The men. The birthing. Our mammy died having Peggy, you know? It can just happen so fast.'

'God rest her.'

I try not to let my face fall. Opening the window to let some fresh air in, we can hear Peggy talking to the cats. I would never have guessed. The mere mention of her mother brings a gloss to Anna's eyes. I suppose we've both said something very personal now. It evens us out.

Then, something catches me: didn't Bill say that their mother died only recently? That was the reason he gave for leaving Miltown, wasn't it?

'Typical, that you'd give anything for a child, and I'm afraid to have one.'

She says, and I laugh, because I only half heard her and I'm not sure what else to do. Poor Peggy, did she never know her mother at all?

'Aren't we hard to please?'

Peggy comes back in saying that one of the cats scrawled her. When I look at her arm, there is nothing there, but still I take her in my lap and give her the attention she wants. Anna and I go on talking about quieter things for a while, and Peggy stays in my lap, her fidgeting hands slowing down. It's lovely, everything feels so soft. Maybe it's something to do with letting things out. The clock in the hall strikes. The lads will be back up from the farm any minute.

'Will you go and find Bill and Tom for me?'

I whisper to Peggy. She yawns and looks at Anna, who nods. And so she gets down and goes out the door for them. I didn't realise she was dozing. To have never known her mother and father. What does that do to a child? When my own mother died, I felt like I had lost a limb. Perhaps Peggy hasn't lost a limb, perhaps she was born without one.

Anna

WHEN PEGGY GOES OUT THE door, something leaves me. My inhibition, perhaps, I don't know, but I say something I'm not supposed to say.

'Jack nearly was a father, in Kilmarra.'

Her eyes widen, but she is too polite to give a big reaction. It's just because we were talking about babies, that's all. And if nothing else, it will keep her interested in us. In me. For some reason, I feel compelled to share it with her. I suppose there is no reason I should be keeping this a secret. It didn't even happen in the end. There was no baby, why hide from it?

Suddenly I feel faint. I turn away to look out the window. And I must be looking out the window for a long time, because the next thing I know, Betty is sitting right next to me, holding my hand, asking if I'm okay. All the power of her touch, resurfacing.

The lads come in the door of the house, with Peggy between them. It's time to leave. I don't have time to explain what I've said.

Tom starts doing his Gay Byrne voice for Betty. I wouldn't have known that's who he was impersonating if I wasn't told. But her laugh sounds genuine. I feel so stupid, standing here listening to them all laughing, smiling, and I have to pretend that it doesn't bother me that

I wasn't invited to watch *The Late Late Show* with them, and that I wouldn't have liked to try American peppers. That I was too busy to be there anyway, but I'm so glad that everybody had a nice time. That I don't feel like a perpetual afterthought.

'Have you all your bits, love?'

Betty asks, and I know better than to think she is talking to me. Peggy answers her, I don't listen, but I see them hugging. Betty looks at me like she wants to keep talking. I have to ignore it. Tom pats the top of Peggy's head, and she shoves his hand away.

'Oh, those boys have no idea about beauty, have they, Peggy?'

Betty says, winking at Tom, and smooths down Peggy's hair. I stand still, watching it all. Unsure how to make myself a part of this moment so it doesn't become another memory that doesn't involve me. Bill mentions the name of an old neighbour that sometimes helps him on the farm, Paddy Murphy, and I sense Tom sharpening. Jealousy. Maybe Tom will try to spook that man away from the Nevans' farm. Maybe the next time he shows up to the farm, he will be limping, not meeting Tom's eye. I try to put myself in the conversation, but there's no room for me. It's time we left.

As we walk out the gate, I hear Betty asking Bill,

'Did you ever hear of a place called Kilmarra?'

We leave, and I feel like she is being taken from me. Walking home, I can't find my centre. I'm sure it's fine that I told her about Jack and the baby. Sure we were talking about babies, weren't we, and when they don't come to be. I'm sure it's fine. I'm sure it won't make a blind bit of difference.

My Betty, unable to have a child of her own. Imagine. I must admit, something about it warms me. And with a jolt I realise how much she has already come to mean to me, and how afraid I would be to lose her. She makes my thoughts feel real. Not like abstract things I can't get a hold of or pin down or make sense of. She grounds me. Maybe she is the centre I have lost. I want to touch her. To hold on to her for just a moment and let her know what her company means to me. Although, given the chance, I couldn't really put it into words.

Jack

DEEP IN THE SUMMER, THERE will be mornings so sunny and bright that I won't feel anything but grateful, and I won't do anything but smile. I hold on to this thought on mornings like this, when the day stretches out ahead of me, intimidatingly empty. Anna has gone out to see Betty Nevan. Peggy is gone to school. Tom is my last chance today.

As he is getting ready to head out to work, I leave what's left of my pride aside and approach him. All morning, there has been tension heating up between us. I'm sure he could guess what's coming. I'm sure it puts him on edge, my looming request. And I'm sure it feels worse than expected when I land it on him.

'I could give ye a hand down on the farm today, if ye need it?'

My throat nearly closes from the embarrassment of having to ask. I stand still, hands by my side. Waiting for a begrudging 'yes', so that I can put my cap on and start my day. My life.

But Tom says nothing. 'Tis often easier to say nothing than to say no. A part of me expected this. Being his brother, I know how to combat him before he has even moved.

'They're awful long days in the house, you know.'

Rattling around on my own, all the time. He can't imagine what maddening length my days stretch to. Uncomfortable. Obviously. We are both uncomfortable.

'Look, Jack, if there was work there I'd give it to you. But Bill keeps cows and bulls. I don't think you'd manage.'

And 'tis often easier to say no than to be kind. Really, I know, Tom probably hasn't the authority to be giving me any work. It's Bill I should be asking.

He leaves the house, and when the door closes, I hear my exhaling echo off the walls. Nothing to be at. Nothing at all to be at. Nothing to look at or to read. Nobody to talk to. Nobody holding out a hand for me.

I catch myself in the mirror, in need of a shave and a haircut. It isn't at all surprising that Tom told me no. This is how he used to behave with Daddy. He had to be the favourite, so I could never be the favourite. I believe one of the things currently plaguing Tom is that if I had the chance, and made a friend of Bill Nevan, I could be asked to take his place on the fields. I could be the one staying late in the Nevan's, watching *The Late Late Show* and impressing Betty. I apply the shaving cream, and imagine Tom acts on the Nevans' farm just as he used to act on our farm. Carrying things that are too heavy, walking too far, working too late. Sweating for approval. All the while knowing that I'm much more like Bill than he is. Funnier, more charming. He hates me for this. He should count himself lucky that I'm not vindictive enough to try to topple him from his spot at the top. I just wish he hadn't made it about bulls. As though he can handle a bull better than I could.

A stack of pages sits under the newspaper, Tom's handwriting. His most recent attempts at poetry and writing. He thinks he's Yeats; but Yeats didn't keep all of his scribblings a complete secret, did he? In an act of kindness to us both, I decide not to look through them.

In the mirror, I start with the razor. And all I can think of is Daddy. As I draw the blade down my chin, my mind races away from the bull. I don't remember much after the time that Daddy died, but those last moments come back to me with more clarity than the moment I'm in. Even with shaving cream lining my nostrils, I can get a huff of Daddy's blood on the wet grass. The strength of the bull, like something I could never have imagined. All the strength I once saw in my father, vanishing. Dilating eyes. Clay on my collar. His futile attempt to fight, and his delayed attempt to flee. A small cut from the razor appears on my cheek.

I blot away the blood and wonder if Daddy would be upset about how little I remember. I get flashes of Mammy sending us out while herself and Margaret and Mrs Hayes prepared the house. And vaguely, Niall Hegarty bringing myself and Tom down to Mahoney's shop to get supplies for the wake. Tom gave me a jaunt on his bicycle. He could hardly steer the thing he was crying so much. I'm sure that he was embarrassed to be crying like that in front of all the men. Maybe that's part of the reason he is always trying to be the big man now. If I could have cried with him, I would have. But I was as stoic as Daddy ever was. You used to always say you wished I would show more emotion.

I appreciate what Niall Hegarty and the other men were trying to do. Maybe they thought that a funeral is the right time to start treating a boy like a man. But I didn't feel like a man. If anything, the whole thing made me realise that I never felt like such a small child. Do you know, a part of me still feels that way. Stuck in Mahoney's shop, shivering but unable to cry, watching as my big brother humiliates himself by feeling his feelings.

That's all I really remember about it. That, and the ache in my arms from carrying back a crate of Jameson.

Right. Come on now, Jacky. Do something with yourself. Switch on the radio and see what's happening out in the world.

Faintly, somewhere within the static, I recognise the noise of The Beatles. Your favourite. I switch it off again. Would I be insane to suggest that the radio is mocking me? I clean the cottage. I feed the pony. I do all the womanly tasks that Anna doesn't bother with, to give some purpose to my morning. Being the woman of the house is a career, I don't know why she doesn't embrace it.

The day is fresh, bright. A good day. Maybe I'll just go down to the Nevans' farm anyway. Tom and Bill will feel too much social pressure to turn me away. I might lie out in the field as Tom comes along with the plough, and have my throat cut by the blade, and be turned into the earth. What a fine thing it would be, to be made into the earth. To be made new again.

'I Feel Fine' gets stuck in my head, even when I only heard a few bars of it. Another song you never heard. I suppose you would have all the words learned by now. You'd be begging me to take you up to Dublin to see them play a concert. You'd be in love with me, and I'd feel fine.

At twelve, I walk through the town, down to Doyle's, knowing there will be a bit of company for me there. I know that Teresa Doyle is probably a bit fond of me, but I pretend not to notice. She's happy to talk to me, happy to listen. Happy to let her eyes melt across me. But I like her company. I want to see her. To let melt her eyes.

When I arrive, to my surprise, I see Tom and Bill, already half a pint in. Bill talking and messing with the black rings from the ring board. The sconces glowing. The fireplace lit.

'Hard at work, I see.'

I stifle a scoff as I sit on the stool beside Tom. Bill is in an animated conversation with another man. Mary is pulling pints, but Teresa comes out from the back when I arrive, and hurries her sister away. She comes to stand with me. Radiant.

'Actually, Jack, Bill is here on business. He's making a deal with that man.'

'Jack O'Leary, nice to see you.'

Teresa smiles and puts a bag of lemon drops before me. She lights a cigarette for herself. Tom tries to ignore her, but I know he is listening.

'Hello, Teresa.'

I smile, hoping she won't notice the cut on my cheek. I can't help but laugh at Tom.

'He couldn't have left you on the farm while he came down for his meeting? You're not a little boy.'

Teresa giggles. Tom rolls his eyes and turns away from us, unwilling to laugh at himself. Recently, Teresa has taken to asking her father to give me a few hours' work. I suppose it's hard for Ger Doyle to believe that I don't have a taste for drink when I'm in the pub most days. Bill shakes the hand of the man he is talking to, pats him on the back and sends him off.

'Job done! Another round please, Teresa. And one for our friend Jack, please!'

Bill says, rubbing his hands together. Whatever deal he has made, he is very happy with it.

'Jack, how's tricks?'

He asks me, and I am at once drawn to and repelled by his charisma. I used to be a man like this. Making deals in the pub, buying rounds, with everyone's names in my mouth. I only ever did it to live up to Daddy, you know. Everyone in Kilmarra expected it from me. It feels good to let it all go for a while.

'Quiet enough.'

I tell him. Tom shifts in his seat, clearly uncomfortable to have me interacting with Bill. His two worlds colliding, here in Doyle's.

'I'm going to ask Dad again today, Jack. Mary will be working less and less now with the baby coming, so we could do with the help.'

I smile, unsure what else to do. This is what she likes about me; I never know what to say, I'm quiet, moody. I don't think she would have liked the old Jack at all.

'Thanks, Teresa.'

Bill leans in, listening to all of this. Wondering, I'm sure, how he could spin his web to make it all work out for me. It isn't that I don't want his help, I just don't want him to think of me as another little son, like Tom.

And anyway, to be very honest, I'm half afraid to be standing on the same side of the bar as Teresa. To be at her mercy. A few days ago, she told me very earnestly that I am something apart from everything that she knows, and everything that knows her. A novelty, I suppose she meant to say. That's the sort of thing that comes out of her when we spend a few hours together each day. What would come out of her if we were to start working together? All our evenings and nights, side by side.

'Did ye see there's a dance next Friday?'

Bill says to us all. He presents this as very good news, which pulls a sigh from me, and a smile from Teresa.

'I saw that alright.'

Looking up at me from his pint, Tom is feeling the pressure to keep up his happy persona.

'We'll be there, won't we, Jack?'

I could terrorise myself with all the awful eventualities of the dance before answering. Or I could just agree now, because I know that I will end up agreeing no matter what.

'We will, please god.'

Tom hops up, suddenly alive.

'Oh, we will! Dancing and drinking and all that carry-on, 'tis good for the soul.'

Teresa is taken aback. I suppose she hasn't seen too much of Tom yet.

''Twould lighten us all up, I suppose.'

Bill says, as though we really need it. As though he knows what we need.

Then Tom claps his hands together, delighted that I am on his side. As though I have ever really gone against him. I feel I need to turn to Teresa and ask her if she's going. I don't want her to feel like she's just watching a conversation, especially when I came in here looking for her company.

'This will be good craic now. A bit of ruaille buaille. There might even be a bit of talent there.'

Tom says, and immediately blushes, realising Teresa can hear. I'm sure he wants to apologise to Bill more than he wants to apologise to her.

'You'll be there, will you, Teresa?'

I ask, and she taps the ash off her cigarette, our eyes meeting.

'I suppose I will be.'

Anna

JUST AS I DRIFT OFF to sleep, I swear I register the sound of a scream. Far-off, like it's wiping past the house, but I swear I hear it. It follows me into a white-blonde dream, this dulled, drawn-out noise. And as I am waking, it almost wakes with me. Becoming more real, a sound so true I could hold it in my hands. But when I look around, I see Peggy and Jack have slept through it. Perhaps there was no scream at all. Perhaps you just want some attention. Are you jealous of my new life?

Then comes silence, and a bright morning. The brightest I have seen this year. The sun has burst across a pale sky. Slowly, wildflowers bud, and the tight beginnings of berries build up the hedges. A chorus of birds sing. And Betty pushes her bicycle up my path. Her blue coat and hat soaking up the light. These days, these moments and seconds, coming from nowhere without warning and filling me with an infinity of reasons to keep going. How violently quick my spirit has been uplifted. It begins with her fingers tapping on the window, on my heart, and her voice calling in the door. A bag of stale bread in the basket of her bicycle. Cooing at Peggy as though she is younger than nine.

'Peggy! Come on and we'll feed the ducks.'

There at the window, she reminds me of myself. Always looking in. I don't even get angry at Peggy for the look she throws me when I follow them. She takes Betty's hand, and I wonder if she's showing off. What I wouldn't give to take Betty's hand. To tell her how she uplifts me. To tell her that she has made my future soft and inviting, where once it was just a far-off and impalpable threat. But I say nothing, and follow them closely.

Betty starts telling us about a man who called to them a few nights ago, with a big horoscope chart. He could read her past or future using the stars.

'It's all to do with your time of birth, I think. It's a science, so he said.'

He was telling Betty and Bill about their own tendencies and proclivities, as though they didn't know themselves. He told them parts of their future that they couldn't guess at. Parts of their past that he shouldn't have been able to guess at. Isn't that interesting? Just another memory that I am not a part of; I hate missing out on these things, even when I fear all of my stars would have been void.

At the lake, Betty gets down to Peggy's height, pointing out a patch of reeds, lifting her dress and letting the bare skin of her knees become dirty with the earth. Isn't she wonderfully uncouth? See her fingers working, ripping the heel of the bread into pieces for Peggy, who drops them into the water. What a gift, to have such a surplus you can allow the bread to go bad. I never felt so grand. Here are the ducks. Amn't I a lucky girl, in a lucky position? To have Betty Nevan elevating me above my own class. Right now, I am so much more than Anna O'Leary. These big, almost oppressive happinesses come on so fast and so strong. I wonder is it Betty bringing them on? When I am with her, I feel I am floating and firmly on the ground at the one time. A big feeling. An almighty feeling. You cannot imagine what this is like. I feel like I came out of the sun to be here. For the first time in so long, I feel the winter is behind me.

'You're going down to the hall next Friday, I assume?'

Oh, every word she utters is an injection of energy into my blood. Do you know what I like so much about Betty? She isn't just humouring me. I can tell that she really likes me.

'I can't go. I've no one to look after herself.'

I say, nodding at Peggy, who seems frightfully close to falling into the lake. Betty draws her back with a hand. How gentle she is.

'Sure drop her down to Minnie Keane. She'll have a few in with her that night, she won't mind at all.'

Solving problems as though they aren't problems at all. Everything is easy for Betty. How lucky I am that she wants to solve my problems. How lucky I am to spend my afternoons with her, breathing in her Imperial Leather.

Would it be bizarre to go down to the dance on my own, without the boys? To enjoy a night by myself, as myself? Imagine, doing something on my own.

Imagine, standing among the hot, damp bodies in the hall, making her laugh. Light trapped in the sweat on her forehead, her waist hot beneath my hand. I have to be there. Of course, I will be there.

'We might get a nice fella for you.'

She teases, and I know she's only trying to have a laugh, but it feels like a slap in the face. I laugh along like it's all fine, but I'm mortified.

'Ah, come on, Anna, you must be ready for a bit of romance now. You're always saying that you're sick of spending all your time up in the cottage.'

She's right, I am always saying that. But I don't remember telling her that I want a man. I shrug.

'I've no luck with lads.'

'I used to think the same thing, until I met Bill. I never burned like that over a man before.'

She speaks so softly that I could be mishearing, but so confidently that she is unmistakable. I've never heard a woman use language like that before. To admit so openly to burning; to express her most private, stirring feelings to me. Why would she bring me in this close and then try to offload me onto some man?

'I wish I could admit to all the ways I've burned.'

I tell her, and I see her pausing at this. It comes naturally, I can catch her off guard.

'Are you nervous of men, Anna?'

She asks me, and I feel ten years younger than I really am. I shake my head. It isn't that I'm nervous of men, not at all. I'm just glad to let them move through the world entirely separate from me. Any man could take a notion to knock me to the ground, to draw blood from me or make a mother of me. Why would I invite one of them around me?

'I was never so nervous of a man as I was of Bill, you know, when we first met. I was afraid of what he might do to me. What he might not do.'

How eloquent. Not like a giddy schoolgirl but like a mature, assured woman, unafraid of her own desire. I have always been building towards a woman like Betty.

'Leave it with me, Anna. I won't match you up with any old dope.'

She makes her way to Peggy and bends down to speak to her. She starts to tell her that she once wanted to be a detective.

'I often think of it. That I'd like to work with the guards, solving things like.'

She says it with such confidence. I don't think she'd make much of a detective, when she seems to think I want a boyfriend and not all of her attention.

'And you're going to be a vet, Peggy, isn't that right?'

I see the flash of every syllable that leaves her mouth and floats into the air.

'That's right.'

I never knew that Peggy wanted to be a vet. I didn't realise that Peggy had ambitions.

The afternoon rolls around us. What a sight she is as I leave her. Rain begins to fall into the lake, but she doesn't hurry away. Instead, she goes back down to Peggy's level and hugs her. And then, getting wetter, she turns to me, laughs at herself, and hugs me, too. The damp of her hat on my cheek. Let the dye run off and colour me blue, please.

The world slows to half its speed, and I hold on to her for my life.

My god, what it is to have her right here, in my arms. Holding on and keeping her dry.

When she turns to go, the rain gets heavier. As though the whole sky has turned to liquid. She is wet, then she is the water. She is glittering blue, and then there is nothing left to see. Only Betty, blue and soaked in the sky. Turning and leaving. Gone.

I wonder if she thinks of me when we are apart. I wonder if she knows she is so deep in my thoughts that she could taste them.

It isn't often I find somebody who likes me this much, who lets me like them this much. Each friend that I've lost was a stepping stone to her. You will remember all the trouble I had keeping friends.

Catherine Jennings. A tall, quiet girl, who I became so close to that I began to voice her thoughts for her. I thought I'd never get over it the day that she left with her family for England. It could have happened yesterday, that's how well I remember it. I was lost without her.

But then, there was Milly Hayes, indulging my daydreams about going to America. I felt like I was one of her senses, that's how well she knew me. It was like she was explaining me to myself. There were countless reasons we didn't remain friends, all of which could be boiled down to the milkman's mere existence. These days, I can't recall it as much more than a story told to me by somebody else.

Then came Aoife Murray, who came into my life around the same time that you met Jack. I thought that we were going to be a little four. But then you and Jack started courting, and Aoife got engaged. Suddenly I didn't fit anywhere. I was so embarrassed over it.

I remember so well the day that she got married. Outside the church, when I couldn't face watching the ceremony, you put your arms around me. Whatever you said to console me, I don't remember now. But I remember the feeling of being in your arms, and of being important to you. It was peace. Broad and complete peace, the likes of which I hadn't known until then, and which I haven't known since. And when the bell of the church rang for Aoife and her husband, I felt happy. Something new had come. Something more than what I had before.

All night through the party, you stayed with me. Even when Jack asked you to dance and told you that I was only looking for attention. Nothing that he tried could charm you away from me that night. The corners of your mouth stained purple by the port wine, widening your already wide smile. And all night I had you laughing. I loved feeling that important, that close to you. I know I was never your favourite, but I think, that night, I got close.

For a long time after, I tried to recreate that closeness. I'm not sure why it never came back. As good as I was to you, it was never the same as that night. Now I wish I could have just enjoyed the memory of us, rather than always trying to reanimate it. Overdoing it, you know.

I'm trying not to do that with Betty.

Betty, Betty, Betty.

A thousand times, Betty.

Everything, Betty.

Tom

'DON'T I ALWAYS TELL YOU, 'tis on the stage you should be, Tom. I'm always telling him that!'

Bill laughs, and Betty laughs along with him. 'Twas only something small I said that wouldn't have even earned a sideways glance at home. But they love me in this house. He throws his hand of cards down on the table, revealing a few eights, a jack and a king. They said it was a simple enough game, but I can't tell what his hand says. Bill could have any cards at all in his hand, he would be winning. He rolls his eyes and tuts.

''Tis hearts I'm playing for.'

And he laughs, and takes his drink.

'Tom wrote poems for me when we were younger. He wrote a few for some girls in the town, I'm sure.'

It's one thing for Bill to think I might have a creative streak, another thing altogether for Anna to confirm that I have made several attempts to be creative. Suddenly I feel I could be sick. If I only had the bottle to tell them I can't follow the rules of this game. That poetry I once wrote was my own soul bared, and it still wasn't very good. Imagine. If I could just tell them to cut the compliments, because I haven't the nerve to take or reject them.

The dark of the night has come, heavier than before, as though a storm is on the way. A box of Fry's chocolates on the table, a bottle of sherry for the women, a bottle of whiskey for the men. A moth dances around the lamp. Nobody is offended enough to waft it away. It's like being underwater, we are so relaxed.

I lean back in my chair. Bill pours another drop out for himself and myself. With every glass, my problems get smaller. It's so easy to forget about Jack and Peggy, at home, asleep. Betty starts talking. It's a nice music that I tune in and out of. Goodness, isn't this goodness? Four little friends, deep into a Saturday night, with no reasons to hurry home.

Betty has been trying to rile us up into a debate all evening. Every now and again, dropping in her opinions about preserving tradition while achieving economic expansion. What debate she's after, I don't know, because it sounds as if she has it all sorted.

'They could do with you above in the Dáil.'

Bill laughs, and Betty starts on about Lemass. She enjoys being a political woman. I must say, right now I enjoy her being a political woman, even when it makes me feel uneducated. Something about being inferior to her feels natural. Betty could tell me that she is joining the British army and I would probably keep gently nodding along, just to preserve this moment. I would go on like this forever, in this rich, dreamy night. Fuelled by drink and the assurance that I am wanted. Dark, and warm, and loved.

A knock on the door, disturbing our melted mood. Bill grunts, rising to answer it. Unbothered by whoever is calling, Betty passes a card to me and goes on talking. I nod along, humming in agreement, trying to keep our gentle night unbroken by this caller.

'Ah, Cathal!'

Bill's voice is perhaps louder than he expected it to be. He is trying to get the young boy to come into the house, although by his face he seems to already know why Cathal is here. Stepping past Bill, he takes off his hat and nods at Betty and Anna. He can't be more than fourteen.

''Tis time, Bill.'

And like that, Bill is reaching for his own cap. Glad to help, ready to go. There is nothing I want more than for him to stay in the kitchen with us, chatting and laughing. To pour a drink for Cathal or to push him out the door.

'Right! Come on so.'

He says in a cheery voice.

'Tom, you might as well come down and give us a hand.'

Bill says, putting on his coat. And I, like a child, unsure of what I am to give a hand in, dutifully rise to pull my own coat on.

And I am led out into the half dark. Leaving the safety of Anna inside. Out with the men. Even with these lengthening evenings, the dark gets so dark. I could get lost in it. How eerily quiet it is. Behind us, the sky is nothing but navy, stretching all the way back beyond the horizon, back to the beginning of time. And before us, a smattering of stars comes through red and orange clouds. Like we are walking towards a great fire. Right into the wrath of God. I stare into it as we move, knowing that if I look away for even a second, the colour will fade and go, and the night will take over. Isn't it always so quick, the movement from sunset to dark?

Anna

A SUDDEN AND DEEP QUIET falls after Cathal has taken the men away. Not wanting to appear immature, I accept the new drop Betty pours out for me. I accepted the first drop without asking what we were drinking, and I feel it's too late to ask now.

My coat and handbag on her chair. My hands around her glass. My body in her home. This might be the first time I've seen her in the kitchen without her apron on.

'It's quiet now.'

How boring, yet I find myself saying it with a little laugh, and wishing that I hadn't. I don't want to bother Betty with such pedestrian observations. I don't want her thinking that the silences need to be filled. I want to be in her silences, as she is in mine. To admire all the ways that we are when we are not speaking, moving or doing. Just existing with each other. How intimate. Betty pretends not to be disappointed that I have commented on the silence; she must like it too. I smile at her and wait for a smile back. I wait for her response. I place each of my delicate feelings between her molars and wait for her to bite down.

'It's no harm to have a break from the lads.'

She says, and I nod. And I wish I hadn't been nodding along so vigorously to everything she was saying about the economy, so she would know I really meant this one.

'It's nice to have a break from everything, isn't it?'

She says, and I cannot tell if she is relaxed or sad or bored. Suddenly, everything stops. It's like time has paused; Betty has paused. There is nothing but me and the texture of her breath. I hear it, and I feel it, warm and ruffled around me. And then everything comes back.

'Yeah.'

I hate that she would ever feel that she needs a break. Her life should be easier. So easy that a break would seem monotonous and unnecessary. What sort of a life would we have if I was to move into her spare room? How long would the bliss last? I wonder could we spend every evening this way. Barefooted, perhaps in nightdresses, drinking with the moths. Without the lads. Close. Yes, barefoot in our nightdresses. Her, in something white, almost sheer on her raindrop body. Something expensive. She makes me feel so expensive. Absentminded, she pulls her hair up and away from her face. Look how the baby hairs lie marbling the side of her neck. Look how her tiny little veins bulge from her temples, ageing her. And then she lets her hair back down. Isn't it good that we are so familiar to each other, that she can expose these parts of herself to me?

Tom

'A CALF IS COMING, TOM.'

Bill says to me as we reach the barn. Softly, and to me only. I feel like a little boy being told that Santa Claus is coming. Half intrigued, half afraid. Man up now, Tom, this will really impress him.

The cow is heard before she is seen. It has been years since I dealt with anything like this. After Daddy's accident, the bull was sold along with all the cows. Now, I've to put on a brave face and pretend I know exactly what I'm at. At a time like this, there would be nothing worse than to ask for help.

'Bill, are ye well? Thanks for coming down.'

Frances McCarthy says, as Cathal leads us into the barn. Bill nods at him.

'I've the apprentice here.'

The men laugh at me, and so, immediately, I laugh with them. Although really, I suppose that I am Bill's apprentice. Not in any trade in particular, just in how to be a man. How to be Bill. It isn't a bad thing to learn.

Calving isn't the gruesome thing I remember it being. For a reason that I cannot name, the mention of calving made me anticipate mass panic, the men racing around the barn as the straw rapidly took the colour of thick, dark blood. This is nowhere near as dramatic as a human birth. The cow is getting on fine without us here. I feel totally unnecessary. What a horrible way to feel. Even Bill might be unnecessary here. But then, the cow cries out. A particular note that I have heard only once before. It is the sound of pure, undiluted pain.

Is it stupid that just the thought of her could bring me to tears?

Anna

MAYBE I'VE HAD ENOUGH TO drink now. It's strange, I feel saturated by everything. It's like I have taken on all the colour in the room, all the humidity and feeling. Something has multiplied my feelings and brought them right up under my skin, so close to the surface that one twitch would have them seeping out of my pores. Everything has been magnified. Somehow better and somehow worse.

And then, I shatter it all by knocking Betty's glass off the table and onto the floor.

'Oh god. Sorry, Betty!'

Don't cry.

Don't cry.

Don't cry.

Don't cry.

Don't cry.

I get down onto my knees to start picking up the pieces of glass before Betty can stop me and tell me not to worry – and she would have told me not to worry, if I wasn't so quick to move. Surely she can see my scalp redden.

Oh, but the glass makes everything worse. Wet from whatever it was holding and determined to upset me, it slices apart the tips of my fingers. Or have I used the glass to slice apart the tips of my fingers?

It's hard to know. Everything is happening so quickly, I don't have time to consider whether I wanted this to happen. Is this unfortunate embarrassment just a cry for attention? Does it matter when the blood is so dark and so much, so suddenly? The drink stings.

A drop falls onto her dress. She hasn't even noticed. Overwhelming, to realise that all that I am amounts to little more than an unseen stain on her dress. Yes, we have had too much to drink. If we hadn't, surely Betty would never have taken my fingertips into her mouth and sucked the blood from them.

Tom

THE COW LETS OUT A roar. It sounds heated. I cannot help but find a piece of myself in the sound. How long ago did this all start? How long was the cow getting up and down for, uncomfortable and crying? She hunches her back, and the hooves of the calf are seen. Where is all the blood? Myself and Frances prepare ourselves. The McCarthys cannot afford to lose a calf, it seems. Frances calls,

'Right, men!'

My eyes widen. Is it possible to be so afraid and so unafraid at once? This is like watching the house burn down and enjoying the warmth of the flames. This is like beating somebody until they bleed and not worrying whether they clot. Alarming, adrenalising, comforting.

Next, a head, a body and long legs. No need for the men to pull at all. A calf drops from the cow. Astonishing. Partly entangled in the lavender and blue of its mother's body, parts that I cannot name.

'Come here, Tom.'

Bill says, approaching the calf, and shows me how to check that it is breathing, how to pull its hind legs apart and determine the sex. And then, the cow licks her own glossy innards off the new calf.

It's only one animal looking after another.

Anna

IT DOESN'T LAST LONG AT all, and yet it lasts longer than perhaps it should. It was only an instinct, really. It's just to be sure that no blood spilled onto the floor. It's just that she wants to look after me. Just that I want to bleed onto her tongue. It's just to feel close, as close friends should. To feel control. My heart hammering so fast that it might shatter.

I tense my hand, which stops Betty. Shameful, to stop such a shameful thing. She does not allow herself to be embarrassed, and just for a second, I let my hand fall on Betty's cheek, leaving a moment of blood there. To feel close. To feel control. And then I go to the sink, alone, to wrap my fingers in a rag. How frightening it is to feel. For a long time after you, I felt like a bruise. Suddenly, she has reminded me that I am freely flowing blood.

It would be impossibly difficult to pretend that it didn't happen. And we don't. There are practical ways of explaining it away. Maternal ways, carnal ways, romantic ways. So many ways that no matter how we look at it, it loses its original meaning.

I am disappointed to realise that there is nothing left in the world to feel after I have felt the pulsing suction of her mouth. Surely there is nothing left in the world to taste now that she has tasted my blood. A quare thing, an unspoken, shared thing.

One animal looking after another.

Something that has been bubbling inside of me for the longest time has suddenly boiled over. It's an injury I sought to cure with you. With Aoife Murray, Milly Hayes, Catherine Jennings. It is the shrill cries of a fox, waking you up from a dream. It is a horse's hoof, firmly planted on your neck. It is a local woman, sucking your blood. It is this: the astonishing joy of a woman's unbridled, unfiltered attention. Something I've so rarely known, something I now have a personal source for. Already I need another dose of it. Of her. What other ugly things can I do to get her to pour her affection into me like that? Oh, what a troublesome thrill. Not even god could touch me now.

Betty

'LONG ENOUGH SERVICE, WASN'T IT?'

Bill puts his cap on. It wouldn't have seemed so long if we hadn't stayed up so late with the O'Learys. The right thing to do would have been to finish the night when the lads came home. Instead, Bill brought the McCarthys back down for a drink. To celebrate the new calf, they said. Although I see now it wasn't the best idea, last night I really didn't mind. The McCarthys were a very welcome addition after Anna cut her finger open. The most awkward hour of my life passed before the lads all burst through the door. With Anna sucking her fingers, not letting her eyes leave me. One minute, she was an adult, the next she was a child. Bleeding, and my responsibility.

Eleven o'clock Mass is something of a novelty to me. I was glad to go late and miss running into the O'Learys. With Bill always up and awake with the breaking of dawn, we never get to sleep late, we never really take our Sundays slow. Today is a nice change, even with a sore head. We pass most of Ballycrea on our walk home from Mass. Eibhlín Quiggly and her girls stop to chat with us. Maybe it's a result of a late night, but I cannot take in a word that she is saying. And I am trying. What captures my attention are the dresses her girls are wearing. Short cut, red and yellow, with white tights. Like little dolls. That's how young girls dress now. It makes me feel old, to look at what young people are wearing and not understand why they like it. I'm sure Eibhlín is mortified to have them walking around the town that way on an ordinary Sunday.

We walk on, I don't let myself feel old for long. In fact, I keep myself in good humour by remembering that Eibhlín is six months younger than me but looks ten years older. Petty, but it keeps me going. Back at home, Bill hardly stops moving before announcing that he is heading down to the farm.

'Ah, Bill, would you not spend the day with me? We could go down to town. Sure 'tis Saint Valentine's Day, isn't it?'

He throws his eyes up to Heaven. It isn't that he doesn't want to spend time with me; it's just that, like most men his age, Bill has to be dragged away from home. He would gladly spend all day and all night pottering between the house and the farm, for the rest of his life. I'm sure that he thought that Mass would be his only excursion today.

'Give me a minute so.'

He will complain for half the afternoon, I know, but he loves coming down town with me. Bill loves to do whatever makes me happy. Look at him grinning as he goes out the door.

A minute, he said. There's no telling how long a minute will last with that man. I read the valentine card he gave me this morning, and then I read it again. If I sit down now I might not pull myself back up all day. I reach the unfortunate conclusion that the best way to pass the time is to clean the place up. Pulling out the chairs to sweep under the table, I see that Anna has left her handbag, in what has become her chair. The clasp untied. The corner of a handkerchief peeking out. And me, very quickly, peeking in.

Only quickly. Only to know what sort of things a girl like Anna carries in her handbag, because she isn't the sort of girl who would carry a handbag at all. And yet, she often has this little thing under her arm. She doesn't smoke, and I've never seen her wearing so much as a swipe of lipstick. What could be so necessary to her that she needs to carry it around all the time?

The handkerchief, monogrammed Kealey, a surname I don't recognise. I hold on to it. A docket from the shop. A tissue. And then two items that shock me almost as much as each other. The first, a Mass card. Yellowed lamination, curling edges. Our Lady on one side, a prayer in ornate lettering. And on the reverse, the name Lillian Kealey. By the dates, only just a year dead. Only twenty-six. And I realise that this is Peggy's Lillian. It must be. The one who would look after her, and make Brigid's Crosses every February, and break Lent on Sundays. Jack's girl, Lillian. Her handkerchief in my hand, her Mass card in my kitchen.

The shock of it is halted by the second item, which somehow scares me more. My blue headscarf. Missing since last week. Suddenly back again.

It's a lot to stumble on at once. My mind is reeling, and doesn't know where to stop, or to start. What I need is to go over to Ciara's house, lay out the contents of the handbag on her kitchen table and connect all the dots with her. She will understand all of this in a way that Bill won't. He'll only overreact. He'll be too concerned and want to confront Tom and Anna before we get any real information. He'll make a scene, and that won't solve anything. I feel hot. I need a minute to think.

I go to open the window to let some air in, and as if by some miracle, Ciara and John are there, in the distance. I know her by her coat. They are coming our way. Ciara carrying something under a tea towel, John a few steps behind her, struggling to keep up. I bless myself as they reach our gate.

'How are ye now?'

John calls, and Ciara rolls her eyes, keeping him a few steps away.

'You're heading down to watch the match, are you, Bill?'

Ciara asks, but it isn't a question. Often, Ciara becomes so irate with her husband that she has to call to mine to vent. When this happens, Bill normally ends up babysitting John.

'I suppose I am.'

Bill looks at John, annoyed over whatever he has done to Ciara that won't allow him to come back home for a few hours.

'You didn't want to go to town, did you, pet?'

'Another time! Ye enjoy the match.'

I smile, knowing that Bill would be more than happy to go down and meet all the boys at the pitch and sink a few pints after. And right now, I would much rather have some time alone with Ciara. Divine timing, all of it.

'Ye better strike, so.'

Ciara says, not turning to look at John. Bill laughs as they go. I've never known a fortnight to pass without Ciara swearing that John is on his last chance.

The lads leave, and my day has changed. Inside, Ciara lays down what she has been carrying, taking off the tea towel to reveal a tart. A part of me wants nothing more than to sit down and listen to Ciara bitching all afternoon, eating slice after slice of sweet tart with her. Warmed by the fire, laughing over our husbands. I want a nice, normal afternoon with my friend. A routine that I understand. But the handbag remains on the table. And I must show her what I've seen. Only how do I start?

'Jesus give me patience and strength, that man has me driven demented.'

Ciara starts, taking cups from the press, making a pot of tea, and telling me that John has lost half their holiday money in the bookies. She sits down, cuts into the tart.

'Anna O'Leary was here last night.'

She pauses at what I've said, unsure why I've interrupted her with something so boring.

'She left her handbag behind.'

I hold it in my hands, showing her that it's already open. Her eyebrows raise, she knows I'm not the type to look through another woman's things. And yet, it's clear I have looked through Anna's things. I don't know how best to tell her what I've found, and so I take her through the exact motions that brought me to the Mass card and my headscarf.

'I was minding Peggy a while ago, and she mentioned Jack had a girl before they arrived here. Lillian. She was mad about her. I thought they had split up or something.'

'I remember, you were saying.'

Ciara says, through a mouthful of tart.

'I was meaning to ask Tom or one of them what happened between himself and Lillian. Well, I'm glad now that I didn't.'

I slide the Mass card across the table. It takes a minute for the penny to drop. Ciara's hand covers her mouth.

'Christ in Heaven, so young!'

She swallows the tart. I hear it in her voice.

'Peggy was talking about her like she was still alive. Maybe she thinks that she is still alive, I don't know.'

Then, before anything settles, I show her my headscarf. Which elicits no reaction, until I tell her,

'This was missing for a week, and then it turns up in her handbag this morning.'

I tap the table while I talk, hoping to hammer some importance into what I'm saying. But Ciara doesn't know what to make of it. And, given a chance to think, neither do I. And so we look at each other a while, trying to make sense of these alarming but banal clues.

'Something is up.'

'Oh, definitely.'

Ciara takes another mouthful of the tart. I do the same, hoping to get to the bottom of it all, fast.

'But what could it be?'

'I don't know.'

A part of me knows better than to say anything bad about the O'Learys, but I let myself.

'I only know that Anna is quare out. And they're keeping this poor girl's death a secret.'

The tart stings at the back of my teeth.

'Ciara, if I had listened to you in the first place. You said they were strange people! Strange doesn't begin to describe it.'

She doesn't want to boast that she was right, so she just nods as I go on.

'I just want to put a distance between us, until I can figure it all out.'

'Sure how will you do that, aren't they always here?'

'They are, I haven't a clue what I'll do.'

But Ciara has. She has several. We talk about getting Anna a job, or involving her with volunteer work, or landing her on another woman. We go around in circles, until something good arrives with us. Didn't I promise her a man?

'Liam Hennessey.'

'Liam Hennessey!'

A young man, without a mother, who recently inherited his father's farm. Not bad-looking, just not good-looking enough to have gotten a girl yet. And so desperate for a wife, for any bit of company, that he'd take anybody we set him up with. And God knows that Anna is yearning for company.

I get the impression that Anna is the sort of woman who is proud to have never been touched by a man. All a bit old-fashioned, if you ask me. I feel sorry for her and her heavy virtue. Maybe this is just what she needs.

Yes, Liam will distract her for a while. In the best case, she will take to him, and they might get married, and I might never need to worry about this again. In the worst case, he will occupy her for just long enough for me to do some more digging and put these pieces together. When we reach a conclusion and plan it all out, Ciara sighs, finally going back to all that John has done wrong this week.

And I relax. It's so good to have a plan in place. It is so good to have somebody to talk to who I can trust. Warm by the fire and eating slices of sweet tart, laughing over our husbands.

Tom

'ARE YE SURE IT'S ALRIGHT to leave her with Minnie Keane? We hardly know the woman.'

Jack asks, fighting Anna for room in the mirror. I comb my fingers through Peggy's hair, because Anna is too busy putting on lipstick to come and do this herself. Peggy wriggles around, trying to pull her head away from my hands. As though I'm running knives across her scalp.

'Yeah, Betty said it's fine.'

Anna says, impatience rising in her voice as Jack stands in her way. It's strange to see what she looks like with makeup on, it's been so long. Strange, too, to see Jack with a bottle of hair oil, preening himself.

'Presumptuous, considering Betty has no children of her own.'

Jack mumbles, as though Anna wouldn't hear him. Of course, Anna hears everything. Even things that we only half think of, she hears. The way that she's looking at him could turn him to stone. Weighted air passes through the room. For days now I have felt a storm impending. I wait for somebody to snap.

But with a cool breath, it all passes, and Anna takes Peggy off me. Positioning her in front of the mirror, she pulls Peggy's hair into two tight plaits. She is more settled with Anna than she was with me. I don't let myself take offence to this.

'Why can't I go to the dance?'

She asks Anna. I decide it isn't my problem. Being left alone is the sort of thing she usually has tantrums over. But she's more than happy to be alone with Betty Nevan, so I'm sure she will get on fine with Mrs Keane. I've met her on the road once or twice. She seems lucid enough.

'Dances are only for adults. You can go when you're grown up.'

Anna roots through her handbag while speaking, not giving her full attention to Peggy.

My God, I was mortified carrying that thing home for her on Monday evening. Betty insisted I took it with me. I don't know why Anna couldn't have just called down for it herself. Even though it was stuffed inside my coat, I was frantic with the idea that somebody would catch me carrying a handbag.

Tying my tie, I watch from the corner of my eye as Anna puts her chin on Peggy's head. Trying to seem sisterly, perhaps. Looking at their reflection, as though something is missing.

'We're more alike every day.'

Anna says. And I hope, for Peggy's sake, that isn't true.

Anna

THE NERVES HAVE MY BONES rattling. I want to get down to the parish hall as quickly as we can, to scope it all out and know exactly what I'm getting myself into. It's as daunting as our first evening here, like going down to John Moore's house all over again. I reach into my handbag and stroke Betty's headscarf, trying to settle myself.

Cold, pale grey air all around me, all in front of me. The sort of foggy night that you might meet Jackie the Lantern in. Before dropping her off at Minnie Keane's, we take Peggy down the sea road to watch the big waves for a little while. She twirls her hair for the whole walk, even when Jack holds one of her hands. Isn't it pretty, the sea? Unpredictable and dark, and so full of life. The ground beneath us mosaicked by crushed mussel shells, blue and white. As the sea churns out creamy foam, I think of England and what I have heard of their seasides; little carnivals.

''Twould put a thirst on you. Seafoam always puts me in mind of a pint.'

Jack says to nobody in particular. The ocean air is wetting us. My hair begins to feel greasy on my neck, behind my ears.

When we get down to Minnie Keane's little terrace house, warm light fattens the windows. Outside, four or five children are running around in the mist. Minnie Keane waves at us from the door, and I realise that she is a total stranger. Something about Betty mentioning her name made me feel like I knew her. Like it would be fine to trust her with Peggy. Well, she is smiling, she seems fine. The other children seem happy, I'm sure Peggy will be grand.

She refuses a kiss when we leave, and I pretend not to be upset by it. I could do with a hug and kiss this evening.

We had to have three conversations with Jack before he agreed to let this woman look after Peggy. Tom called to her house yesterday to check her out and make sure it was all okay. I appreciate that this woman is a stranger, but she's hardly a witch.

'She's not going to eat Peggy, is she?'

I try to make Jack laugh. But with his little Peigín, there is to be no joking.

We turn and leave her, and the mood shifts altogether. How strange. No longer are we three siblings walking down to the parish hall. Suddenly, we are three separate adults, heading in the same direction by coincidence. Each with plans for the evening that don't involve each other. It scares me to think of what they might have in mind for themselves, and so I allow myself to be taken with thoughts of dancing with Betty.

Jack

EVEN THOUGH WE WALK ON without speaking, they feel too close to me. So close that they might as well be on my back. I try to walk ahead, but they catch up. Such a thick silence. Tom must feel the weight of it, too, because he is the one to break it.

'We'll have some craic tonight.'

I hear him from behind me, bolting his words with joviality. I don't bother turning around to give him the reaction that he wants. Unfair, I know. You would have given him a big smile and listed off two or three things that you were excited for. All your endless patience, which I once saw as performative, but now understand as a gift. If I could capture your grace and make it my own. If I could show you how I'm getting on. If you could say to me, 'Yeah, Jack, Teresa is stunning, go for it.'

When we arrive, the parish hall is lit up, almost moving with people. We get in and pay Father O'Brien, and I'm hit with the warm wave of all of Ballycrea crammed into one room. Perfume and sweat. Not far from the carry-on we would have had in Kilmarra.

The single lads lined up against one side of the room, and the single girls lined up against the other. Catching up with each other, pretending they aren't afraid of the other side of the room. Like children. Normally, myself and yourself would have been one of the first couples to break the ice and start dancing. As this thought warms me, I realise I have to send myself to the line of single lads and immerse myself in their nerves. Naggins are pulled from breast pockets and sucked on, even with the disapproval of the women. There was a time I would have joined them for a sly sup. Thanks be to god you grew me up out of that carry-on. I know some of these lads from Doyle's: Jim Ryan and his crew. If I'm lucky, they won't know me. If I'm lucky, I'll get through the night without hearing a cover of 'I Feel Fine'.

There's Bill and Betty, talking to everybody that passes them. As though he is the Lord Mayor and they are welcoming people into their grand home. The band introduces themselves. Some jazz trio I have never heard of but who have stirred up some excitement with the locals. Who will no doubt turn to playing polkas on the saxophone. It's all very familiar, really, and it settles me. No matter how far I go from home, most things seem to stay the same.

Nights like these put me in mind of you. Of course they do. Coming to your door and collecting you. In your nicest dress, in your sister's satin shoes. A vision. Glowing. Goddess of Kilmarra. What I wouldn't give for one more night like that. To feel your dress creasing under my hand. To wear the lipstick off you. It's so sweet to miss you.

Thoughts like this will come to me all night, I suppose. Countless fragments of you, yet never enough to amount to the whole of you. And I'm hit with the fear that I'm only a short sideways step away from becoming like Jim Ryan and his crowd of sad old bachelors, hanging around the hall, looking to snare any young one who is too polite to tell me to piss off. I take a drink, and then I take another.

One of us has to be the first to chance it, so I approach the women against the wall and ask one of them if she will go for a dance with me. It doesn't mean anything. It's just what a man is supposed to do at a dance. I dance with one, and then another. What harm is it to lean into them when they talk? To be closer than is proper, to know the taste of their breath and the heat of their words as they speak. What harm could it really do to let somebody touch me? It's only a feeling. Just to remind me that I am alive. Yes. How easily I forget that I am alive. Teresa approaches me, but I cannot handle the lovely panic her attention would bring me right now. As one song ends, I find Anna against the wall.

'Come on, girl.'

I take her arm as the 'Siege of Carrick' begins. It all sounds good by the jazz band. Better than I thought. It's all going better than I thought. The sweat of Anna's palms warms my hands. We begin, and the blur of the locals wipes past me. Ah yes, I am alive. And how good it is. Anna laughs. The music picks up. I haven't heard this song since I was a boy. Suddenly I remember the feeling of freedom. Suddenly it is summer. You are back for a minute, and I feel fine.

Anna

JACK SPINS ME AROUND AND around. So fast that I feel the soul will be pulled up out of me. A woman passes before me. Behind me. Before me. Behind me. Betty, Lillian, Betty, Lillian. Beautiful, shocking, these terrifying shapes. Blonde to black to blonde. Beauty to beauty to beauty. Passing and spinning away from me so fast that I don't have the time to think of how alarmingly lovely and present they are. I can manage them both for right now. I am a perfect evening sky, balancing both the sun and the moon. I can manage.

Just as I am settling in, the strong arms of Ger Doyle pull me off Jack and spin me away.

'You're some dancer, Anna!'

He calls over the music, smiling a huge smile. Tobacco stains on his big teeth. What a nice man.

Jack takes women in and out of his arms. So does Tom. And for the length of this song, I move without thinking, fitting seamlessly in with everybody and everything. Let's all keep moving this quickly, and maybe everything will stay fine. I like set dances. I feel they are one of the few times when I can be sure of myself and what we are all doing. I am taken into the arms of Michael Fitzpatrick.

Before me, behind me, she comes back again, and I feel as high up as the music.

Tom

YES, TONIGHT IS SOME NIGHT.

It's a long time since I had a night like this. With plans and friends. With loud music and money in my pocket. I catch Anna in the dance, and she is laughing. It's so long since I heard her really laughing. How nice it is, to spin around in circles with my sister. To hear Jack laughing behind me, too. It's so rare that we are all happy at the same time. But look at us now, part of a big dance. Touching everyone, known by everyone. Isn't it enlivening just to be touching somebody?

Dr Desmond passes me by. He smiles and waves as though we are friends. As though we know each other well. And although I'm still half afraid of him, I smile and nod right back at him. As though he was any old eejit.

I see Teresa Doyle catching Jack's arm, and as the music slows, he brings her in closer for a dance. Her dark blue frock and his dark blue trousers. That girl, with her big doe eyes for him. Always with a cigarette in her mouth or a bag of sweets in her hand. Like a child with a dummy. If she wasn't so pretty, Jack wouldn't bother with her, because there's nothing to her besides that. For once I am not jealous of him.

Jack

EVERYTHING THAT WAS MOVING QUICK and unsteady has stilled with Teresa finding me. The curve of her back beneath my hand, her palm against mine. Something I anticipated, and yet somehow did not see coming. And now that we are dancing together, I am not taken over with guilt. Rather, for the first time in a long time, I feel like myself. Dancing with pretty girls was what I once lived for. I am coming back to Jack O'Leary again.

For a little while, I let Teresa lead. Things seem to be happening here that are beyond my control, and so, for now, I let them happen. I let myself melt while this beautiful girl, who is so mad about me, dances me around the room. And I am happy. Limp-bodied, lightheaded, and feeling love from this new friend of mine. She has fallen for me at my worst. Just imagine how happy I would make her if I could get back to my best.

I think I could probably sway with her like this all night. But in the corner of the room, I see Bill Nevan talking in her father's ear. And when our third song ends, Ger makes his way to us. She sighs, and a weight lands on my back. Her father, slapping me up straight. His booming voice and straining shirt buttons.

'Well, Mr O'Leary. You're after a bit of bar work, I hear.'

Bill stands in the corner, watching, pleased with himself for working his supposed magic again. I wouldn't be intimidated by Ger if I wasn't so bewildered by his daughter.

''Tis your Teresa wants me working in the pub.'

I say, trying to laugh, trying to seem like an equal. My hand still holding her back. It seems inappropriate to hold on and inappropriate to let go.

'She's dead right. A man should work.'

I suppose he is sizing me up as a match for his daughter. This was always a risk.

'I'll start you on the days and we'll see how you get on. Come down at twelve tomorrow in a good shirt.'

He looks at Teresa, and then back at me, as though he is warning us of something. As quickly as he arrived, he is gone. She squeals, she giggles. I love these light, girlish noises. For a minute I don't really mind what just happened, because she seems so happy.

'Ah, Jack! This will be so much fun!'

I smile, not only to please her, but because I really can't help it. Her happiness seems to bleed into me. It has been so nice to have a friend. Let's chance it, so. Let's see where it gets us. At the very least, I'll have a wage coming in again, so I can stand on my own two feet a bit more. Okay. It might be good.

The only trouble is I've no nice shirt.

'How nice is a nice shirt by your father's standards?'

I ask, but she only laughs at me.

Anna

ONE OF THE QUIGGLY GIRLS is called up to sing. It's all fine, isn't it? For once, everything is fine. I feel comfortable in the hall. I feel happy. Happier than ever when Betty comes towards me, soft thunder in my ears, white lightning in my eyes.

Behind her there is a young man. Although older than me, I'm sure. A tall, thin man, with fuzzy hair. Betty is all talk.

'Anna, you're looking great! Love the hair.'

A brown suit on him, too short in the arm, too wide on the shoulder. Something comes across Betty's face that I don't really understand. A look you used to give to your friends, a look I have seen exchanged when I come near.

'I thought you'd like to meet Liam Hennessey. He's the only proper dancer in the hall.'

Betty presents him as though she has made him. As though he is something I might be impressed with. Liam smiles, shy but assured, as though he doesn't want to admit it, but he believes that he really is the only proper dancer in the hall. My god.

'This one will put manners on you, Liam!'

Everybody around us has started to dance to the Quiggly girl's song, and we are getting in their way. Betty is acting like a boy.

'Go on, Liam, show her how it's done.'

She nudges him towards me, a huge smile on her face. Surely she isn't trying to set me up?

Liam smiles at me again, wordless, and doesn't ask before taking my hand and waist, and stepping me around the floor. If he is the only proper dancer in the hall, then we're in real trouble.

Looking over my shoulder, I see Betty dancing with Dr Desmond, and she glances over at me. Still smiling, and nodding. Wanting, for some reason, this dance between myself and Liam to go well. If it makes her happy, I'll stick it out.

He's a nice enough man, only that his breath smells of his fish dinner, and he insists on leaning right into me while he speaks. Still, he seems like a fairly safe pair of hands to be in.

After two obliging songs, I look around for Betty, and see that Dr Desmond is dancing with somebody else. I wish I was happy to waltz around the room in the arms of Ballycrea all night, but without eyes on Betty, my throat has closed, and I am faint.

The back of her head, disappearing out the side door of the hall. A moment of relief in catching sight of her, and a surge of panic in her disappearing again. Gone out without her coat into the cold night.

Where would she be going, all on her own, when the whole parish is in here? When I am in here? Where would she be going without me? And what right has she to disappear from me, unexpected and unexplained?

I want to chase her outside, but Liam Hennessey has a real grip on me. He is going to make the most of every last second he has with me. Big rosy cheeks, fish-breathed. Asking me questions about where I'm from and the things I like. But I can't remember the name of the town Tom said we came from. Incessant questions. And the music getting louder. With my palms on his chest, I push him off me, knocking into Mary Doyle and her fella. She is too polite to shout at me.

'Mind yourself.'

Her fella says, and puts his hand on her stomach. Mary Doyle is pregnant. He isn't happy. I want Betty to step between us. But she is outside. I choke out an apology as I run out the side door of the hall.

I want to cry, to fall into her arms. But when I see her, it all goes away. It's just the two of us. Finally, at last. Betty leaning against the pebble-dashed wall, next to a heap of bicycles. The soft sounds of the hedge and the sky. Her face lit up in the dark, she looks up at the stars.

'Why did you disappear?'

I sound more desperate than I would like to. But I suppose I am desperate. Everything inside was too fast and too close, and I need her to bring me back to my centre.

She jumps back when she realises it's me. I didn't mean to scare her. I never mean to scare anybody. It's just hard for me when she leaves so suddenly, without a word. That's what I need to say to her.

'I just needed a break. It's so warm in there. Where's Liam?'

She's looking around me, as though Liam is just behind me. But she doesn't look at me. A tiny little detail that perhaps she doesn't think I will notice. But I notice everything. I feel everything. What would it cost her to just throw her eyes over me? The cheek of her, to come outside for a little rest when all she does is cause unrest. If she needed a break from everything in the hall, that means she needed a break from me. What did I do to make her feel that way? If I just tell her what I feel, everything will be fine. And still that desperate, rough talk comes from me.

'Shake a leg, girl, you're fine.'

My upset is coming out like disgust. Well, I suppose that in some small way, I am disgusted with her. I'm disgusted with myself, with my over-familiarity. But something about Betty wanting a moment to herself is infuriating, and I don't know how to order my feelings. I don't know how to pause long enough to articulate my frustration, to know what is an overreaction and what is justified. I wish I knew how to separate things like that; I wish I knew how to clear my thoughts. Instead, everything melts into one feeling, and I can't speak it without causing damage.

'Come on, Betty, come back inside with me. We could have a dance.'

Something within me is about to crack. I don't know how to make it stop, or how to feel something else. In any other circumstance, with any other person, I could allow a bit of distance. It's just that she seems to know me, to understand me in a way that nobody else does. When you finally feel understood, it's a very hard thing to let go of. I suppose you won't know what that is like, because everybody loved you and wanted you, and nothing for you was difficult.

I just want her to tell me everything is fine, and to come back inside with me. But she won't even look at me. I can't stop myself from talking at her. She is yet to start listening.

'Betty! Would you look at me.'

I had a sense of what I was feeling when I stepped outside, but it's gone now. I don't have any words for this, it's just a flood of feelings. Her arms cross, and at last she looks at me, from the side of her eye.

'Have you been drinking, Anna?'

I hear her speak, but it's like something said on the radio, that I'm not supposed to reply to. The ground under me feels further away by the second. What's going on? I thought that Betty and I understood each other. That she could see me and hear me. Even when I have felt like a supernova, dying in so deep and silent a space that nobody even knows that I am here, Betty knew. And suddenly, that has all gone. Suddenly, she is deciding not to see or hear me anymore. Not to understand.

If she would just smile at me, get up and come back inside with me.

If she would only acknowledge me and let me know that I am still here. Betty, please just give me that smack of attention that I am craving.

'You're as weak as water.'

A woman like Betty should stand up to me, but all she does is look up at the stars. As though if she ignores me long enough, I will go away. As though she is afraid of me. Just looking up at the stars, at a reflection of herself. Admiring her shine, no doubt.

If I could just tell her that I love her. I love her as she is, I love the smell of the dead blood between her teeth, I love the phlegm in her throat. I love her as a woman, and I would love her as a man, as both or neither. Regardless of the form she takes, I love her. It makes no odds to me. If she exists, I love her. Would she look at me then, if I told her that?

It isn't that I need the intensity of my fingers in her mouth again, or my blood on the back of her tongue. I just need a roll of the eyes. My name squeezed into a sigh. To be dismissed would be infinitely better than being ignored.

'Why are you being so boring?'

Grappling for attention, like a child. So embarrassing. But I can't stop. Just as I open my mouth to swear at her, the door opens behind us again.

'All okay, ladies?'

Ciara Moore stands in the glow of the hall. And looking as though she has just seen her saviour, Betty stands up and moves towards me. Close. Closer. Far closer than I would have expected a moment ago. So close now that our cheeks could touch. We share a breath; I have never known something so intimate. From here, I could count the creases that lie against her eyes. I can almost taste the sherry that she drank inside. Almost touching. On the edge of almost everything.

And then she steps back. And the inches between us feel infinite. I wonder if I will ever feel close to anybody again. Just as I think she isn't going to give me anything, her eyebrows worry themselves, and with a hand on my arm, she tells me,

'Cop on, girl.'

Oh, the heat of her words. Isn't this the right fire to be warmed by? Isn't it good to bathe in the flames? I might let Betty burn me alive, just for the thrill of her acknowledgement. She walks past me into the hall. I watch once more as the back of her head moves out of reach. And while I still feel I'm falling, this time I feel I am falling into her. As she dwindles into the crowd, I wonder if she is the jesus that I have heard so much about, and what an honour it would be to be a louse on her scalp, living off her body and blood. She goes inside with Ciara, linking her arm. The best friends. Let them be best friends, I don't want that title. She and I are tethered by the soul. Friendship doesn't begin to describe it.

How strange, that all somehow felt more real than my bloodied fingertips in her mouth. She could put her hands round my throat now, it wouldn't feel as close. She could go right to the centre of me, see my blood while it's still blue, and determine whether or not a soul lingers within me, and still this might feel more intimate.

Just as I think I might fracture into a thousand pieces, Tom puts a hand on my shoulder. I smell him. He is real. He is Tom. Moments later, Betty leaves the hall with Bill. They are going home, I think. It's fine now. I have Tom.

Tom

I ALMOST FEEL ANNA COME back into her body as I lay my hand on her shoulder. Frightening stuff. She can be such a frightening girl. Something comes over me as I see Bill and Betty leave the hall. He turns to wave at all of us. Not at me, but at everybody. And I am compelled to call out after him. To halt him, to catch up to him. Cold sweat on my neck. Cold wind on my face. And tell him that I've never really been anything, but he has made me feel like a man. That I might never be enough to impress him, but that I will always be here.

That woman's husband. It's a funny one. I've had flashes of admiration for people before. Of course I have. Dozens of people. But this is something altogether new. I don't know what to call this feeling, and I don't know what to do with it. All I really know is that it took Bill to find it in me.

I was always comparing myself to Dad, and then to Jack. To any man with his own land or his own woman. Meeting Bill has made me see how wasteful that was. I don't want to compare myself to anybody anymore. I want to stand alone as a singular thing, far away from everybody else, so that his light hits the most of me.

It doesn't matter anymore that I've no land and no wife. I have somebody who cares about me, who wants the best for me, and who is deeply interested in me. There's plenty men with wives who don't have that. Do I want the feeling named? Do I really need it named? Some combination of gratitude and freedom, of ecstasy and lightness. Whatever it is, it all comes from Bill. And he doesn't even drip-feed it, he lets it all flow freely.

Something tells me that I should try to create this feeling for myself. Something else tells me that I will never be able to. He's teaching me how to be a man, how to be smart and happy. Whatever he wants to teach me, whatever he wants me to know, I will take from him.

He walks away with his wife, and I watch him go.

Betty

'GOODNIGHT BILL, GOODNIGHT BETTY! GOODNIGHT!'

Tom calls after us, so loud and exuberant that I can still hear him even after we have gone. There's something about Tom that I can't quite explain. Something pity-inducing, that is endearing and off-putting at once. It's the way that he shouts goodbyes to us in a manner that even Peggy is too old for. Never mind anyway. He isn't the O'Leary I'm worried about at the minute.

I cling onto Bill all of the walk home. Frost takes over the ditches, and I feel unsteady in my shoes. How do I begin to tell him about what happened with Anna?

I look up to see him smiling at me. Oh, isn't he good? Something about the dark of tonight puts me in mind of when we were young. When he would walk me home from dances, with my brothers following us. The smell of his jacket, still the same as it was then. He loves me more than anything. And knowing that gives me the courage to say something that I have been avoiding. Something I haven't wanted to think about, but that comes to me again and again. Which came to me countless times tonight.

'They're a bit much, aren't they? The O'Learys.'

He looks surprised, but he never notices half of the things that I notice. I would have been amazed if he agreed with me. This is why

I've avoided the subject. It's one thing to say that I'm not sure about the O'Learys. It's another thing altogether to begin to explain why. Tom's neediness, Anna's ever-changing moods, and uncertainty of Lillian.

'How do you mean?'

He asks, and I feel already I've started something that I don't want to finish. Still, I swallow back my reservation.

'Just the way that Tom is sort of like a child sometimes, and Anna is such an intense girl.'

Let's leave Lillian out of it for now. There's no point ringing alarm bells for no reason.

'She does nothing by halves.'

He laughs.

'Ah Bill, no, listen, I'd be afraid of her if she wasn't so innocent.'

This is as much as I can say about what passed between us, because I really don't have the words for it.

'Now, Betty, if you're afraid of her it's another story. Why are you afraid of her?'

'I'm not afraid of her, I said I'm not afraid. Sure I've nothing to be afraid of.'

And in convincing Bill, I begin to convince myself. I still haven't told him about the scarf, or about Lillian. It seems the longer I keep it a secret, the harder it is to tell him. I just want to keep it small for now. I feel the smaller it is, the better I'll be able to control it. And perhaps even solve it.

Although I thought that Liam Hennessey was going to solve it. Maybe it's going to take more than I imagined. All the walk home, and all night in bed, I hear her taunting me. Pecking at me, addicted to attention. I wonder what would satiate her, or if anything could at all.

Jack

WHAT A FINE THING IT was, to drink and laugh, and to touch people. To spin around the hall with the locals as though I was one of them. I was so bright in the hall, so full of life. Teresa was full of life. A fine thing indeed. But now, walking home, I feel the sweat on the back of my neck growing cold. Anna is gone quiet. I feel I want to go quiet, too, and preserve what happiness I have left within me.

'You were very cosy with Teresa Doyle, weren't you? I was half jealous of you.'

Tom has been careful all night not to seem drunk, but I can tell that he has taken more drink than what suits him. He isn't the type to admit to the jealousy that he always feels. He is the type to admit to false feelings to please people. Tom pretends to hold back tears at funerals, and breaks into pieces over a deceased person he never really cared for. Recently, he has pretended to be thrilled for Peggy's small achievements in school when I know he struggles to determine her age. I have to wonder how much of the pity and patience he has shown me was put on. It's hard to know if he has any sincere feelings at all.

It's silly, because I'm sure he only said it to upset me, but this is just another reason to feel guilty over the whole thing with Teresa. Tom has never had a woman. He's desperate to have somebody in his life like that. Somebody he doesn't need to share, somebody who will always let him come first, you know? And here I have a woman that I might not even want, throwing herself at me. Oh, but she was pretty tonight. Like she is pretty most nights.

'Era you can have her. I was only passing away the time.'

Isn't that cruel? I am often shocked by how casually callous I can be. Teresa isn't mine to be offering. Remind me, what was it that you loved about me?

'Her mother is dead five years, you know. She might be good company.'

Tom says, as though a dead mother is enough to have in common with somebody. And although it makes my heart twinge for Teresa, I don't let it stay in my head long.

Anna is far enough away in her thoughts that we will probably get away with this conversation. I'm not really sure what Tom wants me to say. Why did he mention Teresa Doyle at all? Does he want me to supply him with some sordid details of what we did? I could be disgracefully honest with him, and still all he would learn is that I am too afraid to move on from you, and even more afraid of my unrelenting urge to try.

He offers the details of his own evening sparingly. Partly, I suppose, because there are so few details to offer. I saw him talking to Linda McManus for a little while, but all the while there was a yard between them. Of course, he hadn't the neck to ask Linda to dance, and so she probably felt her time was wasted. That's only conjecture, now.

I become more free with my account of the evening. Sure I've nothing to hide. I didn't do anything of any real consequence. And still, my stomach sinks when I tell him which women I danced with, and the way he slaps my back in praise.

'So you were dancing with five or six different girls, were you? I'd say you had them all charmed.'

His tone is so false, as if he doesn't believe me. I don't need him to believe me. This sort of chat is so childish, I almost wish that Anna would start listening and give out to us both.

'Sure you have to be charming, Tom, the girls love it. You must know that.'

I speak without looking at him. This carry-on is driving me mad. I want to give him a puck, to tell him he doesn't know a thing about women, and that everyone can see it. Tom loves to say that I'm mad for the women. That I'm a flirt and a playboy and whatever else. The truth of it is, I'm just not afraid of women the same way that he is. And he uses that against me. That's all. Sure you were the only woman I ever had any real time for. He knows that, and so he must know how this hurts me.

'Teresa might have given you a kiss goodnight by the sounds of it.'

He says, under his breath. Maybe to him, this is just fun. Maybe he thinks it's just harmless jeering, and that I am playing along. But I think I'm about to cry. It's as if he has opened me up and looked inside me, chosen to ignore all the space you take up and to illuminate the small space that Teresa has occupied. He is forcing me to confront the piece of me that would have loved a goodnight kiss off Teresa. The part of me that no longer yearns for kisses off you. It's inappropriate. It's tasteless. And just as I pull my arm back to puck the back of his head, Anna interrupts.

'She did not. That girl has more sense than to be kissing an eejit like you.'

Her tone is vacant. As though she doesn't even realise she is speaking. Like snapping at us is just muscle memory. She goes back to not hearing us, ignoring us, whichever it is. Thanks be to god for Anna. We walk on in silence, and I become horribly lost in the complications of kissing a person. Of touching and knowing a person.

'I let a few people know that we'll be having a party for my thirtieth. Just so ye know.'

Tom is almost sheepish when he says this. Not like him.

Minnie Keane is just about awake when we call in for Peggy, who is wide awake.

'Where's my girl?'

I call, maybe a bit louder, a bit more inebriated than I would like to sound. She rushes out to us, hugging my waist. Although she has the energy for walking, I need something besides my thoughts to focus on, and so I carry her home on my back and ask her about her evening. She wants to know about the dance. It's nice to be the older one, so I can dismiss the questions I can't handle. She tells me about the other children that were there, which ones she plays with in school and which ones she didn't know. Her little voice growing tired. As we approach the cottage, she pretends to fall asleep so that I won't make her walk.

'Will you carry me up the hill, Peg?'

I ask her, and fear she can smell the drink off me. She laughs, forgetting that she was pretending to be asleep.

When we get home, we lie down and I pretend to go to sleep. As though the dance never happened. As though we weren't out at all and Tom didn't ask me those questions. Every now and again, he kicks a leg or taps his fingers against his chest. Just moving, I know, but I can't help receiving it as plotting. As menacing. As an attempt to annoy me. Would he not just go to sleep? It's a shame when you get to know somebody so well that you look past the best in them.

Predictably, these sweet and unwelcome thoughts of Teresa come to me. Just about the way that she looked this evening. Curls hardened with hairspray, and the way her cheeks met her eyes when she smiled, creating creases in her powder. Charming, in its own way. I wonder if I will always be confused by feelings like this, or whether they will one day be welcome. I wonder when I will catch up to the life that started the moment I lost you. God, it feels like only a minute ago that you were here with me.

Tell me, where does lust fit into grieving? Things might be easier if I had never met Teresa. Then I might not have been forced into the possibility of moving on.

Perhaps it would be easier if we had been married. Or if I was a woman. Then I could just put on a black shawl and be the Widow Jack forever. I suppose that comes with its own set of problems. I wish I had realised how easy I had it when you were still with me. I close my eyes, and there you are. A strange, liquid light, moving before me. Trapped under my eyelids. Always changing. Always here.

Tom coughs. Do you know what – this is terrible, but – often, when we settle down to sleep, I am overwhelmed by the thought that I will wake up to find the three of them dead.

Betty

'I WAS AWAKE ALL NIGHT thinking about it.'

I tell Ciara, surrounded by the iron smell of stout, with a draft from a small window missing its glass. Jack O'Leary drops a pot of coffee down to us with a wink.

'There ye are, girls.'

I didn't realise he'd started working in Doyle's. Those O'Learys are everywhere. Ciara smiles, somehow drawn in by his little charm. How I'd love to burst his bubble, tell him that Ciara is drawn in by any man with half an ounce of charisma. Sure with her John, how could she not be? We've to wait until he's back up at the bar to keep talking. When I told Ciara what happened with Anna last night, she was so intrigued that she made me tell her a second time.

Part of me feels guilty for suggesting to Bill that the O'Learys are too much. And even worse for saying it to Ciara this afternoon. I don't want to seem like a gossip, but I have to talk about this, because it doesn't feel right.

Ciara is eyeing Jack, waiting until it's safe to talk.

'What did Bill make of it?'

'Sure he didn't take any notice. He probably has it forgotten now.'

I didn't bother mentioning it to him again this morning. What would be the point, when I know he'd only dismiss it? The way Bill sees it, he finally has a big, capable man to help him on the farm, who is too grateful to look for more money and too obedient to do anything but what he's told. Besides, amn't I the one who told him to keep an eye on Tom and Jack in the first place?

'So what are you going to do?'

That's the question. What am I going to do? I keep telling myself that it takes all sorts to make a world. That everybody is different. That I don't have to be friends with everyone. All the things I've been telling myself to justify the odd feeling I get from them. From her.

'I'd cut them out, if I could. But Tom is working with Bill, and suddenly Jack is working in here, and Anna calls up to the house every evening. What can I do?'

Ciara looks at me, defeated. This family has made themselves a part of the town, I can't do anything about that. They have made themselves a part of my life. And I can't do anything about that, either.

I suppose I could ignore them. Smile politely at the market and shake their hands in Mass, and nothing more. But then it hits me. What about Peggy?

'I'm mad for the little girl, Ciara. I'd be devastated if I couldn't look after her anymore.'

I don't want to say too much more about it. It's embarrassing to be so desperate for a child that I latch onto the first neglected girl that comes my way. But something about her feels like fate. She needs parenting, and I want to be a parent. Ciara saves me any pity.

'I would imagine the siblings are a package deal.'

She says, pouring out the coffee, handing me a cup.

'Did you ever think that she might like you? Maybe she's attracted to you, like.'

I scald my tongue on the coffee.

'Ciara!'

She laughs like she isn't saying something outrageous.

'But sure maybe she does! You'd hear of things like that happening.'

It's fine for her, she is only watching this from the sidelines. I'm the one right in the middle of it.

'Not in Ballycrea, you don't.'

But already it's turning in my mind, and I wonder if there might be weight to what she's saying.

'Attraction is perfectly natural, Betty. You wouldn't see an animal repressing its urges the way that we do. Besides, it's everything else about Anna that's unnatural.'

'That's right.'

I don't know what else to say to her. Maybe she's right. But I have enough to be considering without considering all that. Just as I want to ask her what she made of the band last night, Ciara's eyes widen. She is fixed on the door.

Red headscarf. Yellow eyes scanning the room. Here is Anna.

Anna

AMN'T I THE LUCKY GIRL, to come into Doyle's and see both Jack and Betty? Two bright life rings, right here. Today is the meeting of Betty's book club. She told me that I could come along if I had any interest. Though that was ages ago, I hope that she hasn't forgotten. So far, it's only herself and Ciara Moore. I wave to them, and they look at me like they don't know me. Like they aren't expecting me, and I have ruptured their nice time. Hesitating, embarrassed, I wonder if I should sit with them at all. But then Betty smiles and Ciara waves at me. Okay, time to be brave.

'Ladies, hello.'

I sit next to Betty; Ciara has to move to make room for me. That woman, always getting in the way. I'd have her skin for a drum.

Their conversation seems to have been suddenly derailed. Maybe they are just a little worse for wear after last night. No bother, I'll get them warmed up. We will talk like we always talk. About the lads and our mornings, little pieces of news from the town and frocks we saw at the dance. Of course, if Ciara Moore wasn't here, this would be altogether better. But here she is. We have to make the best of her.

'So what's the book this month?'

They look at me like I'm speaking another language. Like they don't realise that's why we are all here. Ciara is the one to remember and takes *Jane Eyre* out of her bag.

'Jesus, I nearly had the book club forgotten about!'

She laughs, and Betty puts a hand to her forehead, as though suddenly realising that is why I am here. I try not to let this embarrass me.

'Have you read it?'

Betty asks, and I smile and nod, when actually, I've never heard of this Jane character. She takes her own book out of her handbag. Ciara's copy wears a greyed plastic jacket, borrowed from the library. Betty's is brand new. Now and again, I glance over at Jack. My safety net for when I fear I cannot keep up with these women. But this is a good time. This is a wonderful, quiet way to live. When things are good, they are amazing. Was that you I saw, just now, from the corner of my eye? No, it can't have been. Just somebody blonde out the window, maybe a sack of flour over somebody's shoulder. Jack drops a box of matches onto the table.

'You'd never light a few candles, would you?'

How embarrassing, to be bossed around in front of Betty and her little friend. But for the sake of appearing calm and agreeable, I do what he asks. Teresa Doyle must be fascinating if he can't even pull himself away from her for long enough to light a few candles. Ridiculous.

Perhaps if I didn't say yes to him so often, he would stop asking me to do things for him. I roll my eyes to Betty, and she laughs along, a little too politely to be friendly. She isn't going to address what happened between us last night. And if she isn't going to address it, then neither am I. Maybe she is just as embarrassed as I am. When my flurry of feelings passed, and I came back down to earth, I felt so foolish – that I always let myself become so reliant on people, that I can't just have a nice time. When the candles are lit, I sit back down.

Betty looks at me stiffly, sipping on her coffee. I can smell it as it pools into her mouth. How strange, I've never seen her at a loss for words. But right now, she doesn't know what to say to me. If she would just put a hand on my knee or squeeze my shoulder. Things she has done many times before, but which now seem as far off and improbable as Jack hopping up on the bar and singing 'God Save the Queen'. Oh, Betty, just touch me. Reach out, I am here. I am ready to receive you.

Ciara excuses herself, heading for the bathroom. Thank god, a moment alone. When she is gone, Betty turns to me.

'I meant to say, we're going to have a little party for Tom's thirtieth soon, if you and the book club wanted to come?'

'Listen, I want to talk to you.'

She stops me. And proving my suspicion that Betty can read my mind, she puts a hand on my leg. Just for a moment. And in that moment, my thigh glows. When she takes her hand away, there is still a luminous mark to show she was there. I feel it, warm. From this close, I can see all the little thread veins on her cheeks. Tiny, lucky little purple lines that get to lie down across her face every day. She takes a settling breath and speaks quietly. Go on, pet. There's nothing to be afraid of.

'You seemed a bit upset last night, I just wanted to make sure you were okay.'

I don't consider what she has said before answering her. I just want to move past it. Without wanting to, I sound overly eager.

'Oh, I was grand! I didn't mind a thing! I just hope I didn't upset you.'

She moves as though she is going to speak, and then doesn't. As though perhaps I did upset her and she doesn't want to say. Look how uncomfortable she is. Where has this come from? I fidget with the box of matches.

'Look, I think you're a lovely friend, Anna. I just think it's time you met a few more people besides me, you know? So you have lots of people in your corner. To stop relying on me so much.'

I can tell she wants to leave it there, but she can't stop herself from adding,

'I just need a small bit of space from you.'

I wait for her to say something nice, to finish it off on a good note. But that's it. That's all she has to say. Somehow, we have become closer than she wants us to be. Unbelievable. I put the box of matches up my sleeve to stop fiddling with it. Betty Nevan wants space from me.

'Fine.'

I say, unable to say any more. She wants me to make other friends. Okay. Alright. I just don't understand where this has come from. Clenching my teeth, I try to understand what I've done wrong. Clearly, she knows that she has touched a nerve.

'Anna, sorry, I didn't mean to upset you.'

I am doing all I can not to lash out. I need to be somebody that she wants close to her, don't I?

'I said it's fine.'

My voice, rock hard. Deep breaths, Anna. Staggered breaths.

'Take Liam Hennessey, for example! He's such a lovely man, Anna, but you didn't give him a chance.'

She is talking to please herself now. As though her sweet, happy voice will make up for what she's saying.

'I'd like you to try and spread yourself out more, you might like it.'

This can't be all about Liam Hennessey. His stinking breath and sweating hands. Is that all she thinks I deserve? What happened to us understanding each other?

'And like today, you'll meet some nice women you might like to be friends with.'

She is talking to me like I'm no more than Peggy's age. Ah, this is hard now. It stings all the way through me. The tears start in my hands and run up through my arms and bulge behind my eyes. Just waiting to spill out. But I swallow it all back, and be the person that she wants me to be, smiling a smile that strains my neck.

'Say no more, Betty! I understand.'

I almost cheer my words, and manage to conceal everything else. Outwardly, it seems to be enough to satisfy her, although I know that, inside, she is not convinced. Just like she will know that, inside, I do not understand.

It's just strange, because nothing about me has changed since she liked me. I'm the very same girl that she stood in her doorway with, watching the men on the field. The same girl she took out to feed the ducks. I can't put my finger on the moment I went wrong. Why am I suddenly not enough? But wait, she must love me in a way that nobody else does, and care for me in a way that nobody else does, because nobody else has ever tried to talk to me like this.

For a moment, she smiles at me as though she never knew me at all. I feel outside myself. And to stop myself from falling to the floor, I squeeze her hand. And she lets me. It seems to be enough to create some genuine feeling between us. For a moment, she knows me very well. Ciara hangs around the bar, chatting to Mary Doyle, and glancing at us in the mirror. When she sees we are done talking, she comes back to join us.

'Mary has only a month left, imagine! That was the fastest nine months ever.'

Fake bitch. How mortifying, to go along with conversations like this, knowing I am unwanted. But this won't last; I won't let it last. I have been here before. And while I don't know exactly what to do to get her back, I know what not to do. I learned that with Milly Hayes and Catherine Jennings, and with you. I won't let this go wrong again. I can't. Three women come through the door and Betty perks up for them. This must be the book club.

They talk in part about the book, and in part about local people and events. I pretend to have an interest in all of it. From the outside, I am doing very well. I'm sure Jack is watching now and thinking that I'm really taking to this. I'm sure Betty is glad that I listened to what she had to say and that I'm giving these ladies a chance. And yet, I cannot help that every beat of my heart comes with the prayer:

I could be yours forever.

I could be yours forever.

I could be yours forever.

I could be yours forever.

I could be yours forever.

Jack finishes a pint and throws a tea towel over his shoulder as though he owns the place. Locking eyes with me, he tenses for a moment. And then he eases off and clears a few glasses for the Doyle girl. Back at the bar, she puts a hand on his shoulder and says something that makes him laugh. The cheek.

An hour passes, and then another, and the women begin to leave. I thank them for including me, wasn't it a fabulous afternoon, isn't it great to get out? All that carry-on. I let them know that I'll wait here with Jack. I let Jack know that I am leaving with Betty. People don't need to know where I am all the time. It's good to be alone. But then, I'm never alone, am I?

As much as I would like to be, I can't be alone. There's always a whisper in the wind, a memory on my mind. I can't remember the last time I really felt I was by myself. I walk through the town, wandering along the sea road. Losing track of time. It's sort of like dancing, I follow a rhythm within me and let my feet take me where they will. Betty has grown tired of me. She wants me to diversify, to have new friends. And while parts of me agree that is a good idea, I can't bring myself to a point where I could follow through with it. I have to wonder if I'm the only loyal woman in the country. I must be the only person who isn't comfortable picking people up and dropping them. Hasn't it gotten dark?

I carry on. A little dancer, floating through the hills. That's what I'm like. The fog comes, and pulls the sun down with it. Mammy's headscarf tied tight around my chin, damp. Barbed fences, almost begging to be grasped. Wooden pillars holding them up, sharpened like pikes.

And although I follow a road I have never taken before, at twilight, I find myself back at Betty's house. The golden light spilling out from her kitchen window makes me realise how dim the evening has gotten. I head down closer. Don't be surprised. This was always going to happen. I am a homing bird. For a while, she was my home.

Purple grey sky. A pale-yellow drizzle, coloured from the light of her blessed kitchen, almost like neon signs you'd see in Cork city, bouncing off the Ford tractor that Bill keeps on the slope down to the field, its tyres caked in mud. Closer, and closer still, I am drawn to her home. I can't explain it. I just need to be near her. I need to be in that kitchen. And it hits me: her kitchen is where I belong. Since leaving Kilmarra, Betty's kitchen is the only place I haven't had to hold my breath to fit into. Her kitchen feels right. She feels right. And without them, I feel incurably wrong.

The stone of her walls against my cheek, cold and rough. I sit under the window, peering in until I catch a glimpse of her. Look how she moves through the room, taking in the air. Laughing, touching Bill's back. Only a windowpane between us. A cosmos between us.

Her hand there, unmoving from his back. His hands on her shoulders, her arms, her waist. Bending her backwards like the stem of a flower. Lowering himself, his face on hers. A cosmos between them, shared as he kisses her. Tender and suave, and nothing at all like the Bill I have known.

Of course, I knew all along that she must kiss her husband now and again. I just never thought I would have to see it. I never thought I would feel my insides rotting at the sight of their meeting lips. I never thought every cell in my body would tremble, wanting to become the cells of Bill. To stand in his place, grey-haired, round-bellied, the farm under my nails. But if it meant bending Betty back gently, and having her so close to me, of course I would want to be Bill. Of course I would.

Kissing. They are kissing. I am briefly tantalised; deeply jealous. The kiss doesn't stop. It deepens. He kisses her as though he means to make love to her. And she kisses him back. As though she means to let him. My blood screams, my tendons tear themselves from my bones. Every part of me thrashes against this. I have to stop them.

It's late, and it's rude, but I hurry to the back door and knock hard. I just want to pause what they're doing. To bring them to their senses and spoil the mood. Any small way of putting a distance between them. Less of him and more of me. Did you ever feel this way?

Her giggling comes to a sudden stop. As though the guards have knocked. I wait. There is some hesitation between them about opening the door. Already, regret is settling within me. I am humiliated, but more than that, I am desperate to see her. The door opens. A flood of her cleansing light washes over me. But it isn't my Betty before me. It is her husband, who looks at me with such confusion it's like he has never seen me in his life. What kind of way is that to look at a guest? He looks flustered, like he has been caught out. He smooths out his jumper.

There was a time when this door would be flung open for me. When my name would be cooed and a drink would be poured before I had even sat down. This evening, I hardly get a smile.

'Anna! How are you? There's no sign of Betty yet, I'm afraid. She's out and about still.'

But didn't I just see his hooks in the fat of her waist? Didn't I hear the falsetto of her laughing? For a minute, I expect him to invite me in to wait for her. But no invitation comes. He lets a tight silence accumulate around us and waits for me to break it. I know she is inside. Turned on and left to go cold. I know she is.

'No worries, Bill! I was only passing. I'll see ye again.'

I give him a big smile and a wave. Like it's all fine. Like I haven't made a fool of myself and he hasn't made it worse. Whatever, it doesn't matter. I put a space between them, didn't I?

'Goodnight so, Anna.'

Without anything else to do or say, Bill closes the door and leaves me in the dark. My pupils, dark and widening for her. Ready to pull her in and drown her. I could crumble to dust, honestly, I could fold in half and drop to the floor. I feel it in my legs. I swear I hear them talking now. Probably saying that she doesn't know how long she can keep humouring me. Wondering whether the moment they had conjured up has gone or can be recaptured. If I only knew what she was saying. If I only knew how to give her what she wants.

I just need a little bit of attention. To remind her of me. Something comes over me. It's more than embarrassment or desperation. It's like shock. It's like I can't catch my breath. I pull the box of matches out of my sleeve. Something in the drizzle sticking my headscarf to my face. Something about being ignored. If I struck a match and touched it to the grass, what then? If I smoked them out, would he keep his hands off her? If the house burned down to nothing, and she came to stay with us while they rebuilt. How could she ever ignore me again after such an act of charity? She could lie across the floor with me at night. I would save her from the fire. Unfazed by the smell of burning hair and skin. She would need me then.

And then I swear I feel your hand on my shoulder. I swear you're telling me it's alright, and that I should go home and dry off. Nebulous blonde, all around me. Your warm hands on my shoulders, saying, never mind, try again tomorrow. I swear I hear you say that you forgive all my mistakes, and that Betty can do the same.

Jack

BELOW IN DOYLE'S, THE EVENING runs away from me. At last, a decent way to pass my time. Half the parish arrives down at the pub on Saturday nights. Young people, old people, married and single, with company and without. Everyone is here, the air thick with bodies, with laughter and smoke. The normal tide of melancholy that comes to pull me away in the evenings has not been able to find me. The small glints of happiness that have been so scattered seem to all be coming at once, shining all around me. I feel a part of the town suddenly; everybody knows my name. For the first time in a long time, life isn't galloping on ahead of me. I can keep up with the pace of things. It feels good.

I finally introduced myself to our landlord, the doctor. I served him two pints of Beamish and a bottle of orange. He's sound enough; I can't see why Tom is so spooked by him. Imagine, I might never have met the man if I didn't take this job. I feel lucky, I do.

'You'd never take out that bin, would you, Jack?'

Teresa asks, brushing past me. Working with her isn't what I expected it would be; her long looks, the suggestive sucking of sweets and the smoke of her cigarettes settling in under the collar of my shirt. Rather, she has taken charge. Calling out orders, not taking it easy on me, paying the customers a mile more attention than she pays me. She talks to the locals as though she invented them. Seeing this new side to her makes me want to show her all the sides to me.

I do as I'm asked. I take the bin out the back, and wonder who will put Peggy to bed tonight, and how well she will sleep without me. Looking out onto the lonely street, I let out a breath, cold and white. And I realise how far I have come. I didn't expect to see you in the empty street, I didn't want to. Isn't that funny? All this time, I've been waiting for you to appear in empty spaces. Lately, I've found that I'm alright with emptiness. Come here to me, darling, if you can call down, then you should. Not so that I can see you, but so that you can see how well I'm doing without you. I think you'd be proud of me.

'Come on, dosser!'

Teresa calls from behind me. A smile revealing her bottom teeth, her hand reaching out for me. Beckoning me back in. Closer to her. The light of the pub snuffed out as the back door closes behind her. The laughter inside, dampened.

The quiet of the night.

Teresa before me. Shrouded in the amber glow of the stained glass of the door. Trembling stars, heavy moon. Softly, she smiles. Look at how far I have come.

A surge of emotion, a gratitude for being alive, a desire to feel her, all come together to pull me nearer to her. So near that I can see the coating the mint humbugs have left on her bottom lip. The earth beneath me softens. I feel like myself, and a night breeze brings me into her. Something that has had a vice grip on me lets go. And I kiss her.

Meeting her mouth, I feel I am the whole night. Each shade of its darkness, the gossamer stretch of cloud and every glossy star. She and I, a small nebula by the bins. Everything twinkling.

And even when she puts a space between us, and you make your way back into my thoughts, the earth remains soft. I remain solid. Not melting into a panic, not collapsing from guilt. I don't merely feel fine.

Rather, I feel alive. I think I had forgotten that I am still alive, and that I must live.

As she heads back inside, she turns to look at me. Teresa, by the light of a Saturday night. Reaching her hand out to me once more, bringing me back inside with her. All night, the stars outside tap on the windows, wanting to be let in. Wanting to be a part of me again.

Anna

NOTHING IS WORKING OUT THE way that Tom promised it would. The person I used to be never gave way to the person I am supposed to be. My trouble was supposed to run off me, instead it has run to find me.

Betty wants space from me. Like everybody always wants space from me. Like you and Milly and Catherine and all the rest of them. Why isn't anybody happy to be close to me? Why doesn't anybody seem to love me on the same frequency that I love them? I want to get it right. I want to move on and live a nice life, like everybody else. All I do now is block out the thoughts of you. Of what happened. The heat with which I needed you. The reasons you are gone. I block them all out, and yet they crawl unnamed across my skin. All the time. Creeping across my eyelids, your hair and body and hands, always just out of sight. Felt but unacknowledged. As though you are still struggling through your last breath. As though I could stop it all.

Tom coughs, attention seeking. I am brought back to the table, where I didn't realise I was sitting. Peggy leaning against my chair, biting her nails. He has something sad to say, I can see by the sad smile on his face.

'I was saying my prayers last night, and I forgot Daddy.'

He almost laughs when he says it, as though it's the only way he could force it out of his throat. Peggy blesses herself. Just for a second, I am grounded. I am sitting with my brother as he tells me something painful, as he tries to make it into something that he can swallow. I forget whatever I was just thinking about. We are together. He forgot to pray for Daddy. Another person wouldn't care much about that sort of thing, but I can't imagine all the ways that it would kill Tom. He hangs onto Daddy's death the most.

'I said my prayers twice last night, don't worry.'

I say, smiling, lying and hoping he will accept it. Better that than to tell him that I haven't said a real prayer in donkey's years. Maybe that's my problem.

That's the sort of admission that would send Tom into shock. The sort of thing you go to hell for, I'm sure. Then, I'm sure I'm heading to hell anyway. Probably myself and Jack and Tom will all end up down there, still looking up at you and Mammy and Daddy. Nothing will really change.

I would never tell Tom this, but hell is of no real concern to me. It's heaven and its furies that I am most afraid of. Never once have I been made to feel like god is decent or clear-thinking. As far as I can tell, god is impossible to please. If I get to heaven, I fear I would perpetually feel like an unwanted guest in his house. No, you're not there at all. You're somewhere altogether better. Somewhere with soft music and honeyed lights. Without rules and without worship. I imagine you are somewhere very free.

Ah, but poor Tom. He's mad for god and praying and all. And once he's happy, who cares? It's probably not a bad thing to have somebody praying for me.

'Can we make some decorations now?'

Peggy asks, leaning into me further. Jack has spent every evening since Saturday down in Doyle's. It's taking a toll on her, not to have him around. It's taking a toll on me, to have to look after her so much more.

'There's paper in the dresser, and Sellotape.'

She goes to fetch them, and against my will I spend the evening with her, making decorations for Tom's thirtieth birthday party. A party that he decided to throw, and which I will do all the cleaning and baking and decorating for.

Tom

THIS IS ONE OF THOSE perfect, blissful evenings. Half the parish here in my cottage. Isn't that lovely? Everybody is in good form, we all have enough and nothing is wrong. An evening that I'm already seeing as a soft memory, tinted gold. An exhalation I didn't know I needed. Relief and sanctuary, right here in my own home, imagine. We've fruit cake. We've bottled beer and music. Peggy runs around with other children. Jack has let his shoulders drop. At eleven o'clock, I will turn thirty years of age. Without my mother and father. Without you. But somehow, with so much more than I had before. For a long time, I didn't expect to see this day. But here I am. Doesn't everything always come around in the end?

Looking around the room, I see nothing but all of the ways that tonight is different from our first night in Ballycrea. Then, when we had hardly a lump of turf for the fire, and we would spend our evenings listening to static on the radio because we couldn't tune it up right, embracing any fuzzy voices that we could catch as friends. Look now: a cottage bursting with real companions who have come to celebrate my birthday. The Nevans, the Moores, all of the Doyles. Con and Mic Harney, endless others. Even Dr Desmond. All wanted and welcome. It all worked out. Imagine that. Looking back, I feel a sweet sort of pity for that early version of myself, who was so lonely, and who was trying so hard.

Finally, I feel like I can stop trying so hard. We are settled now, we are a part of Ballycrea, just like everybody else. Not novel blow-ins from a place nobody has heard of. We make up the community. They have warmed to us.

It happened slowly. It happened all at once. Suddenly we became a part of everything. How strange. How special. Do you know what it is to suddenly feel at home in a place you thought you would always be a foreigner? To feel you could throw your arms around people who once intimidated you, and tell them you love them, and that you're glad ye met? And to be sure that they would tell you the same thing.

How warm the room. How alive I feel. Like something has fallen into place; like something else has fallen away. You know, I never thought I'd say it, but it feels so good to forget about Kilmarra. To move on. Do you know what? I don't think you'd mind me saying this, it feels so good to move on from you. Bill calls me over; he wants a word with me outside. Why does he look so solemn?

Jack

AS THOUGH THEY AREN'T IN the middle of a party at all, Betty sits Peggy down on her lap and takes her hairbrush from her handbag. Ignoring everyone around them, she brushes Peggy's hair like she is taming the waves of the sea. This small gesture, filled with so much love. Gutting. Unbearable. Expensive brush from an expensive bag, in her expensive hands; so much grander than my thin little comb, my calloused fingers. All of Betty's care and attention on my Peggy.

It makes me sick. Just her being here exposes everything that I lack. There is something innately peaceful about Betty. Something that Peggy needs, and that I cannot give her. Although I've tried to stabilise things, Peggy has never stood on firm ground in our house. Betty can give her that peace. But could she ever love Peggy like I do?

Normally, brushing Peggy's hair is a fight. Normally, an adult would ignore her. And normally, Betty would race around the room, engaging with all of the people that want so terribly to engage with her. But they only seem to be interested in each other. They are both happy. Relaxed. As much as I want to call her over, sit her on my lap and assert myself as her parent, I realise that it would be a lot kinder to Peggy to leave her with this woman.

'Ah, you're only gorgeous.'

Betty says softly, and although I wince, it's good to know that she means every ounce of what she is saying.

Era you know, there's an awful lot to be said for those Nevans. Even if I've never really warmed up to them, I can see why the others think that they are what we need. If somebody can breathe a bit of life back into Tom, and anchor Anna down to the ground, and be soft with my Peigín, then of course they must be good. Why, to make sense of the messes that we are, they must be angels on earth.

It appears all Tom's arse-kissing has paid off. Look around the room. He has throngs of friends here. The people really seem to like him; and by extension, they like all of us. I'm happy for him. He got what he wanted. It's about time that something worked out for one of us. I suppose there's a lot here that could work out for me, if I got out of my own way. Did you ever notice that Tom never stands in his own way? There is something in this room that could work out for me, if I let it.

Teresa. The last thing I expected from Ballycrea was Teresa. It's complicated to be this fond of anybody, when I am still so fond of you.

A part of me knows that it would be kindest to let her be, so that she can find somebody who is ready for her. With a fresh head and without a big, dirty past. I wonder would I get away with keeping all her love for myself, at arm's length? Could I let her heal the parts of me that I'm willing to share, while holding back all the parts that I want to keep for you? And how do I find out without hurting her, whether she would be satisfied with only glimmers of me?

She comes towards me. Since kissing her, I have felt adrift. Unable to steady or situate myself without her shore. The way that she walks towards me now – new dress, glass in her hand – glaring eyes, it all evokes something carnal in me. Whenever you moved towards me, I wanted to be a gentleman. Now, I just want to be a man.

'Nice crowd.'

She says to me, and I realise that neither of us will get what we want if a part of me still wants you.

She puts her glass into my hand, and I let her. Her fingers overlapping mine, the condensation slipping against my palm and her pulse beating against my nails. I think what I need is her compassion, but she presents me with the beat of her pulse instead. What am I to do?

A single man, with a beautiful woman handing him a drink. Smiling. The most beautiful woman in the room. Her hand on mine, in front of everybody. What's the problem? Why can't I settle?

'Yeah, really nice.'

Freckled face. Fox-tone hair. Terracotta. Kerr's Pink. Rusted gate. I could love her. With enough patience, I really could.

Teresa is like a Sunday afternoon, you know? I look forward to her all the time, and then when she comes I don't know what to do with her. If anything, the freedom and the loveliness of her are a burden. I suppose it's the effort making, the getting to know someone. Starting again.

Oh, but Sunday afternoons with you. Listening as you hummed along with the radio. Leaning up against the fence with you, as you reached over to stroke the sleeping pigs. I can hear you sucking on a piece of clove rock. I can hear the pig grunting, and you jumping back, laughing. Settling into me. I feel the pulse of your throat under my thumb, still. How do I tell these pulses apart?

The last time Teresa was this close to me, I kissed her. I could take her waist in my hands now and do it again, I don't know if the locals would care much. What would Peggy think if she saw us? I could take Teresa somewhere quiet, away from everybody else. Where I could touch her in the way that I have often wanted to touch her. Somehow, even with you on my mind, I still want to touch her.

Brimming, glistening eyes, looking right into mine. Just close enough to see into the pool of my thoughts, and what lurks within them. Something in her gaze changes. It falters. And I feel sure that when looking in my eyes, she saw you. I take the drink off her.

'You're very good. Did Mary manage to come?'

I say, pulling my hand away from hers, putting her glass to my mouth and swallowing her drink. The cold hardness of it fills me up with regret. I should have taken the chance and kissed her. A glass filling the space where her lips should be.

'No, she's wrecked now with the baby due. I'll be lost without her when it's born. We used be joined at the hip before she got married. Now she's always with himself.'

By her face I know that I have hurt her, but she keeps chatting. As though she isn't allowed to be hurt by me. I'm sure that if I smile in just the right way, she will let me away with it. She lets me away with everything, this girl in love. I think that she sees the sadness in me and likes it. She is one of those women who wants a complicated, dark-souled man, I think. If I could only have an honest conversation with her.

To let her know that I do want her, and that the many reasons I have held myself back are beginning to thin. To let her know that my life has been a deep and endless ache, to see if that would turn her on or off. To ask whether she would hold my hand while I get myself over you, so that we could have a proper start together. Maybe I should say something.

Anna

JUST WHEN I THINK I will have to pull him off her, Jack takes his hand away from Teresa's. Isn't he a divil? It's like he has a measure for my temper, so he knows exactly how far he can push before I push back. He knows just what he can get away with without consequences. The cheek of him, to let Teresa wrap herself around him like a vine when only a few short weeks ago, he was below in the chapel, crying over you. It seems he only misses you when it suits him.

In many ways, tonight reminds me of your final night. All we are missing is that fantastic shrieking, which tore through everything. Jesus, the thought of it is enough to make me sick. I miss my mother. I think I will cry.

But look, Jack's hand is off Teresa. Nothing bad is going to happen. This is nothing like your last night. There are people everywhere, nothing bad could happen with so many people around. Oh god but a tear still runs down my face. Where are you? Is Mammy with you?

I need my darling woman. I need Betty. If I started to cry now, would anybody even turn around to look at me? I have to leave the room. Have a moment alone. I make my way to the bedroom.

Oh, light as rain, her hand falls on my shoulder. Here she is. For a moment, luminous, shrouded in electric light. She looks unlike she has ever looked before. More beautiful. Brighter. Let me soak in all of that light. Singe the back of my corneas, let this be the last thing I see.

How marvellous, that an action as simple as her hand on my shoulder could soothe me so quickly, so intensely. Where we touch, we become one thing. Oh my, I hope she is putting aside her feelings just for tonight. Just enough to revive me, to bring me back to the edge of my mind, away from this swirling mass in the middle which I have been sucked into.

It's a funny thing, normally, she would talk to several people all at once, touching them and looking in their eyes. But now, she is looking only at me. Touching only me. As though none of the rest of the locals even exist. If I only knew what I was doing differently to make me special enough in this moment to receive all of her attention. I never realised something as simple as Betty's hand on my shoulder would fill me with such calm.

'Are you alright, pet?'

How attentive she is. This is my Betty. As I know her, just as I met her. Caring and good and mad for me. Isn't she good to notice me? Her hand stays there a moment. If we were only without reservations, if we were only uncivilised. If we could exist in this moment forever.

'Would you drink a hot whiskey if I made it?'

Yes, a little moment like this. Her, offering me a hot whiskey. I would happily choose to exist in this moment, always. If we could be nothing but an instant, here and gone. Without the time for consequences to reveal themselves, or for emotions to sink in. If we could break free from our flesh and let our souls shiver through the air, touching. Her hand is lifted from my shoulder. The cold of its absence. The world, rushing back to me. Our moment over, so fondly missed already.

Without waiting for an answer, she goes and begins doing what she offered, without offering me much more than a glance. Here and then gone. I realise she hasn't said my name all night.

If I only knew what she counted as special, then I could always be that thing. I want to be the instant of a smile breaking over her teeth. Of birdsong in her morning, while she looks out onto the dew, glistening on her grass. If I could be a moment of bliss, happening and then ceasing to exist. If she could always remember me as a moment of bliss. Somebody drops a glass in the corner. A man whistles. Everybody cheers and laughs. If I was that sort of moment. The burn of a hot whiskey. Glass as it shatters on the floor. Blood sucked from a finger. The throat of a fish, cut.

My eyes begin to sting. With a heavy blink, I find myself alone, in the bedroom. My face turned to the wall. All on my own. How did I get in here? Where has she gone?

My god, it's like waking from a dream. Everything I knew to be reality only a moment ago rushes away from me. There is no hot whiskey coming my way. There was no moment with Betty. Just another something that I imagined. Alright, that's alright. There's nothing wrong with that. It doesn't mean a thing.

I make my way out of the bedroom and into the party, as the little whiskey dream lets go of me. Betty is here alright, herself and Ciara Moore are chatting with some men that I don't know.

'Well, remember now my sister was in Dublin last year doing the Christmas shopping, and she was stopped to be interviewed for the television.'

Ciara tells them all, and I listen, quietly. Thinking clearly again. You can't imagine the burden of thinking and feeling at this rate, when nothing is as it seems. Thoughts come from nowhere, raging with a sort of passion that drags me around in circles and then drops me.

'They were asking her does she smoke, and would she be put off by a man who smokes. Mortified so she was! Imagine everybody at home seeing you on the television, talking about yourself, hands full of shopping bags!'

Seeing Betty here in my cottage, I can't help but wonder if I have finally found the person to keep me still. Even ignoring me, she slows my heart.

'But sure she was too embarrassed to say she didn't want to be interviewed. The shame of the whole thing nearly knocked her down dead!'

They all start laughing, and my vision falls to Betty's heeled shoes, kicked under a chair. Her bare feet on my floor. I can exist peripherally, if that's what she needs.

Tom

'LOOK, TOM, THE OFFER IS there if you want it.'

My ears are ringing. I cannot believe what I have been given. A perfect, unbelievable opportunity. I thought Bill might have been calling me outside for a birthday cigar, or to offer some wisdom for the next decade. A moment just for the pair of us, away from the noise of the party. I didn't expect this. He goes on.

'There's plenty men inside who would jump at the chance. But I thought, no, Tom O'Leary is the man for the job.'

Bill lays an entirely new beginning before me. Even after he gave me a start here in Ballycrea, here he is, giving me another. A job with Betty's brother's company out in New York.

'You could make your fortune over there, more than you'd ever make here in Kerry.'

Could I be one of the disappearing men? Tom O'Leary, vanishing into nothing but a handful of memories, held by so few people. And when those people die, this version of me would die with them. All ties to Kilmarra. All ties to Ballycrea. To my family, to everything. Let go of all the weight I have been holding, and leave. Imagine.

'Did you ever hear of fireflies? They have them in America. Little insects that light up. Imagine, even their insects are glowing.'

He is lit up like one of those fireflies. And while the words are racing up my throat to accept his offer, I stop when I picture myself leaving. As I go, Jack, Anna and Peggy all crumble to the ground. Unable to stand without me. Unable to carry on.

'It isn't that I want to see the back of you, but I want better for you. Do you understand me?'

What would happen to the three of them if I left? Jack would disappear next, he would of course. Leaving Anna to unleash herself. Leaving the past to come into the light. Leaving Peggy without a chance. Peggy has already caused so much damage, it would be a waste to see her amount to nothing.

Would he think I was pathetic if I told him that I'd be afraid to go to New York on my own? If I told him, now that I've found him, I don't ever want to be without him. Do I leave, and pull myself along to glory; or stay, and keep the rest of them from damnation?

'You're so good to think of me, Bill, but I don't know could I go, and leave the family.'

When I die, it will be here, as Tom O'Leary, stuck in a cluster of siblings who will all no doubt draw their last breath at the same time as me. And while I may never make my fortune or achieve my ambition, at least I'll have some control. Now, wasn't this supposed to be my evening, with nothing to worry about?

Bill isn't satisfied with my hastiness to decide.

'Ah, Tom. You'll think about it.'

Okay Dad.

Back in Kilmarra, I would have taken this chance in my teeth and run off with it. How I want to be that selfish. Would Daddy be more disappointed in me rejecting the offer, or leaving the family? Bill tries to lighten the mood by offering me one of the Moores' pups.

'For Peggy, of course. They're old enough to be away from their mother now, and she's mad for the animals.'

My head is spinning. The last thing I need is for that child to have a dog, wrecking the garden, disturbing the pony and barking all night. But I tell him I'll think about that, too.

The weight of my own potential. The fear of a freedom. Doesn't every silver lining come with a big, dark cloud?

Jack

'IT'LL BE YOU TURNING THIRTY next.'

Teresa says to me, smiling as though she has known me all my life and it's funny to see me getting older. I would like to put my hand through her hair. Cinnamon-coloured, somehow cinnamon-scented.

'It will, please god.'

Imagine, she's right. I will be thirty. How little I have to show for it.

I meet her eyes, each an island universe, and I see that I don't just want her carnally; I want the heart of her. I want to start meeting her at the crossroads, taking her arm and bringing her into town. To introduce her to Peggy. To start over again, with her. Teresa would let me take her arm. She would let me take everything. It's always been a case of taking. But suddenly, I want to give.

'Do you think you've the patience to put up with me, Teresa?'

I ask, taking a chance. She puts her hand around mine once more, taking the glass back and finishing the drink.

'I think I have.'

She looks me right in the eyes, inviting me into her universes. I hope she is right.

I look around the room for Peggy. It's time she met Teresa properly. But where is she? I wonder if Teresa would take to her, the way that you took to her. I remember the glow of fire on your face as you lit the fruitcake on Christmas Day. Your careful steps towards the table, cutting a little piece for Peggy, and laughing as she ran outside to spit it out. Another woman would have been embarrassed. But you thought it was funny. You wouldn't let Peggy feel embarrassed. I need to know that Teresa would treat her with the same kindness. The brandy in the fruitcake. The heat in the flame. Peggy is the best in everything. And she needs a good woman in her life.

Tom

PART OF ME WANTS TO go back into the party, so I don't have to think any more about Bill's offer. A part of me wants to stand here with him, forever, talking gently in the quiet of the night.

'Listen, Bill, I'm so grateful for the offer. I'll always thank you for it.'

It's getting cold. He cuts me off.

'Thomas, listen now. Life is full of blessings and opportunity, you know? You deserve a chance. This is your chance.'

Oh dear God, when he calls me Thomas. My chest rises up, as though my heart and my lungs are lining up to leave my body. I believe everything he says. Of course I believe him. After all, wasn't he a blessing that came to me? He keeps trying.

'Life keeps giving, if you're taking.'

What I wouldn't give to just say yes. To be irresponsible, to let things happen, whatever they may be. Life will give if I take. Do I want to be happy or not? It all comes down on top of me. Each of the dark clouds surrounds me. Their silver linings cut me open. It's getting hot. I'm getting hot. Hopefully it's dark enough that he won't see I am biting back tears.

'I have a lot of responsibilities here, Bill. The family, you know, we only have each other.'

What I want to tell him is that I can't manage anymore. That I want to go to New York so that I can stop carrying the burden of being the eldest son. So that I can stop being an O'Leary. So that, perhaps, I could leave your memory on the dock, along with my whole life and everything I've ever done, and become completely new. I don't know whether it's the beer or that I love him so dearly, but I feel I could tell him all this. I wonder if he can hear my feelings boiling within me?

'What does Betty make of Anna?' I ask him. 'Be honest.'

It isn't what he expected to hear. To be honest, it isn't what I expected to ask. But now it's out there, I feel it's worth knowing. If I am going to leave, I need to know there are people here who will look after my siblings. Bill pulls on his collar, uncomfortable, and takes a long drink from his bottle.

'To be honest? Betty isn't mad on her, to be honest. I think "intense" was the word she used.'

I laugh, hoping it doesn't sound like despair. Poor Anna never chooses the right person. Bill goes on.

'Of course, I've nothing against her. She's a lovely girl. And it isn't that Betty doesn't like her! Just that they mightn't be very suited to each other.'

He is trying to cover his tracks. It's fine. I understand. Anna is an awful lot to manage, especially without the benefit of having grown up with her. I knew Anna when she was a sweet, gentle child. Betty has only ever known her after years of disaster. Really, we know two very different people.

Anna has always been the type to have fixations. I've watched over the years as her boundaries waned away to nothing. 'Tis easy enough for me to see her behaviour as passionate. 'Tis easy enough for Betty to receive it as escalated, unpredictable and unwanted.

'It's fine, Bill. I know she's a lot to handle. It's hard on her since our mother died.'

'It's been hard on ye all, I'd say, since yer poor mother died. God bless her and save her.'

He puts a hand on my shoulder, and I remember lies I had forgotten. It comes as a stab to the chest when I realise that Bill doesn't know the real me. He doesn't even know when my mother died. Inwardly, I wish there was a woman here, so that I could be hugged.

This isn't how I felt at the beginning of the night, in the house. When I was proud and warmed by all of our friends, and all I have achieved. I am suddenly sobered by the realisation that there is so much I haven't achieved. So much trouble that I have left to brew, and which is now boiling over on us all. And suddenly, a way out. Bill's offer. It's a siren, screaming.

I want Bill to take me in his arms now. I want him to take it all away. To take me down to his field and put a shovel in my hand and tell me it's all finished. To send me on the boat to America and tell me he will sort out everything here. I am exhausted. I want him to tell me I don't need to be a big brother to them anymore. To tell me I am forgiven, and that nobody is cross.

He brings me back inside. At the door, he pauses, just for a moment. He goes to say something, but stops himself, putting a hand on the back of my neck and squeezing. For a moment, everything is still. I fear this delicate moment is the last true stillness I will ever know.

Anna

TRYING TO REMAIN PERIPHERAL, I listen to Betty as she spills out a story to the two men, something about her aunty being interviewed by RTÉ once. How humiliating, to have nobody to talk to, at a party in my own home; having to pretend that I am deep in thought, worried we are running out of beer or planning when to bring out the birthday cake so that I don't get caught eavesdropping on my guests. I suppose you wouldn't know what this is like.

Betty looks over her shoulder, perfect chin grazing the perfect collar of her perfect blouse. And she jumps back when she sees me. Like I am a big spider on the floor, about to run up her leg. Like I'm something she needs to be afraid of.

'Betty, are you having a nice evening?'

I ask, as though I'm surprised to see her, too. A lost, strained sort of laugh fills a space that she doesn't otherwise know how to fill. She cannot bring herself to talk to me. A fist to my gut.

'Lovely, thanks.'

She finally manages, flustered, her shoulders up around her ears. I know better than to stand here any longer.

As I turn to go, I find Jack in my eyeline again, pouring himself like a glaze over Teresa Doyle. He has a real talent for trapping women.

I wonder if he has told Teresa about you. I wonder if I should; or should I fall into the new regime, where you are no longer a person we miss, but a shrieking secret we pretend not to hear? Shame-tinted. Love-tinted. Your memory has morphed beyond you. Yes, I might tell Teresa about you. She deserves to have the full picture before entangling herself in Jack. Even if it would make me look mad. For years, I have been a woman among men; I'm used to looking a little bit mad.

Jack over there in the corner, edging ever closer to a new future with a new woman. Tipping over the limits of this life and starting something fresh, allowing himself to move on. Tom through the window, his eyes growing as he listens to Bill, finally with somebody who understands him and wants him. Even Peggy, dancing around the room with the other children. And me, an abyss within me that nobody can fill. A longing that cannot be satisfied. All I want is for Betty to hold on to me. Is that so much to ask?

I feel I might as well not be at my own brother's birthday party, because nobody seems to notice me. I should have stayed in the bedroom.

Peggy pulls at my dress. How long has she been trying to get my attention? There are tears in her eyes. Bending down, I take her hands in mine.

'What's wrong, pet?'

She takes a ruffled breath in, about to spill into crying. And then she puts her arms around me. Something she only ever does with Jack.

He is so close to Teresa Doyle that they might as well be one person. So close to Teresa Doyle that he has made Peggy cry. And although she is a world apart from you, right now, Teresa Doyle is filling the space you left. I peel Peggy off me, needing fresh air. Needing anything but Jack and Teresa in my eyeline. I leave Peggy behind, shivering; I have to put myself first. That's what everybody else is doing, isn't it?

Jack

THE NIGHT PASSES. I COULDN'T tell Teresa what I wanted to tell her. About you, and about how I want to move along and feel real love again. I tried, but my throat tightened, my words dissolved. And still, she stood with me. Talking and laughing. Giving me a good time.

The last of them left after midnight. The house is a mess. It will get cleaned tomorrow, please god. For now, we are lying down to sleep. Across the floor, still. Teresa under my eyelids, standing firmly in the dark.

My girl – could she be my girl, really? Will I ever have the capacity to have a girl again? She mentioned going away somewhere together. That if I wasn't settling into Ballycrea, we could go away somewhere else. How bold she is. Her cousins have a farm in Clare, and she said I could work there. Imagine that.

And it isn't that I want to run away and start a new life with Teresa, but I really wouldn't mind running away and starting a new life, with Teresa. To take her and Peggy away somewhere and pretend that none of this ever happened. Sure I'll never be my old self again anyway. I'll never get back the life I once had. So I might as well be somewhere new. With her. It's a funny little feeling that pulls at me. It's hope. Carrying me off to sleep.

In the small hours, stretching across the first darkness of morning, I stir.

Still half in a dream, I turn onto my side, and I'm shocked awake by two eyes, staring into the distance just past me. Anna's marsh-coloured eyes, deep and unending. Wide and unblinking. For a moment, I am drawn into the marsh. I want to walk into her eyes, lie down among the reeds and know what she is thinking. To get wet from the ground, wet from her thoughts, and know my sister again. Is she awake or asleep?

She is cold, and smells of outside. As though she has just come in. But she has been sleeping beside me all night, hasn't she?

Afraid to startle her, I am scarcely breathing. It could be a state of sleepwalking that she is trapped in.

But then something flickers in her eyes. She doesn't move or break her gaze, but she is somehow aware of me now. I feel it.

I put my hand on her forehead, sweating cold. Maybe she has a fever. Maybe she has always had a fever. That would explain her.

'Are you alright, Anna?'

I whisper, barely louder than Peggy's exhaling next to me. But she doesn't answer.

'You're sweating.'

I tell her. Her eyebrows raise, like she is intrigued. Like it's a good thing.

'Go back to sleep, Jack.'

She mutters, in a low-down tone. And like a machine, like a child, I do what I am told.

I turn away from her, and feel her eyes burning through me. Pretending to drift off, I consider how scary Anna can be, but how I am rarely actually scared of her. For all of her strange ways, her swinging temper and unpredictability, for all she is capable of, only once was I ever afraid of Anna. The night you died.

I'll never forget it. All of us drinking across in Finbarr Hayes's house, racing over the road home after Anna burst in screaming. The panic was radiating off her. Honest to god, I felt it as heat coming off her skin. But it wasn't her energy that scared me. It wasn't the drying blood on her dress. It wasn't what Tom told me had happened. It was her eyes. Nothing like tonight's glassy, focused eyes. Jesus no, those were wild, wild eyes. Darting. Flaming. Fixing on something or someone that wasn't there.

The marsh colour of them, illuminated to a shade I've never seen before. As though lightning had struck and set all her reeds on fire. As though a storm was erupting within her. Maybe that's how she felt. Like her eyes were on fire. That's how she was acting.

Yes, for a moment, on that evening, I was afraid of Anna. It hasn't ever come back. But I'll say this: if I ever did see that colour come over her eyes again, I'd throw Peggy over my shoulder and run as far as my legs would take me.

Betty

BILL HAS SPENT THE DAY nursing his hangover. I wanted to leave Tom's party after the first hour, but he would have stayed on all night. I suppose his relationship to the O'Learys is very different from mine.

An hour ago, he finally roused himself up and out to get a few messages in town. It started to rain ten minutes after he left. Good enough for him.

A small knocking on the door. And it's going to be Anna O'Leary. I know it is. Suddenly I realise I don't know how far away Bill is. I'm all on my own. She's going to invite herself in and sit in my kitchen for hours, taunting me. I feel a little panic pricking the back of my neck as I open the door. I'm not annoyed at Bill anymore. I want him to come home.

'Peggy!'

Here she is. All alone. Her little coat darkened by the rain. Not at all who I was expecting. The worst turns into the best.

'Are you by yourself?'

Of course, I don't want her wandering around on her own in the rain, but it would be better than Anna following her down the hill. She looks down at the ground, like she is embarrassed. Like she suddenly regrets coming to my house. I hurry her inside. When the heat of the fire meets her and she breathes in the cake baking, I see her shoulders drop. It's a horrible thing to see a child wound up so tightly.

'Sit down there, pet. Show me your coat.'

Her feet don't reach the floor when she sits in Bill's big armchair by the fire. Something about it drives nails into my heart. Perhaps it's seeing how small she really is. I put a plate of brown bread alongside her. A cup of tea. Butter, jam, sugar, milk. There is a pause before she adds three spoons of sugar to the tea. Alright, that's reassuring.

'How are you keeping, pet?'

She bites into the bread. It's as though I haven't spoken. She hasn't said a word since arriving. Why is she here?

'Do you want to give me a hand outside, Peggy? I've weeding to do. Or we could stay in here and have a little chat?'

Surely she will choose talking over weeding in the rain. Her hair is soaked, the ends dripping onto her cardigan. Who let her out like this? Taking the hairbrush from my bag, I stand behind her and start to work through her tangles. At last she speaks to me.

'Could we stay inside and chat?'

Maybe it's easier for her to talk when she can't see me. Maybe I could finally get some truth out of her about her family. She starts to bite her nails, and I bat her hand away from her mouth.

'How are things up at home? Everyone behaving themselves?'

I begin to braid her hair. I remember my mother teaching me how to do Dutch braids when I was a child. This afternoon, I will teach Peggy.

She sighs, looking at the radio, perhaps for a distraction. Dropping her wet hair, I give her what I think she wants, and turn it on. Some pop music plays: The Beatles, I think.

'Oh, I just love this song!'

Although I've heard this song enough for one lifetime, I keep a happy lilt in my voice, hoping to lighten things up. But I feel her tensing again. Going to speak and then stopping herself, over and over.

'Had you a nice time at the party, Peggy? I bet you never stayed up so late!'

It doesn't work. Nothing seems to work. And I'm made to confront my ineptitude with her; I may be maternal, but I am not her mother. I'm fine for playing, and teaching, and the nice times. But when it comes to all her deep emotions, I fear I am wandering beyond my depth. When her hair is braided, I move around to kneel before her. There are tears in her eyes.

'What's wrong, pet? Did something happen?'

And perhaps knowing that I will not relent, she answers me.

'Do you know Teresa Doyle?'

She says, without looking at me. Ah, this.

'I do. Her father has the pub in town. Her sister Mary is having a baby.'

The tears tremble, threatening to spill. I can almost hear her heart knocking in her chest. I wonder if she can hear mine.

'She's mad for Jack. I saw them together last night.'

I put my hand over hers. Of course, this would be hard for Peggy, when herself and Jack are a little double act.

'Teresa is a lovely girl, Peggy. It must be nice for Jack to have somebody who likes him.'

I stop worrying about finding the right way to respond, because I don't think that there is one. If I'm responding at all, I'm doing more for her than anyone up in the cottage.

'It just all reminds me of Lillian.'

'Do you miss her, pet? Is that what's wrong?'

I don't know why, but it surprises me when she starts to cry. She nods her head again.

'Do you want to talk about her?'

Words are almost bulging from her mouth, but she doesn't say anything. Like she wants to tell me about Lillian, but she won't allow herself to. The rain picks up. A mile away from comfortable, I ask something that I know I shouldn't.

'Did something bad happen to Lillian?'

And I'm half afraid for her to answer. Maybe I shouldn't have asked. But Lillian died so young, and there's obviously something on Peggy's mind. There's obviously something up. And I think this must be at the heart of it all. Unable to speak, Peggy nods. Something bad did happen.

'Go on, pet, you can tell me if you want.'

A big breath shakes out from her. I almost want to stop her, but I need to know what happened to Lillian Kealey.

'We were all mad for her.'

Peggy says, pulling back the crying. Am I cruel to make her talk about this?

'I saw it happen from the bedroom. They all thought I was asleep. But I saw what happened.'

Slowly nodding, I stroke the back of her hand. Encouraging her to keep talking, keeping us both steady.

'You can't tell Jack and Tom and Anna that I said anything.'

Say it, child. What happened to that woman?

I hold my breath.

'What happened, Peggy?'

Bill bursts through the door.

'Only me, dear!'

He cheers, landing something down on the table.

'Jesus, I'm not over the drink at all. Here, you won't believe who Rob Keating claims to be doing a line with!'

As he comes into the front room and sees Peggy crying on the armchair, the volume goes from his voice. And suddenly, his face matches mine. This sort of worried, surprised look. Only he doesn't know what he is supposed to be worried and surprised about. He puts on a happy voice.

'Oh sorry, ladies, am I interrupting?'

He asks, but doesn't leave us. Peggy sighs. She is exhausted. I go and take down the biscuit tin and put it in Peggy's lap.

'Go mad, girl, have as many biscuits as you want.'

I pull Bill into the kitchen, where we have a conversation of very fast whispers. I don't want her to think I'm leaving her alone, but this needs to be sorted.

'Ring Tom there, or Jack, and tell them Peggy is staying here tonight. Say the weather is to get worse, we don't want her walking home. Don't be asking me questions now.'

He takes the phone off the receiver right away.

'She's not ours to keep, Betty.'

Bill whispers, but I ignore him. She's mine for the minute. Clearly nobody is looking after this child properly. I'll have to tell him about Lillian. About my scarf in Anna's handbag, and the way she speaks to me. Maybe Bill will have the other half of the story. Maybe we can sort it out between us.

I go back to Peggy, lift her up and sit her in my lap and put my two arms around her. I put a custard cream into her hand. Even though her eyes are big and shining, she doesn't cry. She smiles at me, backing away from the edge of a revelation. And not knowing what else to do, I smile back at her.

Jack

GRIPPING MY PINT, I SIT all on my own at the big table in Doyle's. A ceaseless rain falls, and with each minute, the pub grows dimmer. The radio catches a broadcast before losing signal again. I pretend not to notice it playing 'I Feel Fine', coming in and out and in. All on my own. This evening, I fear things have reached a breaking point. I have reached a breaking point.

No sign of any customers calling in. No sign of Teresa, either. Maybe she knew the bad weather would put people off and so she decided to stay upstairs. Maybe she knew I would be in another haunted mood, and she has run out of the patience she thought she had for me. She could be out in town. She could be upstairs, wandering right above my head, keeping her distance from me. And this evening, I need her.

She will be along soon, I hope, and she will turn off the radio and put on a record. She will light the room up and make the rain stop, and make me feel better. She won't mind that I've let myself in to drink, not to work. She will still like me.

Ger is outside the back, cutting wood in the shed. I know by the metronome of his falling axe. I suppose if I was any sort of man, I'd go out and give him a hand. The sort of man that Teresa thinks I am. That you thought I was.

For an empty pub, the air is awfully close. I feel the collar of my shirt tightening, choking me. Sharp and sudden, I stand up. So sharp and sudden, I startle myself, and I sit back down again, where the thick air and shirt collar come back around me, and I stand up once more. Heaven forbid Teresa was to come in now and find me this way. Rising and falling to the rhythm of her father's axe.

Right. Stop it now. Stand still a minute, Jacky.

And then the door opens. The lights come on. And she is here. Just as I first saw her, coming in from the rain. Green dress, close to her body, hair pulled into a ponytail.

'Only me!'

She looks at me for a long moment. And I look back at her, waiting for whatever she will do next. Then, catching herself staring, she does as I had hoped: turns off the radio and chooses a record.

'Not a sinner here, on a rainy evening like this! Isn't that strange? Sure what else have people to be doing?'

She asks, flipping through the records.

'What is it you're up to?'

She glances over her shoulder, and I feel I've been caught dossing. But she said it herself, there isn't a sinner here. What else is a man to do in the pub all on his own? I hold my glass up to her. She rolls her eyes as she turns back to the record player. It's all too much. Lately, especially with Teresa, I've found myself experiencing the thoughts and feelings of a hundred men at once.

'Anything but The Beatles, Teresa. I can't hear any more of them eejits.'

She pauses for a moment, and goes back to her selection. I don't have the energy to consider whether I was rude.

If I could only find a way to tell her that there are feelings from last year that I haven't touched. And everything that I've felt since then has just been piling up. All these emotions, building to the point where they are beginning to reach my throat. That I fear if I don't start to let them out, they will suffocate me. And that each moment with her only adds to the pile.

She puts on Roy Orbison. I don't know why, but it's the last thing I was expecting. Just as she sits down at the table with me, I move closer to the window. She's looking down at her hands, it's clear she thinks I'm moving away from her. I don't know if I am.

She takes a deep breath and smiles at me again, and I want so much to smile back at her. But I fear that if I move my mouth, it will tremble and I will tumble into tears. I fear that if I open it to speak, I wouldn't make a sound.

'Are you alright?'

I'm not alright. Not even nearly. It would appear that I have reached the end of my rope. It's hard to find the right words to cut me open and let all the dark drain out of me.

'Grand, girl. I'm grand.'

I wish Teresa would say there is a curse on Doyle's that brings out the worst parts of a man's mind and forces him to confront them. The sort of thing my mother would once have said.

But the trouble is, all of this has been before me, ready to be confronted, long before I ever stepped foot in Doyle's. The trouble is, I have awareness. That's the real trouble. I would give everything to be the sort of man who can tackle his problems head on. Rather, I am the type of man – that most men are – who knows all of his problems are about to surface, and yet refuses to surface with them. Why should I be burdened with all of these bulky feelings and not be shown a way to deal with them?

She sighs. She reaches for my hands, but stops herself, unsure of where she stands. How I am tormenting this poor girl.

She gets up to pour us both a drink. As she moves, I take in the smell of her soap. Her patience has not run out. For the first time in a very long time, that I have found somebody who I could trust with my fragilities.

If she would just start with a few of her own problems, to get things going. The cost of nylons, and Mary losing the lipstick she stole from the dresser. The absence of her father, always choosing the pub over the home. The death of her mother. Her unspoken longing for me.

That soap. The sheen of the nylons. I wonder would Teresa handle me well.

Just as I let myself drift into the smell of her, I am reminded of the smell of you. Of your perfume, your living room, your jam cooking on the stove.

There was a time when I would have died for a catch of your scent in the air. Now, I feel the scent of you is smothering, and I can't get out from under it. I can't get out from under you. Teresa sets two wet glasses of Jameson on the table. The sky outside is lowering and the rain picks up. I feel the oxygen is being squeezed out of the town. Soon, there will be nothing left to breathe but the smell of you. Sweet suffocation. I fear I will never fully enjoy Teresa. I don't think I will ever fully enjoy anything ever again unless I knock it all out of my way. Darling, please, let me knock you clean out of my way, so that I might move forward with my life.

'There's things I never told you, Teresa, about my life before I knew you.'

It looked like an accident, so we treated it like an accident. That's what I want to tell her.

Come on now, Jacky, let's admit it. That was no accident. Denial has never brought me an ounce of peace. It hasn't protected me, and it hasn't brought you back. All it does is accelerate this cycle of sadness that I can't get out of.

Okay. Deep breath. Go for it, boy.

'I had a girl at home. In Kilmarra, not Miltown. I never heard of Miltown before Tom started saying that's where we came from.'

She looks confused, but she's listening. And I think I need to speak to both of you now.

'Lillian Kealey was her name. I had asked her to marry me.'

Teresa's face falls, but she tries to keep it up. As though this doesn't bother her. As though she isn't disappointed.

'Are you going to marry her?'

She asks. And I have to heave to get a breath into me. I shake my head.

'She died.'

Her mouth falls open.

I'd like to tell her it's fine, and that you're in heaven, and that I've made my peace with it. But I can't truthfully say that I believe in heaven, or that god that's running it. I can't bring myself to believe that there is anything but the brief time that we are alive, and the eternity where we are not.

I never questioned any of it until you died. But now that I've woken up from the numbness of the last year, I realise that god isn't available to take issue with. And so I can't comfortably blame anything on him. And so I have to face the reality of everything. This troubles me deeply.

What a strange thing it is, to be questioning heaven, when I've known it. Heaven was the pink of your best dress, and your knuckles on my door. Heaven was butter melting into bread made by your hands and laughter from your mouth. I knew Heaven every day, every time you looked at me. Maybe we don't go there when we die, maybe we live there while we are alive.

I stammer my way through what I've started saying to Teresa.

'I never faced it, you know? When she died, I never processed it. It's always been too awful to think of.'

As suddenly as I felt nothing on the drive into Ballycrea, tonight I feel distraught, enraged, lightning cracking within me and no god to point it at. I'm hit with the realisation that my life was ruined, and I never got an apology. It looked like an accident, so it was treated like an accident. Maybe the reason I've never been able to move forward is that I've been trying to grieve an accident, when I know it all happened on purpose.

'When I met you, I realised I can't ignore it anymore.'

I take her hands, hoping that she is still with me.

'I want to move forward with you, Teresa, but a lot of me is still in the past. With her.'

It might have been fine to go on ignoring things. I might have gotten away with it for years, for the rest of my life. But the inconvenient loveliness of Teresa has awakened something in me. I am reminded of what it is to be wanted, and to want another person. I am reminded of my body, of my heart and what it once meant to me to be a person. She looks at me, eyes wide, with bated breath. How long will she wait?

'What happened to her?'

Let's stop pretending it was predestination. It wasn't an accident, or a divine plan acted through her. It was something she decided to do all by herself.

'It was all covered up, you know? Made to look like an accident.'

As easy as breathing. Easy as loving you. As easy as comparing all the rest of the world to you. Those narrow little stairs. The stone slabbed floor that I wince to think about. No, it was no accident, was it, dear? I'll say it if you will, Lillian.

'She was pushed down the stairs.'

Teresa gasps, puts her hand to her mouth. And then blesses herself and swallows her drink. We are quiet for a minute, and then, just as I think she is going to get up and leave, she squeezes my hand.

'What happened? Who pushed her?'

For many nights afterwards, I heard Tom talking things through with Anna while they thought I was asleep. Piecing it all together, writing the story. Walking through the whole thing without me. As though it had nothing to do with me. As though you weren't my girl, just somebody I knew in passing. An accident, that's always been the official line. That you slipped and fell. Sure it was easy enough to come up with. But I know that isn't true.

'I only know what I was told.'

'What were you told?'

'That it was Anna.'

Teresa is shocked. Of course she is.

'Jealousy, I think it was. That's what I was told anyway.'

She sits back in her chair, and probably won't even hear the rest of what I have to say.

'The guards believed it was an accident. The coroner didn't.'

That's the only reason that Tom told me what Anna had done. The coroner insisted it was foul play, and I suppose Tom knew that it might end up in court. He said it wouldn't be fair to your father or your sisters, to drag them through all that. He was keen to protect Anna. To eliminate any chance of questioning. He only told me what she did so I wouldn't push for an investigation.

'The whole thing was handled all wrong. The guards in Kilmarra weren't trained for that sort of thing.'

They moved you before anybody official had come to have a look at you. In the end, it was easy enough for Tom to convince everyone it was an accident. The whole thing got thrown out. Nobody even looked at Anna.

I have chosen to believe that it really was an accident. And although there are times that it builds up within me near the point of violence, her involvement is something that I try to keep in my back pocket. Unsaid, unacknowledged.

'Everything happened very fast. I think I was in shock until after the funeral.'

Tom insists that we have to look after Anna, that she's fragile. When I was waist-deep in grief, I agreed without even considering it. But it doesn't make sense anymore; my life revolving around her, submitting to her. You know, I would walk out on her in the morning. Let Tom look after her. I would take Peggy and never come back, if I only had the means to do it. Money, and a house, and all of the other things a child needs. All of the love I have for Peggy has trapped me at home, with Anna.

I always thought that facing this would break my heart beyond repair. But now I've faced it, and my heart isn't broken at all. And I'm not sure what to do with that.

'Oh, Jack.'

Teresa says, and for a second I see her hesitating, perhaps even afraid. But she moves closer.

I always hoped that admitting this would set me free. But now I've admitted it, and I'm not free. Now, I'm a man without his woman or his god or his sister. I wish I could take it all back. I wish that I could believe in Anna's innocence, in Tom's good intentions, in heaven and the soul; because if anyone ever had a soul, and if anyone ever deserved salvation, it's you, Lillian.

There is a hesitation between us. Teresa wants to kiss me, but isn't sure if she can. Somehow, I want to do the same. She leans her forehead on mine. A moment of stillness.

The telephone shrieks, and she gets up to answer it.

Anna

I SIT MYSELF AT BETTY'S kitchen table. The smell of fresh bread fills the room, the warm sunlight coming in the window. It's like a dream. She is close to me. Right next to me. So close that I am wetted by the condensation of her breathing. So close that we are one fluid thing. At last, thinking one line of thought. We touch, the velvet of her fingertip against mine. Her hand against mine. Hip against hip. Rib against rib. Bone against fat. Where we touch, we burn. We become a star. Burning so brightly that we set the kitchen alight. At last, I am home.

Tom's hand comes to my shoulder.

'Okay, Anna?'

Oh. I'm at home. Not in Betty's kitchen at all. A daydream that got out of hand, again. How dour it all seems now, the pale light of a cold sun barely meeting my windows. The smell of nothing. The feeling of nothing. It's unsettling how quickly it all changes. It was all so vivid, perhaps too vivid; I should have known it wasn't real. These days, my thoughts are like rushing water. They come and go so fast I can hardly even see them. How am I to make sense of anything like that?

'Anna?'

Tom tries again. There's something short about the way he's speaking. His voice cuts, like he doesn't want to be talking to me at all.

I smile, my eyes wet from the daydream.

'Yes, sorry! Just thinking about the shopping. I've to get a few messages tomorrow.'

In truth, I don't know what I'm doing with myself tomorrow. I have nothing to do and nowhere to go. Nobody to be with, now that Betty wants her space. I have to stop letting myself drown in deep thoughts. I have to stop talking about what I want, and get what I want.

Tom

AFTER MASS, BILL DROPS PEGGY home. She is in his geansaí, the sleeves rolled up to half their length. I forget sometimes how young she is. She wriggles in his hands as he ushers her in the door, like she doesn't want to come home. And by the way he stares at her, he doesn't want her coming back home, either. I have something that Bill wants. There is something that I take for granted that he is jealous of. I never expected that.

'Betty would have kept her again tonight, but I said she better come home.'

He doesn't believe what he is saying. When he is sure that Peggy is settled, we walk down to the farm together, in somewhat of a silence. He wants to ask me something, I can hear it ramming against his teeth, dying to get out. But in the end, I have to be the one to bring it up first.

'Look, Bill. About New York.'

His shoulders drop when I mention it, but he seems occupied by something else. I wish he would just tell me what. If I could tell him how tempted I am to accept the offer. To disappear and leave every hideous part of myself behind. To become something new, unmarred and promising. He pats me on the back as we walk.

'That's alright, Tom. We'll talk about it another time. Alright?'

Bill looks ahead, deep in thought. If I only knew what he was thinking.

How I hate the separation of our two minds. All his thoughts, half formed opinions and desires, trapped, unsaid. The uncontrollable unknown. I hate it.

He tries to do some work on the farm, but in the end, he ends up going back to the house. Captured by the thoughts that he will not share. Leaving me with the grass and the earth.

Without him, I don't allow myself to think of much. All I've done lately is get caught in sharp, spiralled thoughts. New York and the offer. The admission that Betty doesn't like Anna anymore. The burden of Peggy. The ineptitude of myself.

There was a time, very recently, when I'd call into their kitchen after a day's work and find Betty and Anna talking the ears off each other. My God, how easy we had it then. Anna is never down there anymore. Well, maybe they have just run out of things to talk about for the minute. 'Tisn't anything, I'm sure. So I won't allow it to amount to anything in my head.

She is such a sensitive girl, my sister. I hope that Betty hasn't done anything to upset her. It's the last thing Anna deserves. Such a terrible girl, my sister.

Three o'clock comes and brings rain along with it. This is as good a time as any to stop. There's been no more sign of Bill all day, I don't think he's too worried about any particular work getting done.

And knowing that Anna won't be here, I call into Betty. Just to check on everything. Just in case there is something I don't know. I might see the thing keeping Anna away, filling Bill's head.

But it is only Betty, alone. Without him. Black hair melting into the dark room around her, as she stares into the fire like a cat. I saw this look a few times in you, I remember now.

'Goodnight, God bless, Betty.'

I say, poking my head around the door, not wanting to appear as an interruption to her thoughts. Fully knowing I have shattered them. But with some urgency, Betty hops up off the chair, and she takes a loaf of bread from the side and puts it into my hands.

'Mind yourself, Tom. We'll see you tomorrow, please God.'

Her voice is as deep and as serious as the grave. And only when her door is closed behind me, I realise that her urgency was to get rid of me.

All the walk home, I don't think of Anna once. I don't feel as weak as cobwebs. And I don't think of the instability I showed Bill on Friday night. Not imagining all the ways in which my life is about to fall down around me, or the mass of unknown thoughts occupying the Nevans. Not of the reasons that Betty might think we cannot make our own bread. Not of the next steps, or an exit strategy.

Honestly now, all I'm thinking of is how perfectly kind Betty is to make us this bread. Especially when she knows that we are perfectly capable of baking our own bread. How perfectly it will pair with our tea this evening, and what a perfect life I have made for us here in Ballycrea. Unpuncturable perfection.

Up at home, I am met by Peggy playing outside. All on her own, in the grey evening. I feel a deep streak of guilt for not letting her have one of John Moore's pups.

However, this guilt is never long lasting. There is always something more pressing that demands my attention. In this instance, it is Anna's face at the window. Pale, watching us.

Anna

IN TOM COMES, WITH – is that a loaf of bread under his arm?

'That's from herself.'

He doesn't dare say Betty's name. It's like he knows that something has soured. Is it so obvious? He leaves the bread on the table.

All day long, I've sat here. Rejecting my every instinct, holding myself back so that I don't run to her. All day long, I've imagined the smell of her mouth, and whether it would be cold or warm inside. I've allowed the distance between us to grow, just to keep her happy. And yet, she sends Tom home with a loaf of bread for me. What does that mean? Softly, she is rubbing at our boundaries. Blurring them away to nothing.

Surely the bread is a message. Something to let me know that she is thinking of me. That she wants me to be eating, and that she doesn't hate me. Perhaps it's her way of beginning to close the gap between us. Our slow migration back to each other. Back home.

'Had they any news? Did they ask for me?'

A pathetic thing to ask, in a pathetic tone of voice. But if there was ever anybody I could be authentic with, it's Tom. He has guided me through the most vulnerable parts of my life. He will guide me through this, too. After a thoughtful pause, he answers both of my questions at once.

'No.'

No news. Nobody asking for me. It's hard to know what Betty wants me to do next. Maybe she is like this with everybody; one minute behaving as a summer breeze, the next as a toxic fog. Whatever sort of air Betty is, she has seeped into every crack in my house and every pore on my skin.

Perilous hope begins to bubble deep within me. I hate it. And I am drawn to it. I must chase it until I catch it and bite into its neck, draining all the blood from it. Until it isn't hope anymore, just a ruined chance. I'm afraid I can't do anything by halves.

'Come here to me, Peggy!'

I call outside, and we set to work making a cake to send down to Betty in the morning. It wouldn't be my preferred way of communicating with her, but it's something. It's a nice evening.

I wake to the smell of Daddy's pipe. Tom standing in the darkened doorway of the house, the rain coming down like bullets. Jack standing beside him, hands in his pockets. Both mumbling and sighing into the wet light of the stars. This seems to be the only way that Tom can have a sincere conversation with anybody. How many nights have I stood in doorways with Tom, listening to his lectures as everybody else sleeps? The smoke of Daddy's pipe, propelling him through whatever difficult thing he needs to say.

As I linger in a place between awake and asleep, things come back to me. Things that I have rejected all year long: the day I learned you were pregnant, and the uncontrollable pangs of loss I felt. Mammy in her bed. Counting down to the New Year, everybody cheering and kissing. The day Peggy was born. And the scalding seconds when you were falling down the stairs. My hand reaching out for you, as regret burned up the last of the small light within me. Tom's shouting. And later, his quiet voice, telling me we had to be careful. Telling me things I had done but couldn't remember.

A sudden rush of understanding finds me on the floor. All the friends I ever tried to have but couldn't hold on to. All of the ways I loved them. All of the ways I loved you. And the awful burning I feel for Betty. I understand, at last, what I am.

I swallow it all down and fall back into a dreamless sleep.

With some hesitation, Tom takes the cake away with him in the morning. And with the same hesitation, he comes home in the evening and tells me that Betty was delighted with it. There is no loaf under his arm, but I don't take it to heart. I know better than to leave our entire relationship to bread and cake. We are taking little steps back to each other. I wonder how to accelerate these little steps. How to shake off the heavy thoughts that came to me last night, and share the truth of them with her. To get her back on my side. Right by my side. Stitched to my side, if necessary. No, I cannot bear our slow crawl between certainty and uncertainty.

If there was a way to make her understand me. To let her know that my life isn't right for me, and that I need to get into her life, with her.

I can't feel like this any longer. I'm going to sort things out now. While the lads are still asleep, I lightly get up from the floor and let myself outside.

The smell of rain on grass, February becoming March. The earth, soft and damp under my feet. Mammy would kill me if she caught me; barefoot, outdoors, at this hour.

'A lady always wears her shoes.'

She would say, even when I was a little child, when no other little children were wearing shoes.

'Sorry, Mammy.'

I whisper to her, and tightly fasten her headscarf under my chin. The red darkening once more as it touches the sweat from my forehead, the damp from the air.

Down at the Nevans' house, all of the lights are off. No noise from the farm. No stars left in the sky. Quietly, I make my way to her window. I am not here to disturb anybody. Just to bask a while in her liquid darkness and think of a way to pull her back to me. A way to knock the barrier between us.

I settle on my knees before her window, watching. The thin glass pane, marbling her body. Stone-still asleep. So unlike the vivacious creature I have known. Right now, softer than anything I have ever known. How steady her breathing. How still her body. Mesmerising. A gift to have seen her this way, this soft.

So soft that I feel myself burning up from the inside by watching her. Through the mottled glass of the window, her skin is the pale yellow of a fish's spine. How soft. Like a kiss on the cheek. Like steam from the bath. Look how she sleeps. No sweat; not a tremor. Like warm seawater in the summer. Like cold air in October. Like all I would ever need to sustain me. The only thing sweeter than this perfect, sleeping Betty is the waking Betty, taking me as she needs me.

And I realise that without me, she would go on being as perfect as she has been with me, because I do not alter her. I have never altered her in the way that she has altered me. I don't make her a brighter, better, happier person, the way she makes me. She does not love me the way that I love her. In truth, I know, she hardly loves me at all. What a horrible thing to realise. Where she is a warm, guiding light, I have just been dull, dead air.

A new night rain begins to fall. I don't mind getting wet. Let it fall. Let all the blue of her sky pour down on me. Let each of her stars melt and cover me. Yes, if she is the blue night sky, then let me be the day. Let her colour and consume me until the day is no more.

'Don't forget me, darling.'

I whisper, and hate myself for letting my own voice cut through all this precious silence. I make my way to the back door to let myself in and sit in her kitchen awhile. For the first time in so long, I feel I can breathe easily.

And just as I am settled, I see it. My heart seems to disappear from my chest. The breath evaporates in my lungs. My cake, in the bucket of chicken feed. Thrown away. Like it was poison. Like it didn't mean a thing.

The softness runs off. Emptiness comes with hard edges and fills me. Physically, I feel her forgetting about me. How does she do it? Why did nobody ever teach me how to move on from things?

Somehow, she is reverting to the person that she was before she knew me. Bill's wife. Ballycrea's favourite. Gleaming, glorious Betty Nevan, who never needed me at all. Isn't it cruel, that to me, all this time, she has felt like coming home? And to her, I have just been an inconsequential stop.

It's clear she is no longer interested in looking after a blow-in. There may once have been something mysterious about me that was worth learning about. Gone now. I am human, like the rest of them. The light coming in through the kitchen window illuminates how endlessly ordinary I am. Once, I basked in that light.

To look at the cake a second longer will kill me. And yet, I cannot tear my gaze from it. I am drowned by the utter humiliation of knowing I have outstayed my welcome in her world, and unable to stop myself from clawing my way back in.

Hours go on, and eventually I move my eyes off the cake. Don't worry, I'll be gone before she wakes up.

And in the dying dawn she stirs, as I linger on the bog road. A field and a half between us. That cosmos, between us still.

The shrill sound of her cockerel. Unending lavender morning. I hang around, unable to let go of the hope that she might see me and remember how much she liked me. To meet her on her morning walk. To be seen as a drop of falling blood against her early sky.

There is Tom now, a definite shape on the horizon, heading down to the farm. Where he is a welcomed, wanted presence. I wonder did he notice that I was missing this morning. He looks troubled. But doesn't he always?

Here she is! My god, it sends a stroke of lightning through me to see her up and about. Moving and living, out of the house to greet Tom.

And suddenly it lands on me. Such lovely manners. If I called down to the house, Betty would be far too polite and kind to ask me to leave. Even as another rain begins, and I realise I am surely going to catch my death, I'll wait until the men go, so I can have her alone. Mammy's headscarf is soaked.

Time passes, I couldn't say how long, and while I wonder about lying down in the hedge to sleep, Tom comes out of the house with Bill. Whatever they talked about for so long seems finished with. Such lovely friends. Bill is such a lovely supporter of my Tom. A bit like you were. And I wonder, are you the barrier that stands between Betty and me?

With the pair of them making their way down to the farm, I slip back down the hill, to the house I spent half the night in. Only this time, I want to be known. I don't want to be something that Betty could ignore. Not anymore. Look, she sharpens when she sees me. All her muscles jump and tighten. She is ready for me.

'Look, I know you wanted to keep a distance.'

I begin to close all of the rancid space that she has laid out between us. If she really wanted me to stay away from her, she would at least take a step back from me now, don't you think? An awful shame that she has let it come to this.

'I just wanted to talk to you.'

A big, defeated sigh. She steadies herself against the wall of her house and nods to me. I suppose she's all too aware that the cake I made for her is in a bucket of chicken feed inside. I won't mention that I've already seen it.

She is ready to listen. How best do I tell her that where once I wanted to be a flicker of light, I now want to be a wildfire, avidly burning everything around me to keep her warm? I move closer to her. I only want to be near her. What salvation it would bring me, to feel her breathing, to know she is breathing. To put myself into the air that she is breathing and be within her.

'I just wanted to let you know how much I appreciate your friendship, Betty, and how good you've been to me.'

I love you so much I want to be you, is what I wanted to say. But I'm doing very well at making all of this palatable.

'I think I've been a bit much for you. I just want to explain myself.'

She looks down at the ground, pausing on my bare feet. Suddenly I am embarrassed. I want to let her know how deeply I have loved in the past, and how cruelly each of those women has been taken from me. I want her to understand that I love her, and that when she takes herself away from me, it causes my earth to shake.

Betty

THE MOST UNNERVING THING ABOUT Anna is how unpredictable she is. Out of nowhere, she has appeared, barefooted, soaked. Looking as though she has slept outside all night. Maybe she has. Maybe if I'd had five minutes to prepare for this, I would handle it all a little bit better. But she likes to spring herself on me, and whatever was keeping me involved with her – sympathy, or patience, or being a good Catholic – has run out. Just as I start to tell her that I don't want to talk, she cuts across me.

'Do you remember I told you that Jack was nearly a father in Kilmarra? Her name was Lillian.'

Jack's girl. Lillian Kealey. I try to keep the look of intrigue from my face. What else am I going to learn about that poor girl? Why is she telling me this now? My breath comes in ripples. I nod my head, hoping it will be enough. Don't cry now, Betty, keep it together.

'She was amazing. I'd never met anyone like her before. I loved people before, but never as much as I loved her. And she died.'

I am reminded of Ciara, asking if Anna might be attracted to me. I brushed it all off before. But now I don't know if I should have. Is that how she loved Lillian Kealey? Perhaps a moment too late, I put on a look of surprise. I can't let Anna know that Peggy has been talking; all that I already know about Lillian. And although I have been itching to find out what happened to her, suddenly I am petrified to know.

The morning sun is faint. She peers her head down to try to look in my eyes, and then lets out a heavy breath. As though preparing herself.

'I had blocked it out of my head, but last night it all came back to me. The way that she died.'

Take it back. I don't want to hear it. It's none of my business.

Why has she chosen me? Of all the women in Ballycrea, why has Anna targeted me?

She reaches a hand out, and I dodge it. It hurts to treat her like this, when she so clearly needs some empathy. But I can't give it to her.

Anna

MY HAND FALLS AWAY FROM her. It feels as though it will fall forever without anybody to catch it.

I really need her to listen now. To be on my side. This is the nearest I've ever gotten to what happened to you, to how I really feel, and I need her to look after me while I carefully unravel it all. The truth isn't something I have been able to reach for a long time. It stands somewhere, always, around a corner in the back of my mind. In a place that I can't get to. Always running parallel to me, and now I am turning to look at it. Whether I tell a lie or the truth now, I need Betty to hold me up while I do it.

'It was a nightmare.'

If pressed, this is all I have ever been able to say on the matter.

Bloodied floor. Bloodied hair. Yes, I remember all of that brutal, feral night.

Her face remains stiff, unchanged as I expose you entirely. All of the ways that Jack loved you, and all of the ways that I loved you. The shape you took at the bottom of the stairs, the rapidly changing colour of your skin. Jack crying about the baby, and Peggy trying to run out of the house. Tom wrapping me up in a blanket; I still feel how tightly he wrapped me up, as though I was about to fall apart. How strange it is to tell her your name. Betty. Lillian. Two beams of light, intercepting each other.

'Tom told me what happened, but I don't know if I believe it. I haven't stopped thinking about her, and how much I loved her.'

She won't look at me. I press on.

'I've realised that I love you in the same way.'

For a moment, she is quiet. If we could only exist as this moment. This silence. All the pressure relieved. All her mercy before me. At last, her voice. I feel it vibrate through the air and shake through my body.

'Why don't you believe Tom?'

The lovely, trembling journey of her voice through my body stops. My admission, ignored. My love, unwanted.

And I have to consider what she has said. Why don't I believe Tom? I'm always drifting into daydreams, talking to Mammy, thinking of the past; when I'm told something happened I tend to believe it, because I'm so rarely in the moment to witness it. But something about this, I can't believe. A deep, churning regret forms within me. I miss you. The birds sing. She meets me with a look of uncertainty.

Betty appears to be making her own sense of this. The last thing I wanted was for her to interpret this information for herself. I want to tell her a very solid version of the truth and have her understand it exactly as I tell it.

'Because it never felt right. What he said doesn't seem like something that I could have done.'

Oh Tom, oh Jack, always thinking of me, putting me first. Jack always curled up with Peggy against the fire, warming her little feet in his hands. Tom always looking after me, watching without blinking, as though to miss even a second of me would be punishable. Betty is frozen. This isn't about Lillian, it's about love. I want her to understand my love. I cannot be misunderstood any longer.

'I'm not sure of any of it, Betty, except how I feel about you. I'm sure of that.'

And suddenly, she is attentive.

'Right. Okay, Anna. It's okay, you're okay.'

Okay. I'm okay. This is all I wanted. Betty on my side, telling me that everything is okay. She isn't trying to shut me up, she understands me. I knew that she would.

I am coming near her again, at last. Oh, to be nearer to Betty.

I've never known such astonishing relief. I've never known such still, pale air; all that separates us now. The sun breaks over the hill, white light fills every space between us. Let me show her what this relief feels like.

Taking a risk, bringing myself to my home, I kiss her cheek. Secular flesh made holy. And I kiss the bone of her jaw. A silent, fat tear travels down the almighty curve of her cheek, and I welcome it into my mouth. Oh, yes, her tears are made of stars. Let me eat those stars. Her lustrous, salted eyes.

Wet grass against my ankles. Far-off sounds of a tractor's engine. Her lips tighten. I kiss their corner, their centre. At last, I am within her cosmos.

Bliss, right before me. Not kissing me, but there to be kissed. Close to bliss, alright. You will never understand what this is like.

I know I must go before Tom catches me. It's hard to leave, but no harder than any other time I've gone. She hurries me off, not wanting me to be caught, either. When I ask if I can come back soon, she smiles.

When I am gone, out and up the hill, I hear her saying my name. I hear her rejoicing, shrill, running down the field to tell Bill that she has just spoken to me. It takes everything not to turn around and wave at her.

Betty

AS QUICKLY AS SHE APPEARED, she is gone. A little smudge on the hill. Frozen, I pray to God that she will not turn around. I pray to God that whatever Anna is going to do next has nothing to do with me.

I run my teeth down my tongue and spit onto the grass. The cold of her lips on my face, now burning.

She loves me. A crush, I could handle. If it was a crush, grand. But she said that she loves me the way that she loved Lillian Kealey. And look where Lillian Kealey ended up. What was it that Anna swears she was incapable of, that Tom swears she did?

Where is Bill? I need him. But I am stuck with the fear. I cannot run to him. And so, I remain with my back against the house, waiting for somebody to find me. Dreading to know who it will be.

And there on the horizon, I swear I see a tiny smudge of red. And I am sure it is Anna in her headscarf, settling in somewhere to watch me.

With a jolt of nerves, I stand up and run.

Tom

IMAGINE MY HEARTBREAK WHEN I see Betty hurtling towards us. Half demented, her hair still in its rollers, running through the field. Shouting Bill's name. Recoiling when I try to reach out for her. As though she hates me. She falls into his arms like she is about to collapse.

Imagine how it feels to have the people I have regarded as my saviours looking at me like they don't know me. Betty is crying. I never thought I would see a woman like Betty Nevan crying. And yet, something has brought her to tears.

She murmurs into Bill's chest, and I want so badly to push her out of the way. To put myself in Bill's arms, and for him to hold on to me. To shush me and promise me that I will be alright.

And then, glaring at me, Betty regains some strength. For the first time, looking her age. Like a dog, she snarls at me.

'Tell me now, Tom, what did Anna do to Lillian Kealey?'

Exasperated, your name in her mouth. Something I never planned for. I am completely, totally lost for words. What happened to Lillian Kealey. Where did she learn your name? What do I say to them, Lillian? What do I tell them now? I stammer, I cannot even begin to speak.

'I don't know what to tell ye.'

I am breathless. Caught off guard and facing you. Bill stands up straight, as though he is going to have to threaten me. As though I am a stranger. Maybe I am.

Betty looks almost ready to strike me. Right now, I am much more afraid of what she could do to me than of Bill.

'Did ye kill her?'

Betty

LATER ON, I'M SURE I will be shocked that I had the nerve to ask him this. But now, I feel I could stand before God himself and question all He has done. Something comes over Tom's face. He is shocked himself. In disbelief, disappointed.

'Betty, no.'

He says nothing more. Not begging me to believe him. Not afraid of what I will say next. Something in the shock and sadness of his tone makes me believe what I am told. Bill's hands tense around me. As though he needs to protect and restrain me at once.

'So what happened to her? Did she even exist?'

I ask more softly. Breaking away from Bill, I face Tom. Look at him shaking, like a child caught out. Later on, I will feel sorry for him. Tears in his eyes, then tears on his face. He tries to speak, but can't.

'You better start talking.'

Bill tells him. And immediately, like a trained dog, he answers my husband.

'It was Anna.'

Tom

NO. WAIT. WHAT SHOULD I have said? It was an accident. That's the line, isn't it? All the lies I've told fall down before me. I can't unpick them. Bloodied wool. Mammy in her bed. Miltown and New York. A year of lying; I don't even know what Bill thinks he knows about me anymore. What have I told him? What have I done?

All I've done is prepare for moments like this. But now that I am faced with it, I feel an unexpected wash of defeat. Of absolute exhaustion and nausea. Isn't it always the way? You prepare for the worst, and when the worst happens, the preparations go away to nothing.

For a moment, they are quiet. Taking in what they have been told. I see Bill joining up the dots. Understanding that perhaps Anna has always been dangerous, and that I still choose to leave her alone with Peggy; and I let her be alone with Betty; and that I have never had any control over her at all. I could have left that lie in Kilmarra. That was the plan, wasn't it? But I can't take it back now. They heard me.

I expect to be hit. I expect to be pushed down into the soil and kicked and left. But Bill stays calm.

'Go down and get dressed, pet, and we'll follow you.'

He tells Betty. I expect he will want to speak more frankly when she goes. It isn't fair to make her go down to the house on her own. But Betty goes.

And once more, my expectations were wrong. Every time Bill starts to speak, he falters, beaten by the gravity of it all. I wish I could think of a way to talk this away, to erase what I said. I wish he could ask me to hold him. To make it all better, the way he is always making things better for me. This is something I know how to navigate. I could show him, if he wanted to be shown.

'Our mother used say that Anna was born during a storm. That was the reason for her swinging moods. For years, I believed that was true.'

I am trying to channel my mother now, who could talk anything down to nothing by a turn in the wind or an itch on the palm. Yes, the truths we are facing could be talked away, if I find the words.

'I feel like my whole life revolves around her. I've to have a constant eye on her and her endless, delicate emotions. 'Tis cruel like, I don't even know does she realise how much damage she's done to me.'

Bill looks over to me, stony-eyed, as if to suggest his patience is up. It's time to stop garnering pity. The jig is up, Tom, you're caught out. I have to pull the veil off and reveal the hideous face of my family. Knock down everything I've worked so hard to build up.

'Lillian Kealey died. And 'twas Anna killed her.'

I pray he will believe me.

My humiliation, my total and absolute heartbreak, and my greatest joy, when he says,

'We'll get this sorted out.'

I don't know what to say to him. There were few times in my life I felt more fragile than this.

'Do you believe in God, Tom?'

He asks me, and places a hand on my shoulder. He is touching me.

He is not afraid of me. But what a question to ask. In a moment like this, how could I not believe in God? When is He more present than in our guilt, or humiliation, or fear? At His kindest, God is nothing more than a reminder of my failings, of my inability to be glorious. He comes to me often.

'Of course, I believe in God.'

'Then you had better pray for that girl.'

Given a moment of thought, I realise that since I met him, Bill has stood in as my God.

Anna

THE EVENING FINDS ME. AT home, I am sewing curtains and waiting for a call to be brought back down to Betty's house. She didn't kiss me, I know, but she didn't turn me away. She might need time. I won't entertain the idea that it was all in my head. It wasn't. Not this time.

Jack is out at Doyle's. I'm not sure where Peggy is; I never really am. It was such a shame to have had to leave in a hurry this morning. Tom bursts in the door. He slams it shut, the cross falling off the wall. The windows shaking in their frames. Clearly ready to strangle me. Let him try.

'Were you down in the Nevans' this morning, girl?'

He asks me, trying to be gentle. But I hear the heat in his voice. I know better than to answer him. Tom is in his saviour mindset now, where he knows exactly what is best for all of us, and any deviance from that is criminal.

'I'm fit to kill you, Anna.'

A cold streak runs through me, but the anger thins out of his voice before he finishes his sentence. He half chokes, as though he is going to cry. He doesn't want me to answer, I know. And yet I cannot fight the compulsion to further upset him.

'I don't know why you're always putting Bill Nevan before me. It's like he's your god, or your daddy. Tommy, you're nothing but his employee.'

Disappointed, and angry, and then, as if so bewildered by me that he has been left without any other option, he wipes his hand down his face; in defeat, he blesses himself and drops down to his knees and begins blubbering out a prayer. All pointed at me.

'When are you going to buy us beds?'

I hope that hurts him.

I get on with my sewing. When it seems he has prayed himself to the point of exhaustion, he takes Daddy's pipe and lies down to sleep. That's it then, he isn't going back to work. He isn't having the rest of the evening; he is skipping straight to tonight. It seems that he hasn't much regard for what upset him so much before.

It's all too much for him. I suppose I should be deep in thought, too. Creating a counter to all of the moves he is planning. He mumbles a little plan to himself, but I know that I have time. Tom's problem is that he needs to have his plan thought out before he can execute it. He never just acts. So I have time to do something myself, before he goes out to get Jack. Before he finds Peggy. And before he secures the details of a plan that the three of them will enact against me.

'Sorry, Tom. Sorry, Jacky.'

I whisper, as I slip out of the house, undetected. Into the depth of the night.

I have to get back to Betty, to keep talking. To find how my love has settled in her, and whether it has sparked a mutual feeling. She might let me sleep at her house; I could tell her that Tom is fit to kill me.

It isn't the nicest walk down to her tonight. The weather has turned. It seems we cannot catch up to the spring.

When I arrive, I don't want to go inside. The idea of mentioning you again makes me sick. I don't want to disturb you anymore. I just want to watch her awhile and gather my thoughts.

And so I take myself as far as the window, where her perfect sleeping form faces me, warped by the thin glass. Breathtaking. I want her always sleeping as softly as this. Unharmed, unharming. If I cannot have her alive, I will wait for the day when I can be her grave. When she will sleep this gently forever, and I will wrap myself around her. Imagine, Tom wants me to let her go. As though I could ever let her go.

And then, as if by some horrifying miracle, her eyes open. And she looks out at me. A moment of just her and me, suspended in time. Just eyes meeting eyes through the glass, through the night and all that has passed. And I know that all of the things that I feel for her are real. I know that. It doesn't matter what anyone thinks of it, or if I feel differently one day. I love her. I know it. I love her.

She whispers something, and then she says it aloud, and I can only just make it out. It sounds like crying.

'She's outside, Bill.'

She kicks back like a mare, waking her husband, who darts up to catch me, too late. I am gone, part of the night again. Part of the hedges. Part, perhaps, of her dream. Only a flicker of the light, something that briefly fascinated and terrified her. Existing only as a moment. Let her catch me on the horizon, running out of her husband's reach.

I wonder for a moment about leaving my scalp here for her to find. Doesn't she always say she loves my hair? Well, then she can always have my hair, and know I came for her tonight. Oh god, suddenly the sky is so low. I fear I might have to crouch to walk under it. The dawn is coming on so quick.

And then, a smear becomes a clear shape, and I see Tom coming towards me. Racing, like a bull. Shouting my name. Once more, I am reminded of the night you died. Oh god. For a moment, I remember it all so clearly. How deeply I loved you. The veins at Tom's temples, bulging. Like Mammy all over again. That's what he said. Unmarried and pregnant and his problem. I should never have told him you were having a baby. I should never have trusted him with my feelings. He knew that if he pushed Jack, then Jack would push back. But if he pushed you, you would just fall. How easily he knocked you back down the stairs. Maybe he wanted to get rid of the baby. Maybe he wanted to get rid of the pair of you. My hand, reaching for you, a moment too late. I remember it all now.

Tom catches my arms. Once more, in complete control of me.

Don't forget me, darling.

Tom

I CATCH HER. I SEIZE her. That girl has done enough talking. She won't be sharing any more secrets with Betty Nevan.

It takes all I have not to crack her head off the stone wall and leave all the madness to drain out of her. I squeeze her as tightly as I can, and I don't care if it kills her.

It isn't the first time I've had a thought like this. I had it all planned out. How we would do it, where we would put her. The alibi and all that. I'd know how to talk to the guards. It all worked out in my head, except for the guilt. It was the only thing I couldn't explain away. So I left it.

I fear that intending to kill her is every bit as foul as carrying out the act. For a moment, I had every intention of her ending up dead. You might say there was a world of difference between them, but really, having felt what I did, I'm not sure.

At home, the drizzle starts again. Let it pour rain now, I don't care anymore. Jack comes out of the cottage with Peggy. His hands on her shoulders. Her bag packed. And she rubs the pony's nose. She looks so like Anna. Have I just seen this for the first time? I'll say it to her when I see her tomorrow morning, down on the farm.

'All okay?'

Jack asks, hardly stopping.

'Grand now. Everything is grand.'

I pat the soil down with the shovel. I pat her on the head. Tomorrow, please God, I will plant a tree here. Something that will grow eighty feet tall, with flowers and fruit.

Jack

TOM COULDN'T COPE WITH THE damage Anna was doing to our reputation. When a man has so little, that is a lot to take away from him. I'm trying to justify this. We couldn't have let her carry on the way she did; obsessive, scaring people. Getting too close to people. And I suppose it wasn't doing Peggy any favours to be raised by somebody so uneven. Anna's is the last influence I'd want on Peggy. Are there any reasons that explain it away?

I suppose all I have is an honest reason: I am not the good man that I once was. To be frank, it got to the stage where I couldn't stand to hear Anna take another breath. She had exhausted my patience. I had exhausted every other option.

I believe it's fair to say that Anna took a great deal away from me. In ways, she took my life away from me. And there have been times that I was worryingly tempted to take her life, too.

To put the kitchen knife to her neck while she slept softly beside me. To watch all that kept her alive suddenly reduced to nothing but a stubborn stain on the floor. Yes, in my most extreme and obscure streams of consciousness, these ideas came to me. When Tom told me how carelessly and gladly she pushed you down the stairs, it was only natural I would want to do the same to her.

But then I would always realise that she would only be another thing that haunts me. Another bout of grief to mount within us all. If she had already driven me to these thoughts while living, imagine how intensely she would torment me when dead.

And so, I had no real choice but to let Tom take care of it. I stayed in with Peggy, and he took Anna out. I'm not sure what he did next, but he came back alone, after it was gone dark. Whatever he did, where he left her or what his plan was, I don't know.

I didn't say goodbye, just in case she came back. Maybe she will, one day. Maybe one day, I will ask Tom what happened. I know he's done a lot wrong, but I've never been more grateful to Tom than I have been these last few weeks. Taking care of the hard things, like always.

Without Anna around, things have gone silent. The peace and quiet isn't anywhere near as soothing as I had hoped it would be. I never thought I would feel anything as terrible as losing you, and yet I feel this. Teresa calls up to the cottage to see if I want to go to the pictures with her. I send her home. 'Tis quare liberation alright.

I'm afraid that feeling this way about Anna means that you and I are well and truly over. We have finally reached our end, Lillian. I know, because you would never have been with a man so bitter. Over the last year, too much has changed to sustain the dream of you and me. You, changed into some celestial being, far out of my reach. And me, changed into a man you would not recognise. I am only an abstraction of an abstraction of the man you once knew. Once loved. If we were to meet for the first time now, we wouldn't fall for each other at all. But I will always know what it was to love you. Darling. My darling. I think it's time that I let you go.

Go on, pet. I might see you again.

Tom

BILL PUTS A CUP OF tea in front of me. Somehow, it's a nice morning. It's the first morning that it feels like spring. I feel a little bit of hope. He spoons sugar into my cup and stirs it for me. Endlessly generous Bill – I cannot put into words what he means to me. He looks after me. He takes the pressure off me, just for a minute. In all of this grief and misery, Bill is an answered prayer.

Let this be the end of it now. Let this be the last sadness that ever passes between us. Let's get over this as quickly as we can, so we can go back down to the field and enjoy ourselves. He can tell me I'm not like the other men in Ballycrea, and I can gather the courage to recite a poem while we work. Let us always work the land together. Living in an everlasting afternoon.

'You were right, Bill. About Anna.'

There's a lot of men wouldn't dare cry in front of people. Well, if I could cry now, I would love to. At present, I'm afraid, I can't feel a single thing.

'I brought her to the convent back in Cork. We'll go and see her when she's settled.'

His face softens, and he reaches out, puts a hand on my knee and squeezes it.

'You did the right thing, Tom. They'll sort her out with what she needs. I was half thinking you'd put her in one of them lunatic asylums. Frightening places.'

I did the right thing. My God. I will let his voice echo around in my mind forever.

I did the right thing.

I did the right thing.

I did the right thing.

I did the right thing.

Betty comes through the kitchen with bedsheets in her arms, making up the spare room. She pauses, wanting to say something to me, but moves on. That woman doesn't look at me right anymore.

Betty

THERE ARE SOME THINGS THAT I cannot forget. Even when things have worked out quite beautifully, there are things I cannot make peace with. The false smile smeared across Jack's face when he dropped Peggy up to us. The maroon dirt that stayed under Tom's nails for a week. Hard to look past, aren't they?

Bill painted the walls of the spare bedroom pink, and it became Peggy's bedroom. He bought her a new bed, and she came with me to Flannery's to choose her bedding. And still, those first few weeks, she cried, wanting to sleep on the floor. But she is settling. When Bill sits in his armchair by the fire in the evenings, she sits on his lap, and she likes his help with her lessons. We took one of Ciara's puppies for her, she has a new fiddle and we'll get her whatever she wants for Christmas. She comes home to me every evening after school. She needs me. I suppose I got what I wanted.

There was a little while when Tom would call in to see her after work. Peggy would be feverish to see him, and half afraid to see him. Last week, Bill dropped him to the boat. He will write to us when he meets Declan, Michael and Joe. Although he promised that he will send parcels to Peggy when he can, a part of me hopes that he won't.

The odd weekend, Jack and Teresa come back from Clare to see Mary and the baby, and Ger Doyle. When they call to us, Jack stands back from Peggy, mostly. His eyes glossed, making small talk as though he doesn't know us. Asking her about school and her friends as though she isn't his. Politely complimenting her manners as though she is mine. Each time they call, I expect him to usher her into the car and take her away with them. It's clear by the way he looks at her that he wants to do nothing more. And yet, he leaves without her every time.

Anna has never come back. For a while, I was on constant alert, nervous to walk into the kitchen in case she was sitting at the table. Every knock on the door, every letter through the postbox, every flash of red in town was Anna in my mind. Peggy has been asking about her less and less. One day, when she is older, she will stop asking about her altogether.

By then I might be able to explain things to her a little bit better. I might have been able to make some sense of it myself. By then, I might have stopped mistaking the car headlights for Anna's glowing eyes. I might look out the window without expecting to see her headscarf. I might have recovered from her.

When tucking Peggy into bed tonight, she catches me off guard with a question.

'Will Tom ever come back from America?'

She looks so small in her bed. Based on my own experience, brothers that go to America don't ever come back. I wish that somebody had told me a long time ago not to expect their return; I might have been a little less disappointed by it all.

'I don't think he will come back, pet.'

And she surprises me by smiling, and turning away to fall asleep.

'That's good.'

She sighs. Once more, I have a burning urge to ask her what exactly happened to Lillian Kealey. To ask whether she was afraid of Anna, and if she ever trusted Tom. But her breathing is evening out. She is falling asleep. I'll ask her when she is older.

Acknowledgements

I would like to say a big thank you to Northbank Talent Management for all of their hard work and help. Diane, Natalie, Martin and the entire team are a wonderful group to work with. A special mention to my agent, Elizabeth, for her unending enthusiasm and support. From early conversations about this novel to the final manuscript, she has been a joy to collaborate with.

Thank you so much to everybody at VERVE Books; I'm delighted we have been able to work together for a second time. The dedication, energy and passion from Ellie, Sarah, Lisa and Demi has been wonderful, and makes the process of publishing really fun and exciting! Thank you especially to Jenna, my editor, for her guidance, kindness and expertise. Thank you also to Dominique for your keen eye and excellent suggestions!

Thank you to the team at Turnaround for championing my books. Thank you to all of the amazing booksellers for their brilliant work.

Sincere thanks to all of my lovely community of readers. From those who loved *Sunburn* and have celebrated it online, to those joining for the first time with this novel. I am so grateful to you all.

CHLOE MICHELLE HOWARTH is an Irish writer who grew up in the West Cork countryside and is the author of *Sunburn* (2025). The landscapes, culture, and people of rural Ireland have served as an inspiration for her writing in 2015, she moved to Dublin to study English, Media, and Cultural Studies in IADT Dun Laoghaire. She currently lives in Brighton.

Darling, let me knock you clean out of the way . . .

Scan to see and hear more from Chloe Michelle Howarth